The Mother-of-Pearl Men

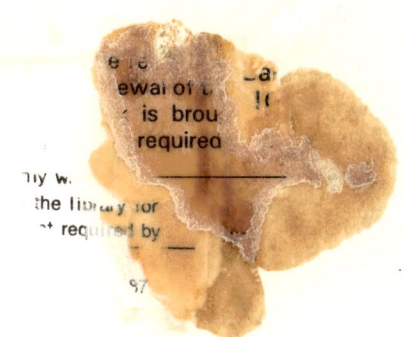

MARK FRANKLAND

The Mother-of-Pearl Men

JOHN MURRAY

Maps on pages 189–91 by Dorothy Couzens

© Mark Frankland 1985

First published 1985
by John Murray (Publishers) Ltd
50 Albemarle Street, London W1X 4BD

All rights reserved
Unauthorised duplication
contravenes applicable laws

Typeset by Inforum Ltd, Portsmouth
Printed and bound in Great Britain
by the Bath Press, Avon

British Library CIP Data
Frankland, Mark
The mother of pearl men.
I. Title
823'.914[F]   PR6056.R28/
ISBN 0-7195-4221-9

*for Nguyen Dang Thuong
and my Vietnamese friends*

In the province of Thua Thien,
The boys are wise, the girls beautiful,
The mountains blue, the water violet,
The palaces of jade, the rivers crystal.
There is a seven-storey pagoda there,
An Imperial temple and the Lord's pagoda.
How greatly are they to blame who have nourished duplicity in
    their heart,
And who for foreign money have betrayed the poor people's
    trust!

Old Vietnamese popular song

According to Vietnamese legend the Vietnamese are children of King Kinh Duong Vuong, a descendant of Dragons, and an Immortal called Au Co. One day the King said to his wife: 'I am from the race of Dragons, you from the race of Immortals. Water and fire destroy each other: it will be difficult for us to live together. So we must separate.' Half the children returned with their mother to the mountains and the rest followed their father to live by the sea.

from Le Thanh Khoi's Le Viet-Nam

Prologue

This story would never have been written if I hadn't rediscovered the Vietnamese tray. I work for an overseas bank, and when I was in London recently between postings I brought some suitcases and boxes out of storage; on earlier visits home I had packed them with old letters and papers and souvenirs.

I didn't recognise it at first. All I could see at the bottom of a cardboard box were strips of dark, almost black wood, each about a foot long. I took one out and only when I turned it over in my hand saw the prancing and swaggering little figures. They were made of mother-of-pearl and set into the dark wood – horsemen waving long swords in both hands, foot-soldiers carrying dragon-tailed banners, battle-axes and spears.

I picked out another piece of wood and there were more of the little men, this time four horsemen fighting in front of a castle wall. One horse was leaping as his rider swung back over his head a scimitar-shaped blade set into a pole. Another horse had fallen and the rider raised his lance as if to ward off the leaping horseman's blow.

There were four of these strips of wood and they formed the tray's deep sides. At some point in my travels it must have been broken and reduced to these pieces. I laid them out in a line across the floor and the figures, frozen in their martial leaps, shone back at me with an unworldly green and pinkish-purple light. I tried to remember where in Saigon I had bought it. As I looked at the figures, each no more than an inch tall but carved in restless detail, the faces came back to me.

Mr Ba, puzzled but always refusing to admit defeat; Maurice, so smooth on the surface but underneath as nervous as an animal; the enraged Colonel Dinh; Father Lam, who looked anguished even when he laughed; old Do grinning stupidly as he beckoned us on to yet another disaster; and the soldiers, both the 'other gentlemen' who were so quiet and the government's men who were almost always noisy. Gruson, too, belonged there though he wouldn't have thanked me for placing him in such company.

They were the figures on the strips of wood, condemned to chase and fight each other for ever. There was so much energy in the tiny, aggressive men that I felt as though I was looking at a film that had been stopped. It might start at any moment. The figures would move and the horses spring forward, the weapons clash and the chase would begin all over again.

I had seen none of them for over ten years but they seemed as vivid as if I had never left their bewitched country. I could feel the heat of those days at the end of the dry season when the climax was reached and each morning I woke to find myself trapped deeper and deeper within the circle of intrigue that had become habit for them. I felt a brief, almost physical pain as though I, too, had lost something in my encounter with these mother-of-pearl men and the mysterious missing limb throbbed. Most people in my world consider me a successful husband, father and businessman, but looking at the shattered tray reminded me that my life has something about it of a cripple's performance. Most of the time it is so excellently done that I take even myself in, but something was destroyed in Saigon.

One face was missing among these pigmy warriors: Thai's, half child, half old man. Perhaps he truly did not belong there, for he was exhausted, burned out, to keep the others going. And so although it happened several years ago in a country that no one cares much to think about any more I decided to put down Thai's story.

I

I first met Gruson at a party at the British ambassador's. I was talking to a colleague from the bank when a short man with a red, shiny face came up to us. He greeted my friend, whom he obviously knew, and then turned to me.

'You must be our new banker. Well, I can tell you one thing. This place needs more than money to save it.'

His name was Peter Gruson and he was a surprise. I'd already met several of the British diplomats. They were for the most part pale, cautious men. Gruson had a rich Oxbridge accent but there the similarity with them ended. He talked at the top of his voice and obviously enjoyed saying things that shocked people. He didn't hide his lack of respect for the ambassador.

'H.E. may not understand the first thing about Vietnam but he knows how to give a good party. It must be his daughters' influence.'

He leered after a pretty, fair-haired girl who had just gone by, the youngest of the ambassadorial daughters. My bank colleague giggled and Gruson's eyes gleamed as he turned from surveying the drawing room to see what effect his remarks were having on me.

What struck me most about him that night was the way he moved. He would pirouette to the left and then the right on the heel of one foot and the toe of the other as though he were doing a drill, part military, part ballet. And when he left us he raised his glass in salute and turned about in one quick, neat movement. Later I saw him talking to a large American. The Yank (I discovered later that he always called Americans Yanks) had his hand on Gruson's shoulder. Gruson was listening to the American, amused contempt plain on his face though the American seemed not to notice.

About two weeks later I got a note from him asking me to lunch the following Sunday. The address he gave was not far from my house on Nguyen Du. Most of the foreign community lived in that part of the city. It was very pleasant there, with handsome brown-tiled villas built by the French and tall, smooth-trunked trees along the streets. It was beautiful in the early morning when the light was gentle and the air was grainy and smelt of charcoal fires. I had taken to walking then along Nguyen Du towards the square where the Roman Catholic cathedral stood. It was a large, red-brick building with two tall steeples topped with crosses. Outside the entrance there was a Virgin Mary made of white stone, holding in her hands a large orb that looked like an old-fashioned anarchist's bomb. There were little stalls on the side of the square in front of the post office and even at that time of the morning people were already eating snacks. But there was little traffic and Tu Do Street leading towards the centre of the city and down which the calm white statue gazed was still quiet. Later it became clamorous and stayed that way, with a break for the noon siesta, until evening. On those early morning walks I felt as though I were walking into the dream of the Frenchmen who had built the city and planted its trees. I began to understand how seductive it must have been, this chance to combine Europe with the tropics in a kind of beauty the earth had never seen before. But the dream did not last, just as those minutes of tranquillity after the dawn were soon forgotten in the noise and harsh sunlight that spread over the city.

On Sunday mornings the cathedral square filled up with neatly dressed Catholic families and troops of Boy Scouts appeared to play well-disciplined games under the trees in the middle of the broad avenue in front of the presidential palace. But by the time I set off for the lunch the streets were deserted again, except for one untidy policeman leaning on a traffic light and picking his teeth. The villa was hidden from the street by a white wall that had been heightened by adding metal sheets to the top. The gate, also made of metal sheets, was open and as I turned into the short drive I saw Gruson, very white-skinned below the glowing face, a round belly sticking out over his swimming shorts, just about to dive into a tiny pool. He had surfaced by the time I got out of the car and shouted to me from the water.

'Welcome, my dear chap. You see we've all the comforts here. No need to rub shoulders with the bloody Frogs at the Cercle Sportif.'

He got out of the pool and, thin arms swinging vigorously, marched me towards three people sitting at a table under a tree.

There was a big blonde girl who worked at the embassy and a middle-aged Australian couple. The man had a bad-tempered, handsome face and was a colonel of some unspecified sort. His wife was heavily sun-tanned and chain-smoked American cigarettes. The lunch was good, a salad with olives, anchovies and eggs that Gruson announced he had made himself, followed by cheese, and plenty of white wine. But the conversation between Gruson and the colonel was better still.

My first post with the bank had been in the Persian Gulf and had bored me. I'd resisted the wish of my father, a brigadier in the Gunners, that I follow him into the army. After school I had almost gone to agricultural college, knocked around a bit courtesy of friends and relations and then hit on the bank as the right compromise between my father's idea of respectability and my own hesitant inclination for a more adventurous sort of life. I say hesitant because I think I sensed that my modest middle-class skills were poor equipment for a world no longer in awe of the British way of doing things. In the Gulf I'd seen little outside the British community and in Saigon, too, I had so far found the native life and the war in the countryside no more than a vague backdrop to a business and social life conducted largely among Westerners. No one talked much about the war except to say that it was going better – that was how it seemed at the time. The stir abroad about the war seemed pretty unreal in Saigon where the fighting and the Vietnamese quarrelling were taken as part of the ordained order of things.

But Gruson and the Australian talked as though they both knew and cared about the war and the Vietnamese world, though perhaps even then I realised it was an odd sort of caring. They were like two doctors discussing a sick man, indifferent to the patient but fascinated by the disease that was destroying him. They argued a lot, mostly, as far as I could understand, about whether the communists would be able to win back land they had recently been losing and whether the government now really controlled the villages that had once belonged to the other side. Gruson said the government didn't have proper control. The Australian said it had. Gruson made scathing remarks about the 'Yanks'. He didn't have much good to say for the

Vietnamese either. He complained about the feebleness and dishonesty of the government. He even complained about the language. 'Like ducks quacking,' he said. He seemed obsessed with the idea that there was no Vietnamese aristocracy. The Australian thought that was a good thing but Gruson would have none of it.

'That's a typical pseudo-democratic digger attitude but it's absolute bollocks. What can you expect from a country that has never had an aristocracy? Where is it to learn its manners from?'

The Australian laughed and Gruson got angry, but in a way he enjoyed.

'You know damn well what I mean. Manners, the social and civic virtues, they have to be learned from someone, you know. The best the South has ever come up with is a middle class and they are either pansified French or Asian bourgeois, which means greedy and selfish to a degree that's self-destructive, only they're too stupid to know it.'

The Australian went on protesting but he was no match for Gruson whose face was getting redder with the wine, his long nose twitching with pleasure whenever he said something he knew the less agile colonel would particularly object to. The only people Gruson talked of with anything like respect were the communists although he invariably called them 'those bloody little men' and seemed especially excited when discussing ways to kill, trap or defeat them.

Gruson and I were left alone for a while when the Australians decided to swim and the embassy girl disappeared into the house with the remains of the lunch. He started to ask me a lot of questions. Why had I joined the bank? Did I find the work boring?

He seemed pleased when I said yes. I sometimes wonder now if some ancestral memory was at work, if the ghost of great-great-great uncles who had made minor and unscrupulous fortunes in a vanished Empire weren't irresponsibly whispering in my ear to ape them. A Bishop had been involved in the scandals of the East India Company. Another had built a fine house in Sussex on the profits of opium though he died of typhoid in the South China Sea before he could enjoy it. But surely the mischief had long ago worked its way out of the family together with the money. I seemed a prisoner of respectability. The bank had turned out little better than a bureaucracy. The cautious tropical clothes I'd bought at Austin Reed before leaving for Saigon were as restraining as a uniform.

I realise now that Gruson's question was a shrewd one. My answer to it, I believe, suggested that I could be of use to him. Of course he was far closer to my enterprising ancestors than I was. To this day I sometimes imagine him in eighteenth-century wig and breeches. They suit him very well.

His last question was practical. Did I speak French? My answer didn't please him, though I couldn't understand what difference it made to him.

'Schoolboy French is not enough,' he said. Then the Australians came over to us and the party broke up soon afterwards. Gruson, though, stuck to the matter of my poor French like a terrier worrying a rabbit hole. He stuck his head inside the car as I was about to drive off and said, 'Remember to do something about your French. It's in your own interest, you know.'

I was amused by this persistence and smiled but by the time I had got back to Nguyen Du I was, in spite of myself, beginning to feel like a child who has been set an unwelcome piece of homework. I knew that I ought to speak better French but I'd calculated that I could do my work with the little I knew because all the Vietnamese I dealt with at the bank spoke good enough English. But I sensed that Gruson wouldn't forget and that one day he would check up to see if I had made any progress.

2

The Oriental and Commercial Bank had its office off a wide street called Ham Nghi that started at the railway station and ended at the Saigon River. Westerners, Chinese and Vietnamese came together here to do business and make money, beginning on the street pavements. I was struck from the first by the ill-tempered energy of the streets. Buyers and sellers seemed to regard each transaction as a fight, voices rose and faces grimaced though all that was at stake was perhaps a tin of American army food. There was a sweet, rotting smell from the piles of rubbish and from a rail track running down the centre of Ham Nghi that was used as a lavatory. It appeared to be a convention that anyone squatting there was invisible.

Inside the bank it was another world. The building's exterior was unimpressive but the interior conveyed a calm dignity that was just as soothing as the cool, conditioned air to anyone coming in from the hot, restless streets. It was one vast hall in faintly classical style where the employees worked together at desks like students taking an exam. Only the manager had a private office, the four other British members of the staff being scattered among the natives as though to prevent cheating.

I soon discovered this wasn't so far from the truth. The manager was one day explaining something about the office's organisation to me. We were standing outside the door to his office when he pulled me inside, smiling.

'By the way, there's one rather important principle of organisation that we don't talk about too much though everyone understands it perfectly well. I don't know if you can tell the difference between a Chinese and Vietnamese but I suggest you try to see if you can spot the difference between the people working in the cashiers' office and everyone else. The cashiers are Chinese. The Vietnamese do the paperwork. The two can't stick each other's guts and so it reduces the chances of fraud pretty well to zero. A crooked Vietnamese wouldn't be able to get at the cash, you see, and a crooked Chinese never has a chance to cook the books.'

When I was at my desk and watching the bank at work I found it hard to believe that a calculation about racial distrust was one reason for its calm. But it wasn't long before I realised that the bank worked another alchemy out of unpromising materials. The ceremony and routine of its daily life tranquillised the people who worked there. Inside the bank nothing was hurried and no one raised his voice. The old messengers who wore white shirts and trousers yellowing with age moved about as cautiously as officiants at a church service. Most of the Vietnamese secretaries wore cardigans because they found the air-conditioning too strong. Putting them on gave them a different, more substantial and European air. I had no way of knowing what they were like outside the bank but it was not long before I began to suspect that their real life was closer to the bad temper of the streets than to the bank's calm. This started, I suppose, with an uncomfortable evening I spent at the house of one of the senior Vietnamese members of the staff. At work he was efficient, reliable and never seemed agitated. But that evening, his wife silent but carefully watching our faces, he let himself appear as a man on the point of drowning. He was one of the refugees from the North who had come to Saigon at the end of the French war when the country was divided into two. He talked again and again of their early days in Saigon when his wife had had to help keep the family by making soup every night and selling it the next morning on the streets. He seemed to look upon his prosperity — a little villa, a Peugeot, large diamonds in his wife's ears — as fairy gold that might vanish at any moment. He asked me all sorts of questions about the Americans and the war which I couldn't start to answer. The next day I watched him at work in the bank, his calm restored and seemingly a different man.

At the time I didn't find this particularly interesting. In fact I had soon become bored by the routine at the bank and was starting to think with horror of the three or four more years in Saigon that were before me. Then one morning my telephone rang and it was Gruson asking me to have dinner with him. We fixed an evening and he gave me an address on Phan Thanh Gian which struck me as odd because that wasn't where I had had lunch with him that Sunday.

It seemed even odder when I was trying to find it. Phan Thanh Gian was a long street leading from the foreigners' part of the city towards the Chinese quarter of Cholon and I was soon in a Saigon that I had scarcely seen before. It reminded me of the day I arrived in the country and had been driven to my house through streets crowded with cars, motorbikes and people, all in a frustrated hurry and ignoring everyone else's haste, like a colony of ants that had been disturbed. I passed a theatre with large billboards painted with the pictures of unnaturally plump actors and actresses. The space in front of it was crowded with stalls selling food and customers squatting on low stools in front of them. There was a row of furniture-makers carrying on their business as much on the pavement as in their shops. Children were shouting, running and crying, as though put on edge by the nervous adult life around them.

Gruson's house looked out over this clamour from behind a wall and high hedge. It wasn't big. A garage took up most of the ground floor and you had to go up a flight of stairs to get to the front door. A Vietnamese girl in shiny black trousers and loose white tunic answered my knock. She said something that sounded like 'plee' and pointed to a half-closed door. I pushed it open and found Gruson talking to a tall, grey-haired man.

Gruson didn't seem pleased to see me and he hesitated before introducing the other man cursorily as 'Broadbent'. Gruson then made it plain he expected Broadbent to go but the latter ignored him.

'There's another thing, Peter. That young Scots lad who's just joined the tobacco company. I had a drink with him the other day and he seems solid enough. I think he could be useful. He'll be getting round the country quite a bit.'

There was a hissing sound from Gruson. I looked at him. His face had gone a deep red and he gave a little hop of what was clearly vexation. He half-hissed, half-shouted something that I didn't understand at first but then realised was French: *'Pas maintenant. Pas maintenant.'*

Broadbent didn't seem to find this at all disconcerting. He picked up his drink and slowly finished it before saying 'All right, old boy, another time.' He waved his hand at me and left. Gruson gave a sigh, which seemed to indicate diminishing anger, and offered me a drink. He made no attempt to explain his outburst.

The house was as much of a surprise as Gruson. The bar he led me to was made of rattan and the stools in front of it had bright red cushions. There was a lot of red in the room: red curtains, more red cushions on the rattan armchairs. Behind the bar were shelves backed by a mirror and full of bottles. The walls were white but broken up by lines as though a child had run a rake through the wet plaster. The effect was like a bar in a cheap Mediterranean holiday hotel.

'Had it done myself,' Gruson said. 'Always do when I'm abroad. Get the landlord to allow me to do the place up as I like and then I sell all the stuff back to him when I leave. Makes sense, don't you think?'

He didn't obviously expect an answer so I asked him who Broadbent was. He looked at me for a moment, his head on one side.

'A bloody idiot. He's also one of the British police advisers who are trying to get the white mice into shape.'

I knew 'white mice' was foreigners' slang for the white-shirted local police but I didn't know anything about the British training them. Gruson gave me a short lecture.

'My dear fellow, the Yanks know nothing about real police work. What do you suppose a Texan cop who's spent his life getting a fat arse in a patrol car could teach the Vietnamese? They need straight old-fashioned police training. But getting that simple fact home to the Yanks is not easy.'

He did one of his pirouettes, turning away from me towards the window.

'You don't think it's wrong for us to be doing this, do you?' he asked, and turned about again to watch my reaction to his question. I said I didn't see any reason why we shouldn't. I didn't tell him that as far as I was concerned everything to do with a war that was invisible from the life I led in Saigon was unreal. The answer seemed to satisfy him and he proposed that we go out to a restaurant to eat.

We went in my car and following Gruson's directions arrived at what looked like a block of flats. We took the lift to the top floor, went through a door with 'Chez Asterix' written above it in black paint on a piece of wood, up some stairs and onto a terrace. A large man with thick arms came over to us. Gruson broke into a fast French that I could not follow. The Frenchman seemed pleased to see him and called him Pierre. He showed us to a table overlooking the street and when we'd sat down didn't produce a menu but just said with an upward flick of the eyebrows: '*Le couscous?*'

'*Bien sûr,*' Gruson answered, his eyes shining with pleasure. When the Frenchman left us Gruson looked around and then lent towards me.

'He's an ex-legionnaire from the old days and the most awful racist you can imagine. But his food's decent. And there's something rather piquant about eating the food of one ex-colony in another ex-colony, don't you think?'

Gruson was enjoying himself, but then I didn't know anyone in Saigon who enjoyed himself as much as he seemed to do. I thought that he probably even enjoyed himself when he was getting angry.

We had almost finished the *couscous* and the effects of several helpings, the heavy red wine and the still hot evening air had brought sweat onto Gruson's face. He produced a large silk bandana to wipe it away and as he put his hand in his pocket he gave me one of his cold looks and asked if I'd be ready to help him. My surprise obviously showed. It was the last thing I expected from him. I had never met anyone who seemed so in control of the world around him. I was beginning to envy him and also to want to share in the excitement he got even from such simple things as ordering a *couscous*.

'Do you remember, at school – a Vietnamese boy called Thai?'

The first thing I thought was how did Gruson know where I'd been to school because I knew I had never told him. Then I remembered a thin boy shivering on a football pitch in a winter drizzle. I'd forgotten his name was Thai because he was older than me, but he was the only Asian at the school so everyone knew him. My elder brother had known him quite well. He once told me of a fight Thai had got into after he'd been taunted with a particularly miserable performance on the football field. There'd also been some schoolboy racial jibes – yellow belly, slit eyes – that sort of thing. They had to drag Thai off the boy who'd needled him but not before he'd bruised him badly round the head. No one ever mentioned the colour of his skin after that. Football field apart, I remembered him as a composed, almost adult figure by comparison with the raw pupils of a minor public school. Of course we knew nothing about Vietnam but we could sense he already knew things we couldn't even guess at. He was clever too. His name was on the school board of honour which was something that I never aspired to. I didn't think much beyond football and cricket and my favourite reading was *Wisden*.

Gruson showed no surprise when I said my brother had been Thai's contemporary.

'Exactly,' he said. 'Now what you may not know is that Thai's father at that time was number two in the South Vietnamese Embassy in London. The old man's retired now and still lives in Britain. And what you also probably don't know is that three years ago Thai went over to the other side.'

Gruson sensed he had lost me. He gave a sigh of irritation, then fortified himself with a mouthful of wine.

'Christ, I'd forgotten you don't know anything about this country. All right. Here's a quick history lesson. When the little men in Hanoi launched the Tet offensive in 1968 – you've heard of the Tet offensive I suppose? – they created a front organisation with one of those fancy names the Reds love so much. The Alliance of this, that and the other. You know, one of those long names they pick to bamboozle silly sods with. Well, this Alliance was supposed to show that non-communist intellectuals were rallying to the winning cause. They got an old Saigon lawyer to head it, kidnapped a Buddhist monk or two and put them on it together with the odd hopeless old opium smoker as decoration. They got your brother's friend Thai as well. In fact he was one of their best catches. You see, when he came back here from London he became rather famous as a student leader against Diem but then I don't suppose you've heard of Diem. That doesn't matter – but you might as well know that he was a bloody-minded little man who was also tough and honest. He might just have kept this country going if it hadn't been for the hysterical Yanks who found him too complicated and had him bumped off by some second-rate generals who then made this mess for them.'

He waved his hand towards the street and the city beyond as

though it were one big rubbish dump. The Frenchman appeared bringing coffee in cups that had what looked like metal hats on top of them. I tried to lift mine off and burned my fingers.

'You don't do it that way,' Gruson said with an unkind smile. 'Haven't you ever seen *café filtre* before? The hot water drops through the coffee in the metal container into the cup below. You take the container off when the water's all out. That way you don't burn yourself.' He spoke slowly, as though to a child; and then, with satisfaction, 'Christ, you've got a lot to learn.'

I began to stutter. It had been a problem when I was younger but I'd learned at school to control it. At moments of confusion, though, it returned and, shamed by the business with the coffee cups, I felt I would never be able to force out the 'sorry' that I had so foolishly tried to say. Gruson's reaction was odd. He made as though not to notice but at the same time I was sure I caught in his eye a quick spark of interest and even satisfaction.

There wasn't much more to the story of Thai. He had disappeared from Saigon shortly after Christmas in 1967. A British diplomat who knew him slightly had seen him on Christmas Eve in one of the Chinese grocers' shops that sold French food. Thai was buying cognac and *marrons glacés*. It had caused quite a stir in Saigon when his name appeared on the first appeals made by the Alliance during the communists' offensive. But now that they had been beaten back and the government was doing better the Alliance had been almost forgotten, and Thai with it.

Gruson finished the wine in his glass. He looked at me over its rim before putting it down.

'We feel we owe Thai's father a favour. He's helped us quite a bit one way and another over the years. And he's worried about his son. He feels the communists may not trust him any more. The point is, will you help?'

I looked puzzled and Gruson put the glass down on the table with a slap.

'Good God, man! Help. Help. Help find Thai and then help get him out of this wretched place.'

3

Of course I said I would help. 'Of course' not because I liked Gruson – even then I knew that I didn't – but because he was offering me a chance to enter his world which seemed so much more vivid than any I had known. I was, then, only twenty-seven and a conventional young man. I had been brought up to accept hierarchy and to believe elders were better. Gruson, twice my age, belonged with my masters at school and the retired army officer friends of my father. He even dressed like them. That night he was wearing trousers of cavalry twill, a cream-coloured silk shirt with the sleeves rolled down and heavy brown shoes. He too didn't seem to doubt for a moment what my answer would be. He had barely waited for me to say yes before telling me that nothing might come of the idea and that for the moment I had only to wait. If the plan did take shape he would get in touch with me.

As matters turned out, I only had to wait a month and it was just before Christmas that I found a letter at my house asking me to meet him for lunch at the Cercle Sportif. I had already discovered the Cercle for myself. After that Sunday lunch with Gruson I had, as he suggested, found a French teacher. She was a middle-aged Vietnamese woman whose French husband, it was said, had left her for a young Cambodian girl, the fact that she was Cambodian being thought particularly humiliating. Perhaps for that reason Madame Larose had cultivated an air of put-upon respectability. She wore Western dresses of neat, modest cut and was shocked that I was not a Catholic. She also had a daughter, Jeannette, who turned out to be one of the group of Vietnamese and *métisse* girls who hung around the Cercle's swimming pool. It was because of Jeannette that I started going there at lunch-time. It was the sort of place that made Englishmen of my father's generation concede that while the French might not have known how to run colonies they at least knew how to live in them in style. There was a large clubhouse with a brown-tiled roof built in the style of a rubber planter's mansion. Inside it had not changed since the time of French rule, with no air-conditioning but fans in the ceiling, old copies of French newspapers and huge armchairs designed for European bodies. The Vietnamese tennis-players, slumped in them after a game, looked like children playing at grown-ups. The terrace of the clubhouse gave onto the tennis courts and the swimming pool was beyond them. The carefully planted trees, the hibiscus and bougainvillaea gave the impression of a tame tropics. For a child of two worlds like Jeannette it was a perfect setting. She would lie for hours by the pool, her skin dark gold from both blood and the sun. Here at least Europeans did not make her look too fragile and she was not clumsy by the side of the Vietnamese.

I went to the Cercle earlier than usual on the day of Gruson's invitation so that I could swim with Jeannette before lunch. I was in the water with her when I saw Gruson and another man come up onto the terrace restaurant by the side of the pool. Gruson ignored the waiter who tried to intercept him and walked quickly towards the furthest, most private table. I climbed out and went over to them. Gruson introduced the other man as Roger Byrne.

'He's a journalist, but don't let that worry you.'

'Very funny,' Byrne said.

I'd read in books of people snarling but Byrne is still the only person I've met who really did snarl. He snarled when he said 'very funny', his upper lip lifting to show long teeth. He had a pale, slightly yellow face and black hair. He was wearing an open shirt and there was thick black hair on his chest up to the base of his neck. He looked at me with distaste as I sat down.

A waiter gave Gruson a menu.

'The food here is French in concept and Vietnamese in execution,' he announced, studying the piece of paper as though he had been handed an unsatisfactory school report. 'The way the Vietnamese have attacked the decent old colonial standards of this club is an excellent measure of the state of the country. The day you order some respectable French dish and it is quite unrecognisable you'll know that the Vietcong have reached the kitchen.'

Gruson and I ordered the local beer. Byrne snarled and said it was buffalo piss. He drank ice tea. He wore a heavy gold identity bracelet on his right wrist and it clicked against the glass. Gruson, I noticed, had chosen the seat with the best view and his small eyes moved backward and forward over the other lunchers. Apparently satisfied by what he had or had not seen, he lent forward so that his head was below mine and looked up at me.

'Byrne is going to introduce you to a man, a Vietnamese who can help you get in touch with that person I mentioned the other day. Byrne knows the story. Two things, though. First, you're going to have to speak French because this chap hardly knows a word of English. Second, and this is vital, you must only tell him that your brother wanted you to get in touch with the person in question. Nothing about me and nothing about helping him to get out. The man you're going to meet is called Ba and if he asks how you heard about him you can say that Byrne and his journalist friends (a snarl from Byrne) told you that he has the reputation of knowing a lot of people. In fact Ba is a pretty hopeless character who hangs around doing odd jobs for journalists but he did know the man we're interested in rather well and he also has ways of getting in touch with the other side.'

Gruson was in good spirits for the rest of lunch. He gave an imitation of the ambassador not wanting to believe that a Vietnamese official he had just met was notoriously corrupt. He pointed out some of the other people at the poolside all of whom, according to him, were rascals of one kind or another, except for the Americans who were just 'stupid Yanks'. Byrne said little except to curse the waiter for his slowness. The man, who was thin and old and wearing a very stained jacket, put on such a fine show of being weak-headed that even Byrne, after a snarl or two, was compelled to leave him alone.

The meeting with Mr Ba was fixed for the next afternoon. Byrne was waiting for me in the foyer of the Caravelle Hotel at five o'clock and without a word being said by either of us we crossed the square to a café. It must once have been a smart place. It had large plate glass windows and a wood and brass bar. There were a few Americans and Europeans but most of the customers were Vietnamese. Plump parents, their faces reminding me of the actors and actresses on the theatre billboards by Gruson's house, were feeding ice-cream to wide-eyed children. Girls were talking quietly to young army officers, whose rolled-up battledress sleeves revealed childishly thin arms and wrists. There was one table of middle-aged Vietnamese men. They were all talking loudly and interrupting each other, and every now and then one would turn away in apparent exasperation at what another had said. Their table was in front of a double glass door that was loosely closed by some string round the door handles. On the floor, in between it and the middle-aged men's table was a pile of cake boxes holding *bûches de Noël*, those log-shaped French Christmas cakes covered with brown icing. As Byrne and I sat down I saw a street urchin poke a stick through the opening in the doors and under the lid of one of the cake boxes. He prised the lid open, rolled the stick in the icing and then withdrew it through the doors and sucked it clean. He then began the process over again. The men noticed nothing although it was going on just a few feet from them. Even when a waiter saw the boy and rushed at him with high-pitched shouts of anger they broke off their conversation only for a moment, looked at the little drama around them but without taking it in, and started to talk at each other again.

Byrne nodded towards a small man at their table. He was sitting on the edge of his chair, elbows on the table, and taking short puffs from a cigarette which he held between his thumb and forefinger. He wasn't saying much and had the look of a child that is day-dreaming.

'That's Ba,' Byrne said.

The idea was that Byrne would try to get Ba over to our table and then leave the two of us together. It seemed good to me for I had no wish to be with Byrne any longer than necessary. When Byrne went over to Ba and tapped him on the shoulder the little man came to life. He jumped up and gave a series of slight bows. As he listened to Byrne he kept saying over and over again '*Oui, oui, oui*', '*Oui, oui, oui.*' Almost before Byrne had turned round Ba came bustling towards me. The impression of a small boy he had given when he was sitting down did not entirely disappear when he stood in front of me. His face had an eager but slightly puzzled expression. It also looked stubborn, for it was long and the mouth and chin jutted forward beneath the nose. I could not easily tell Vietnamese ages but I supposed he was about fifty. He was thin, and only as tall as my shoulder.

Byrne in French that even I could easily understand made the introduction and left at once. I asked Ba if he would like something to drink. He shook his head impatiently.

'That gentleman told me you need someone who knows the country well. *Moi, je le connais*, not like those other journalists.' He jerked his head at the table he had left. 'They never go out of Saigon.'

He laughed. For such a small man it was a surprisingly deep 'Ho! Ho! Ho!'. I had no idea how to put Gruson's plan to him in a natural way so I asked him outright if he knew Thai.

'*Moi, je connais*,' he said at once, not the least bit surprised at the question. He said he knew not only Thai but his wife and baby son whom Thai had not seen since he had gone over 'to the other side'. He also knew Thai's mother, '*une femme formidable, ho! ho! ho!*' who was a collector of diamonds and the friend of powerful generals. This, he said, had come in useful when Thai had got into trouble with the police in his days of student protest.

I told Ba about my brother and how he had been Thai's friend. He didn't seem to think there was anything odd about that or about my interest in seeing Thai. Looking back on it I think he was anxious to show me that there was little he did not know or could not arrange. He said of course he had some friends who could get a message to Thai. He wouldn't hear a word about money. He looked at his watch, gave the glass a tap with his finger and said he must be going. He waved at the table of journalists who were still too deep in their arguments to notice and hurried out, pausing at the entrance to give an uncertain look to left and right before vanishing among the early evening crowds.

One evening about two weeks later he turned up at my house. That had been the arrangement but I hadn't expected to see him again so soon. I wasn't convinced by our first meeting that he would really be able to make contact with the other side and I was sure that if Gruson had met him he would have been even more doubtful. The more I thought about it the less likely it seemed that even if Ba did make contact it would result in a meeting with Thai. Why should he want to meet me just because I was the brother of someone he had known several years before, and even if he did want to why should the communists let him?

These questions didn't worry me much because at that time Jeannette had become a satisfactory distraction from the boredom of the bank. We had begun making love though out of deference to her mother's principles she would not sleep the night with me. Gruson's schemes and my meeting with Ba had been amusing but I no longer cared if nothing came of them.

But I had underestimated Mr Ba. About nine o'clock in the evening I heard a motorbike turn into the gravel drive and then a rattling at the door. When I opened it Ba moved quickly into the hall as though the few moments he had been standing there had stored up energy that had to be used at once. He was dressed as he had been in the café: a short-sleeved white shirt, its pocket holding a mixture of pens, and dark green trousers that were too loose for him and which every now and then he pulled up. We went onto the terrace at the back of the house. He wouldn't drink anything and began talking as soon as he sat down.

His friends had contacted Thai who was not far away from the city. They – Ba's friends – had been suspicious at first. They wanted to know why I wanted to see Thai. Ba said he had had to be *rusé* and gave his laugh.

'You see, Monsieur Bishop, these people are never going to believe that someone is telling all the truth in a business of this kind. So I said that I thought you might have a message from the British government.'

Ba smiled happily as he described his cunning. Oh God, I thought, what would Gruson say about that? But Ba didn't notice my dismay. The day before his friends had been to see him and said that they could arrange a meeting. The best time would be during the Tet new year holiday in two weeks' time. 'The gentlemen from the other side,' as Ba's friends called the Vietcong, would probably ask us to celebrate the holiday with them. It would mean a two-hour drive to a rubber plantation north of Saigon. There was no guarantee that we would see Thai but Ba's friends thought it very probable.

The next day I sent a messenger from the bank with a letter to Gruson. The answer came in an unexpected and not particularly welcome form a week later. I had gone in the afternoon to the post office with some letters for my family. I'd noticed a change in the city as the Tet holiday came nearer. The street life seemed less irritable and people less dissatisfied. Even the girls at the bank were smiling more. They brought me and my English colleagues little paper bags of delicacies: water melon seeds dyed red that they cracked elegantly between their front teeth to extract a tiny kernel, and yellow candied lotus seeds the size of raspberries. Walking over to the post office that afternoon I discovered that the approaching holiday had also put its spell on the square in front of the cathedral. Men were selling goldfish from little wooden carts. Each fish was in a transparent plastic bag full of water and they hung side by side glowing like lanterns in the mellowing afternoon light. Little boys chewing on pieces of sugar cane stared longingly at the fish.

Even the post office, usually a bad-tempered place, seemed in a happier mood. One of the girl clerks was showing off her baby son. He had a gold bracelet around each wrist and wore a white smock embroidered with blue flowers. The mother, who was very pretty, carried the child from desk to desk. Each time she put him down she nudged him and the child made a military salute. The other girls laughed and kissed him.

I was watching them when I felt a tap on my shoulder. It was Byrne.

'What luck,' he said. 'I was on my way to your house to fetch you. Gruson wants to see you. He'll be at the Caravelle in half an hour.'

I walked down Tu Do street with him, answering his questions about Jeannette as unhelpfully as I could. He had seen us together the day of our lunch at the Cercle and Jeannette had noticed him too. She was particularly struck by the hairiness of his arms and what she had seen of his chest and that hadn't pleased me. I hadn't had enough success with girls to be sure of my hold over Jeannette and I didn't at all like the idea of Byrne as a rival. There were more beggars than usual on the street, perhaps because of the coming holiday, and Byrne snarled at them all, even the pathetic boy whose legs were shrivelled and caught up behind him like a trussed chicken. Byrne's room at the Caravelle was chill from the air-conditioning, an appropriate atmosphere for him, I thought, and I wasn't looking forward to making small talk with him in that enclosed space. He was more bearable in the open. Luckily Gruson soon appeared. He was wearing his heat-defying cavalry twill trousers and had a bright yellow bandana round his neck.

'Well, you seem to have fixed it,' he said encouragingly. In my note I had told him none of the details of the trip Ba and I had planned and I went over them, but leaving out Ba's improvisation about bearing a message from the British government.

Gruson listened with approval, Byrne with an indifference that I was sure masked irritation, and I found myself enjoying both. Gruson's plan might also help keep Byrne off balance where Jeannette was concerned. I imagined with pleasure Gruson's applause at the successful conclusion of the mission and Jeannette's admiration for I had decided I would eventually tell her about it too. Before I left Gruson produced a letter from his pocket.

'It's from Thai's father,' he said. 'Give it to him. All you have to say is that you can help him get out. It's as easy as that.'

4

The evening before we were to leave Ba brought round to my house the motorbike he had hired for me. It was a Honda, like his own, but when I sat on it I felt I was astride a tiny pony while Ba gave the impression of a jockey on a racing horse. The next day, when I was riding beside him and could see how he screwed his eyes up against the wind which flattened the hair against his head his machine seemed an extension of his restlessness and delight in movement. We did not have to set off early, for the instructions were to arrive in the village in the late afternoon, and the city streets were still crowded with people doing their last shopping for the holiday. Ba led the way, turning round every now and then to make sure I was keeping up with him. When we reached the motorway that went to Bien Hoa he slowed down so I could catch up with him and started talking, though against the noise of the engines I could hardly hear him. We passed the big military base that I had already seen when driving out to the sea coast at weekends. Ba gestured towards it and shouted.

'*Les Américains sont forts, uh?*' but the expression on his face was not that of a man who was deeply impressed. Americans had only a ghost-like existence for him. They were a flock of exotic birds who by some chance of nature had broken their flight in Vietnam but would not stay for long. He often commented on them but never suggested that they would ever change anything that was important in his life and thinking.

We left the motorway and drove through a string of villages, each with its own Catholic church. Some of them were elaborate, with gothic towers and steeples. Outside were plaster-white Christs with outstretched arms and sinister-looking grottoes made of stained and crumbling concrete that hid Italian-faced Virgin Marys. Others, where the houses were poorer and made of reeds, had only huts of wood and corrugated iron marked with a cross. We passed a priest in the road, heavy set but old, like a struggling insect in a black soutane so worn that it shone blackish green.

'*Beaucoup de prêtres et beaucoup de Viets.*' Ba shouted and laughed, waving his hand at a church and then to the scrubland beyond it. But if there were Viets, guerillas, there we saw nothing of them though even without Ba's remark I would have found it an unsettling landscape. Much of the land had been abandoned and the vegetation, though meagre, could have hidden scores of men.

We stopped only to drink coffee in a village and eat sandwiches made by Ba's wife. Shortly after that the landscape became more reassuring. Tall rubber trees, planted in rows and with the ground clear beneath them, gave it the sedate air of a park. We drove by a planter's house, large and handsome with its heavy tiled roof and terracotta walls. Small white children were playing around a swimming pool and there were the same luxuriant but tamed plants and shrubs that you saw in the gardens of Saigon. To find such peace and order after the threatening landscape we had come through was as calming as a pleasant dream and Ba shook his head at it in disbelief. Our road took us on and down a track through tall trees between which the afternoon sun was pouring its mellowing light. The village where we were to meet the Vietcong turned out not to be a village at all. It was two lines of identical huts with cream-washed walls, green shutters, and brown-tiled roofs facing each other across the red dirt track. They had been built by the plantation for its workers. Here too everything was calm, the tall rubber trees on all sides as reassuring as the columns of a cathedral.

A man wearing yellowing shorts and a dirty tee-shirt was standing by the door of a large hut a little away from the others. He beckoned to us.

'The overseer,' Ba said. 'He's the man we have to see.'

The man smiled knowingly as we approached and took us without saying a word into a room where there was a plastic-covered sofa and a table littered with dusty glasses and empty bottles. A large cupboard stood against the far wall, on top of it the family's shrine: a plate of bananas and a few incense sticks inserted into an old Budweiser beer can. The overseer was plump and soft-bodied and he smiled all the time. Before Ba said a word he told us that 'the brothers' were expecting us and that they would be in the village before dark. Only when Ba started to ask questions did he stop smiling and instead pushed two dirty glasses towards us and poured out some bitter yellow tea. The silence was broken by his wife, a discontented-looking woman who appeared at the door suckling a baby at a long withered breast. Life was difficult, they had twelve children, they did not want to be involved in the war but the communists came and then the Americans came . . . Her words made an angry buzzing sound, and as she talked the baby just as relentlessly pulled at her nipple. The overseer smiled but after a few minutes cut her off and suggested we went to wait on the track between the huts.

The sun was going down and children were playing in front of the huts. As soon as they saw us they ran up shouting '*Ong My! Ong My!*' Some of them pulled at the hairs on my forearm and shouted even louder when I pushed them away.

'They think you're an American,' Ba said. 'They're calling you Mr American.' He spoke to the children for a moment, his voice rising in anger, and they quietened down.

'I told them you were French. It's better like that.'

It was then that I turned round and saw two men walking towards us along the track. They were already only twenty yards away. One was dressed entirely in black, the other wore a khaki shirt over black trousers. Both had black and white check scarves round the neck and a collection of little packs and satchels strapped on their chest and back. Ba half-ran, half-walked towards them. He shook them by the hand, smiling all the time, and then introduced me. Both men had very firm handshakes. Ba talked rapidly and they listened, smiling almost as much as he and making soothing 'aah' sounds. The man in black who seemed to be the leader replied to Ba in a very quiet voice. He was tiny, about five feet, and elf-like. He had curly hair, sticking-out ears, a pointed chin and a tight mouth. His eyes were lively but tired and his neck as fragile as a child's.

Now that it had happened the whole business of the meeting seemed stupidly simple. There was just enough light from the sun to illuminate Ba and the two Vietcong, like figures caught in a golden spotlight on a darkened stage, but there was nothing dramatic in the scene. It was peaceful and entirely unthreatening, until I realised that other figures were moving towards us from all sides. Some were between the plantation workers' huts, others advanced through the trees or from each end of the track. They all carried rifles and wore the oddest clothes. There were black, green, khaki and blue trousers and shirts; wide-brimmed hats like Scouts wear or little pork pie hats of the kind sharp street boys in Saigon favoured. All of them, though, wore rubber sandals that had been cut out of motor tires. The villagers who had come out of their huts to watch us talk to the two leaders paid no attention to the arrival of this silent little army. Village boys who had started playing basket ball behind the huts went on playing. As they got closer I saw that some of the soldiers were no more than schoolboys themselves. They carried their guns anyhow, and a few had tied red cleaning rags around the barrel. Most of them smiled at Ba but a very small boy wearing a scout hat stared suspiciously and frowned.

Ba, who seemed not to have noticed these new arrivals, whispered to me 'They say we are to have something to eat and then they will come and talk to us. Then they want to invite us to the party they are giving the villagers to celebrate Tet.'

'What about Thai?' I asked.

Ba looked evasive. They hadn't actually said anything about Thai, and it wouldn't have been correct for him to bring the matter up so soon. We had to be patient. I didn't feel patient. The arrival of the boy soldiers had reminded me that we weren't simple travellers enjoying the tropical countryside. What if government troops came through the village? The overseer's wife had told us that both they and the Americans had been there several times. In Saigon people talked with awe about the battle skills and cunning of the Vietcong but I couldn't persuade myself that these boys would be able to defend Ba and me.

One of them came over to us. He wore a cowboy hat, with blue and white flowers embroidered on the front, and was carrying an AK47 in one hand and a Sony transistor radio in the other. He led us to the barn where the raw rubber was stored and pointed to a small room at the back. We were to eat and rest there. Before he closed the door on us he grinned and said something to Ba.

'He says he's going to be our guard and that we can be calm because we are now under the protection of the National Liberation Front.'

I looked out of the open window. The boy was sitting on the ground, his rifle beside him. He had turned on the radio and was holding it close to his head, listening to what was unmistakably a love-song.

With nothing else to do we brought out our food; bread, tins of sardines and pineapple chunks, the latter courtesy of the American army and bought by Ba on the black market. This refinement of military life impressed him more than any elaborate piece of American weaponry. While we were eating he lectured me again on the pointlessness of trying to hurry the communists. I couldn't detect whether he was surprised or not by the silence about Thai. Our guard brought in an oil lamp. I tried to sleep on a hardbacked chair but couldn't. I watched with envy as Ba, after cleaning himself like a cat with a damp flannel he produced out of a plastic bag, lay down on the table to fall to sleep at once.

It was about ten o'clock when the guard came in again to tell us that the two leaders were coming. He brought another lamp as they arrived, one carrying a tin canteen of tea and glasses, the other biscuits and pieces of sugared coconut wrapped in a Saigon newspaper. We sat down and the man with elfin ears poured the tea carefully. Then he sat and looked at me as he drank from his glass with noisy sips before delivering a short speech. Ba translated it gravely into French, and to my relief I found I could understand this. The elf wanted me to convey the greetings of the Vietnamese people to the British people. In particular he wanted to thank Bertrand Rool for his support of the Vietnamese people's just cause. Who? I whispered to Ba. He looked startled and repeated rapidly 'Bertrand Rool, Bertrand Rool.' Still whispering and feeling stupid I said I didn't know the name. 'Isn't he famous in England?' Ba asked, even more surprised. I shook my head and Ba and the elf chattered at each other for a couple of minutes, at the end of which Ba smiled.

'He means Bertrand Russell.'

Feeling that I was at fault not having divined at once who was meant I could not bring myself to tell them that the great philosopher was dead. I was also constrained by the audience we had gathered. While the explanations had been going on I'd noticed that some of the young guerillas had gathered round the window, their faces lit dramatically by the oil lamps. I also noticed, behind them, the overseer's wife. They had all nodded their heads at the mention of Russell's name and watched me expectantly for a sign that I was similarly impressed. Invoking his name in the thick, warm night air amid the rubber trees was for them like lighting the incense sticks in the overseer's shrine. It did not matter if he was alive or dead.

It was obvious to me, but I hoped not to them, that Ba's tactic with the two leaders was flattery. He encouraged them to talk about the guerillas' patriotism and suffering.

'The spirit of the revolutionary overcomes all difficulties,' the elf said and the number two man, silent till then, added:

'The Americans think their lives are valuable and do not want to die. But we Vietnamese consider our lives to be nothing. We are not afraid to die.' They looked very pleased at that.

Ba kept the conversation going when I had run out of the questions they seemed to expect from me. It wasn't easy, for my mind was on Thai and I had to fight off a feeling that we were running a pointless risk. I was grateful when Ba had the idea of getting them to show us the equipment they travelled with. The elf began to pull things out of his pockets and pouches and lay them carefully on the table. There was a green toothbrush; a tiny lamp made out of a little glass bottle filled with oil, the wick set in an empty cartridge case; a net hammock; a water bottle; a tube of toothpaste called Hynos that was advertised in Saigon by pictures of a black man with large white teeth; a safety razor and nail clippers; a comb; an American army tin spoon; anti-malaria pills; a spare black shirt and trousers; a small piece of khaki plastic used as a rain cape and a larger piece for covering the hammock.

'That is all we need to win the war with,' the elf said.

'*C'est formidable*,' Ba said, nodding not just to please the guerillas. He seemed genuinely impressed.

It was after midnight and time for 'the party' they had promised us. The two men went on ahead and Ba and I were guided to one of the village huts by soldiers with electric torches. The hut consisted of one room and was brightly lit. Two tables had been put in the middle of the room and round them sat the overseer, still smiling nervously, and some other men from the village. The overseer was wearing what Ba said was the old Vietnamese dress, a long black robe and black turban. The other men were in pyjamas. Three women were sitting in chairs against the wall, each holding a young child, but the overseer's wife was not among them.

A large Vietcong flag had been hung on one wall and banners with political slogans on another. A large Sony radio stood on a small table beneath the flag. There was a vase of plastic flowers on one side of the radio and fresh orange-coloured flowers like marigolds on the other. About a dozen soldiers squatted against the back wall talking quietly amongst themselves and some-times giggling. For the first time I noticed that two of them were girls. The leaders made us sit down at the table with the overseer and the village men. They poured out tea for us and handed round the same biscuits and sugared coconut they had brought to us earlier. They themselves didn't sit down the whole night but stood watching to see if anyone's glass needed refilling with tea.

At one o'clock the Sony was switched on so that we could listen to Radio Hanoi celebrate the arrival of Tet. The young soldiers leant towards the radio, looking very serious. There was music, a short speech and then the Sony exploded in what I first thought was a burst of static. The guerillas started laughing and clapping.

'They're letting off firecrackers in Hanoi,' Ba whispered and he looked so happy that I could not bring myself to remind him that the night was almost over and we still had not heard of, let alone seen, Thai.

One of the boy soldiers got up and announced that there would be a concert. The youngest of them was pushed forward to sing. He began and then, forgetting the words, covered his head with his arm and rushed to the darkest corner of the room where he stayed for half an hour before they could coax him back. Others were more successful. Ba lent towards me. 'They are very sentimental, these young people.' He started to translate the words of a song one of the two girls was singing, his fingers tapping on the table to its rhythm.

'I go to market to buy cotton for a handkerchief. I shall embroider it in red thread with flowers and two swallows and I shall give it to my lover. When he uses it to wipe away the sweat and when he eats his rice he will think of me.'

As she finished someone pulled up a chair behind me and I felt a hand on my shoulder. An almost English voice said 'You must be Michael Bishop.'

I turned round to see a thin young man in a khaki shirt. He had large eyes, deep in their sockets, and the skin around them was unnaturally dark. 'We must listen to the songs,' Thai said, 'and we shall talk tomorrow morning.'

I woke up very stiff after sleeping on one of the tables in the room at the back of the barn. Ba was already up and giving his face careful, cat-like wipes with his little damp cloth. Thai had disappeared before the end of the party and I had gone to sleep thinking gloomily that I would never be able to get to talk to him alone and give him his father's letter. Ba, as we walked back to the barn in the early morning, said he had asked the soldiers about Thai but they could tell him nothing except that he was 'a brother from another place.' They had never seen him before. He added that Thai was much thinner and that he looked *'angoissé.'*

There was a knock at the door and the elf in black came in with a teapot and his perpetual smile which I was beginning to realise he used to keep people at a comfortable distance. The night before he had used it on the assembled villagers as well as

Ba and me and they had responded only with cautious, fleeting grins. As he put the teapot down Thai, too, appeared carrying something wrapped up in big green leaves. He was taller than the guerilla leader but just as thin. His long neck, the large tired eyes and large forehead gave him the look of a grave, exhausted child. He was wearing khaki trousers and shirt and the inevitable rubber sandals. He grinned and waved the green thing he was holding.

'This is a special cake for Tet,' he said and started to peel back the leaves to reveal what looked like a roly-poly pudding from which he cut off thick rounds with a piece of string. It was made of sticky rice wrapped round lentils which in turn were wrapped round what looked like a core of lard. A Vietnamese swiss roll, I thought, to encourage myself. The others started eating with obvious enjoyment. Thai looked at me and smiled when I took an apprehensive bite.

'Thai is going to talk in Vietnamese,' Ba said, 'and so I will translate as usual.' Shit, I thought, what on earth could we talk about with the black elf listening in? They were expecting me to begin and so I said something about my brother remembering Thai well and that when he'd read in a paper about Thai joining the communists he had become curious about the war and what the Vietcong were really like.

What Thai said in reply sounded like a story of religious conversion. As he spoke he stared straight ahead as though he was concentrating his gaze on something he could see but we couldn't. He had been against the Saigon government when he came back from England but he had not had the courage to join the resistance. At one time he had even been influenced by some Americans who had encouraged him to go into politics to clean up the government and make it more effective. But he had soon realised, he said, that they only wanted him to be their 'puppet'. It was only before the communists' Tet offensive in 1968 that he had summoned up enough courage to make contact with the Vietcong and ask if he could join them. Now that he was with them he was learning more than he had ever done in his life. His teachers were the peasants and soldiers with whom he lived. The revolution, and here at last he did turn and look at me, had already saved him and in the end it would save the whole country.

I could read nothing in his eyes when he made that final declaration of faith. The guerilla leader gave his final 'aah' of approval and there was a long silence which Ba of course found unbearable. He started fidgeting and then asked me if I had any questions but I could think of none, or at least none that I could ask until I was alone with Thai. Luckily one of the soldiers put his head round the door and said something to the leader who laughed and followed him out. Ba, whose interest had also been aroused, went after him. I don't believe I stopped to think even for a moment. I almost slapped the letter down into his hand so anxious was I to get rid of it.

'It's from your father. And look, if there's anything I can do for you I've written down my address in Saigon.'

'What do you mean?'

'I can help you get out. Get out of Vietnam.'

Again I could not judge what he was thinking. He looked at me but I could detect neither surprise nor anger. He said quietly 'I think we should go outside' but he put the letter and the piece of paper on which I had written my address in his pocket.

To my surprise I found myself trembling, whether from fear or excitement I still don't know. Even when I went out after Thai I could not properly take in what was happening until a grinning Ba came over to me. He pointed to a man who was holding by the hand two little boys dressed in blue pyjamas and broad-brimmed jungle hats made out of a leopard spot camouflage material I had seen Saigon soldiers wearing.

'The man's from another village,' Ba said, 'and he's brought his sons to give Tet greetings to the Front.'

The children opened their eyes wide when they saw me but their manners were so good, or they were so awed by the occasion, that they said nothing. Thai went into the barn and came back with two thick slices of the Tet cake and gave them to the boys. Then he looked at his watch and said they would soon be leaving. He pointed down the track to where the village ended. The guerillas were standing in a ragged line. I asked Thai where he was going. He smiled and said he couldn't tell me. The leader came over and shook my hand and then beckoned Ba to translate for him.

'He says he hopes you will remember that the Front is fighting for the freedom and independence of Vietnam and that it accepts as friends all foreigners who understand that.'

Again I looked at Thai and again I could catch no reaction. He just shook my hand and said thank you quietly in English. The two of them walked away towards the rest of the group which, without any orders being given, started to move down the track in single file. When they reached the place where the track turned left and disappeared between the rubber trees Thai and some of the boys turned and waved. If they hadn't been carrying guns you would have said they were boy scouts making their first expedition into the forest.

5

Gruson was furious.

'Good God, man! How on earth can you have let that opportunity go? You had him there alone and you didn't manage even to get a hint out of him whether he wanted to leave or not?'

Byrne had arranged the meeting. He was now sitting on one of Gruson's red bar-stools looking at me as though I made him feel sick. I wondered if he had seen Jeannette while I had been away. Gruson walked up and down, his brown brogues clicking on the tiled floor.

I was puzzled more than anything else. I couldn't understand why Gruson was so angry. He hadn't told me to try to persuade Thai to leave. I'd assumed that if he didn't want to we would let the whole business drop. But Gruson was making such a fuss that it was obvious to me now that he had wanted Thai to say yes, get me out. Why he wanted this if he was only interested in doing Thai's father a favour – as he had told me that evening when he had first asked for my help – I did not understand. Nor did I like having him rage at me in this way.

His bossiness had been tolerable up till now because I'd accepted it as the price for taking part in the amusing game he'd introduced me to. But to my displeasure I'd noticed how I'd tried to win his approval by the way I recounted the meeting with Thai. I'd made a lot of the way Thai had put the piece of paper with my address in his pocket. If he'd had no interest in getting in touch with me, I'd said, he wouldn't have done that. Gruson wasn't impressed.

'What else could he have done with it?' he asked sarcastically. 'Dropped it on the floor for one of the other little buggers to see?'

It had been, I remembered, the same when I had reported back to him about my first meeting with Ba and the ease with which I had arranged the trip to the plantation. I'd taken pleasure in winning his approval.

But this time Gruson himself seemed less impressive than before. He was wearing his cavalry twill trousers and a blue linen shirt and together they exaggerated the narrowness of his shoulders and the width of his bottom. As he did his pirouette turn at the end of the room he looked almost comic. He seemed to guess at part of what I was feeling and his manner changed at once, becoming the amusing friend with whom one could joke about the idiocies of the world.

'My dear chap, look, it's not your fault. These people are just bloody. They've got the war they deserve and we are probably crazy to try to help this fellow Thai or any of them for that matter.'

Just before I left, though, he became business-like and told me what to do in case Thai should somehow get in touch with me. We would have to move fast, he said, so I must let him know at once. Ba might come in useful again so I should also stay in touch with him.

That part of the instructions proved easy. Since we had got back from the plantation Ba had started to call at my home one or two evenings a week. I would hear his motorbike and then the impatient rattling on the front door grille and there would be Ba, tense as a runner at the start of a race. He had apparently decided to take me under his wing and to help me 'understand the situation' as he put it. This meant telling me the latest Saigon political gossip, a jumble of names, rumours and intricate theories of plots and intrigues. The lessons began the moment I pulled back the grille. He would give a casual greeting and then announce, while still standing on the doorstep, that 'General So-and-So was very angry with the President' or

'Monsieur So-and-So (usually a politician of whom I had never heard) had excellent information that the war would end next year.'

After a few such evenings I realised that Ba was not really a guide at all. He was too much like the metal ball that is batted and switched backwards and forwards across a pinball machine. His day began with a rush of enthusiastic curiosity and ended in confusion. He would call on a cousin in the army to hear military gossip, stop at a Catholic church or Buddhist pagoda to sample the latest theories of the men of God. By the time he reached the café in the late afternoon to gossip with the elderly Vietnamese journalists who gathered there and with whom I had first seen him, his mind was a tangle of contradictory facts and opinions. I think he liked coming to me because he knew he would hear no more gossip. He found my foreignness and ignorance useful. He could use me like a torch to cast an impartial beam of judgement on the latest rumours and theories. When he left me he was calmer, his mind cleared in preparation for the next day's excitements.

Ba had also been pleased by our journey together and seeing Thai again. I couldn't make out his attitude to the Vietcong. I knew he had been on their territory before and there had seemed something genuine in his desire to please them during our meeting. But when I asked him if he thought Thai was all right he looked worried and muttered that the communists were *'très durs'*, very tough.

One evening about a month after I had told Gruson of the unsatisfactory result of the encounter with Thai there was a rattling at the front door. I hadn't heard a motorbike but I was sure it was Ba for he hadn't been round for several days. I was wrong.

'Monsieur Bishop', the Vietnamese man on the doorstep said in very clear French, 'I think you know my nephew.'

He held out his hand. The cuff of his shirt was frayed but it was held together by heavy gold links. I noticed a thin, elderly tie and baggy grey trousers kept up by a narrow belt around a very slim waist. The man's hair was glossy from some dressing and brushed straight back from the forehead. Both costume and manner suggested a stubborn jauntiness.

I must have looked puzzled.

'I'm so sorry', the Vietnamese said. 'I had forgotten that you didn't know that Thai had an uncle. He has, of course, several, and I am one of them. His father's youngest brother.'

I asked him to come in but he shook his head and smiled.

'No. I would like to take you out. You see, I am what the English I think call the "black sheep" ' (he said the words in English and they came out as "blek ship") 'of the family. I have to live up to my reputation.' He took me by the arm. 'Come along, I have my car outside.'

The car suited him. It was a long black Citroën, the kind you see in old French gangster movies. The body was beautifully polished and the walls of the tyres were painted white.

'Now what should you call me,' he said, as though talking aloud to himself as he started the engine. 'My real name is Tran Dai Tan but many people know me as Maurice or Maurice Tran Dai Tan or even plain Maurice Tan. It must sound complicated to you but then, Monsieur Bishop, you are beginning to get involved in a very complicated business.'

He had driven down Tu Do and then turned off into Nguyen Hue where he parked expertly. He called out to a small boy standing on the pavement. He said something to him and the child nodded gravely.

'In the old days that boy would have been watching over water buffaloes. I am not sentimental. I expect he would find the buffaloes much less interesting.'

He laughed. There was something of Thai about him; the same broad forehead and thin neck. But the cheekbones were higher and with the glossed back hair he reminded me of photographs I had seen of fashionable Vietnamese taken in the 1930s which was when he must have been a young man.

He took my arm again, and we walked towards a neon sign that said 'Pink Night'. A man selling cigarettes from a small trestle table on the pavement saw us and waved at Maurice who smiled back. The man came over with two packets of Gitanes. Maurice paid him and sighed.

'You see, I am very well known here.'

A boy in a white uniform with gold braid and buttons opened the door and bowed mockingly low. It was dark inside. I could make out a small and crowded dance floor. Most of the tables were occupied. There were some very pretty girls and several officers from the Vietnamese army. A short and fat head waiter hurried up to Maurice and took us to a table in the corner. Without a word being said another waiter appeared with a bottle of Scotch, ice and glasses. Maurice poured us each a stiff drink, drank deeply from his and sighed.

'It really is hard to know where to begin. Obviously I have heard from my nephew about your little journey to see him. What I can't understand is why you want so much to help him.'

At this point the band started playing so loudly that I almost had to shout to make Maurice hear me. I looked at the people at the nearest tables and was relieved to see they were paying us no attention. Nevertheless it struck me as an odd place to hold a conspiratorial meeting. Maurice, though, did not notice what must have been my very obvious unease. I told him almost what Gruson had told me: that Thai's father had appealed to friends in the British Foreign Office to help extract his son. I didn't mention Gruson, an omission that Maurice at once spotted.

'But presumably someone at the British embassy asked you to do this?'

Instead of denying it I said that this had to be confidential, and as soon as the words were out of my mouth I knew that Gruson would be angry at my admitting the embassy's involvement rather than denying it.

Maurice looked pleased.

'Of course I understand that. But you must try to understand my point of view. We – I mean the Vietnamese – are suspicious people. We do not even trust each other. To tell the truth, we particularly do not trust each other.'

He was leaning towards me with his elbows on the table and I could hear his high, clear voice quite easily in spite of the band which was now playing Beatles tunes that every now and then slipped into odd Eastern dissonances, whether intentionally or not I could not guess.

'Let me give you an example,' Maurice said, 'a particularly dramatic example, it is true, but it happens to be an important one. To you all the people here look like Vietnamese and so shouldn't I feel at home here? But I don't. You see, most of them are Northerners. To me, they have hard voices, even these pretty girls, and their accent sounds to me like the buzzing of a fly.

'I remember very well when the Northern refugees came to Saigon in 1954 after the communists had won the war in the North. Southern families like ours were becoming impoverished because we had not been able to get income from our land during the war. Most of the Northerners arrived with nothing but they opened up little shops and sent their wives out onto the streets selling soup. We were shocked by this. We laughed at them for doing things we would never dream of doing. But they got rich while we got poorer. And when the Americans came it was the Northerners here who learnt fastest how to get on with them. One of our cousins who was a general until he annoyed the president told me that most of the American agents here are Northerners and I believe it. They are selfish and cunning. We are also selfish, but too proud and lazy to do much about it.'

I couldn't understand why he was telling me this and I felt embarrassed by such confessions. So I tried to make a joke of it and asked why he came to the nightclub if he didn't feel at home.

'Perhaps because I get a perverse pleasure in feeling a stranger in the city in which I was born.'

The whisky had turned his face pink. He took a cigarette-holder from his trouser pocket and vigorously screwed in a Gitane.

'Well, don't believe everything I say. We are a melodramatic people and, besides, we like feeling sorry for ourselves. Take my own case. I am a very interesting specimen. I am an Asian who had the chance to change his skin. You see, my father took French nationality. That is why I was baptised Maurice – he was a Catholic too. Thai's father is Roland and our eldest brother is Bernard. You probably do not know that he is in Hanoi where he is someone of importance. Our house in the village where we had our riceland was very modern, very Western. My father was one of the first Vietnamese to own a motorcar. One of our neighbours had his own aeroplane – all this was long ago of course, before the second world war. You know I still have some of the menus of the dinners that my father used to give. They are beautifully printed – in French, of course.

'Did I say I had a chance to change my skin? Of course I meant my soul. Well, you understand what I mean.'

He seemed carried away by what he was saying. He inhaled his cigarette deeply and stared at the smoke as he let it slowly escape from his mouth. The band had now been replaced by three singers, two men with slicked-back hair and small moustaches and a tall, handsome woman in a long Vietnamese tunic and white trousers.

'One had intimations of it at school in Saigon,' Maurice went on as though he was talking to himself as much as to me. 'Some of the teachers sent out from France were really very good, you know. But it was at university in Paris that I nearly lost my soul. That marvellous, clear reason; the way we were taught to cut through problems with cold analysis. But most of all there was that intoxicating feeling that man can change the world if he will. It was another planet from the Vietnamese world I had been brought up in. I'm not thinking of our superstitiousness and ignorance, though there was plenty of that even in a family like ours. It was mostly the sense of powerlessness, the feeling that we were at the world's mercy. I learned in Paris that that need not be so. But I was too lazy to do much about it. Yes, if I hadn't been lazy I would have been lost – to Vietnam at any rate.'

He laughed.

'Listen to that music. That's what happens when you try to bring the West to the East and it serves you right.'

The woman in white trousers had begun a solo. Her voice swooped and trilled. She put hands together as in prayer and fluttered her eyelids, her head on one side. At first I could not place the music for it was both familiar and strange. The audience listened with obvious admiration.

'Isn't it astonishing?' Maurice said. 'After one hundred years of Western civilisation we have learned how to turn the *Blue Danube* into a ridiculous song.'

His face had now turned from pink to red but he was far from being drunk.

'I'm sorry I've talked so much about myself but I wanted you to know a little about our family. You see, Thai does want to get out of the *maquis* and there would be all sorts of problems if he just came back to Saigon. To avoid being put in prison he'd have to come over publicly to the government side. They would want him to do propaganda for them and that would be very disagreeable. Very likely there would be people on both sides who would find it simpler if he were dead. So your offer of help is interesting. But you'll forgive me if I say I can't believe it is quite as pure as you make out.

'I mean I can believe the British government might like to help my brother in London and do him a favour. But this is rather a big favour, don't you think?'

I said I didn't follow him.

'My dear young Monsieur Bishop, in order to get this one not so very important Vietnamese away from the Vietcong the British government is apparently ready to . . . Well, let's make a list. First, it's ready to risk a scandal with the government here because it of course regards my nephew as a traitor. And yet you say the British would be ready to spirit Thai away without telling Saigon anything. And lastly you say this is just a British affair, which means the Americans know nothing about it. But I don't believe that anything of importance happens here without the Americans knowing about it. And if they know about it . . .'

He didn't finish for at that moment the woman brought the *Blue Danube* to a loud climax and there was enthusiastic applause even from the most languid of the pretty girls in the audience. The singer looked pleased with herself and after bowing several times sat down at a table next to an army officer.

'I think you should look carefully at that man,' Maurice said, nodding towards the soldier.

He was a stocky man, of a quite different race, one would have said, from the bamboo-like Maurice and Thai. He wore a tight-fitting camouflage combat uniform and his hair was shaved to the top of his head where it had been allowed to grow into short spikes. The face was that of a pugnacious schoolboy. We could just hear his voice from where we were sitting. He was talking excitedly and every now and then it rose to a fiercely high pitch. When that happened the sides of his mouth turned down and he looked like a boy who has been frustrated and is about to cry or shout from rage. The singer and the others at the table listened to him deferentially. He was not, I realised, angry, just putting on a show to make them laugh, but the performance seemed designed to remind them that he was capable of real and frightening anger.

I asked who he was.

'He is a colonel called Dinh. He is the man who catches the Vietcong in Saigon and would be very pleased to get his hands on Thai. He comes here a lot. I thought it would be instructive for you to see him. Does he frighten you?'

I said I didn't see what he could do to me.

'Oh, he would be most unlikely to arrest you. And of course if he didn't arrest you he couldn't torture you. But he could quite easily arrange for someone to throw a grenade into your car or your house. I am not trying to scare you – just to make sure you understand what you are getting involved in. Dinh isn't a bad fellow really. I went to school with his father. Their family had more luck with their land than we did. They were able to rent some of it to the Americans for a military base. But you see, even Dinh isn't really sure what's going to happen here. He looks like a tough colonel but he feels like a man on a raft in the middle of the sea and so he does very nasty things to anyone who he thinks might overturn it.'

The whisky had turned Maurice's face a darker, almost brownish red.

'I remember when I was in the *maquis* fighting the French – yes, I did that for a year or two, all of our family did though with differing degrees of enthusiasm. I was in a village just before a battle. I knew the place rather well. It was a big, lively village not far from our land. It had large, handsome houses with tiled roofs. But the day before the battle the villagers sensed that something was going to happen. They were burying their valuable things, locking their doors and escaping into the paddy fields. That village was like a condemned man waiting for the guillotine blade to fall.

'You are probably too young to understand that the world you know and that seems so steady can all of a sudden slip out of your fingers. But it can, you know. Sometimes at dawn I walk down the street outside my house and it is deserted like that village and I look up to the sky expecting to see the guillotine blade. It hasn't fallen on me yet, but it could, at almost any time. Dinh knows that too. That is why he is nervous and also very dangerous.'

He looked at his watch and said it was time to go. As he got up he said:

'I've taken a long time to come to the point. Thai wants to get out. But before we make any arrangements I must meet the man who is in charge for – you will forgive me, young Monsieur Bishop – it is obviously not you.'

I said nothing and he looked at me for a moment enquiringly. I imagined Gruson's reaction when I told him everything depended on his meeting Maurice Tran Dai Tan and shuddered. Outside Maurice gave me his card and told me to telephone to arrange the meeting. As we got into the car the boy he had asked to watch it ran up and I gave him some coins. The boy looked at them angrily. His mouth turned down at the corners as Colonel Dinh's had done and he threw the money on the ground.

'Better nothing than not enough. That's a real Vietnamese for you,' said Maurice and laughed.

6

The next day I telephoned Byrne at the Caravelle but the desk clerk said he was away for a week. Gruson had said that if I couldn't get hold of Byrne and I needed to get in touch urgently I could go round to the embassy. The important thing was not to telephone him or to go to his house.

I hadn't given much thought to this precaution at the time. If I had, I suppose I would have considered it rather pointless. But the evening with Maurice changed that. It had nothing to do with Colonel Dinh for I didn't believe he could harm me. It was Maurice who set me thinking. At first he had struck me as tremendously self-confident. But when I got home from the Pink Night what I remembered most was his wariness and the remark about waiting for the guillotine to fall. He seemed to live in a different, infinitely more disturbing world than mine. I couldn't imagine anything falling unexpectedly on my boss at the bank, let alone on the Oriental and Commercial. And yet I felt as though I had put a foot over into Maurice's world. His wariness had infected me.

I made an excuse to leave the bank early in the afternoon and drove over to the embassy. If it hadn't been for the Gurkha guard at the gate you could have mistaken it for one of those hotels on the Costa Brava where the plumbing isn't finished before the first package tourists arrive. The ambassador's sand-brown Jaguar was parked outside but it looked as though it had been put there for a publicity photograph and would soon be driven away never to return. I was shown into an empty waiting room where I had hardly time to examine colour photographs of the Queen and Concorde before I heard familiar footsteps. Gruson raised his eyebrows. I told him what had happened the night before. He folded his arms and put a finger to his chin. He was silent for a moment and then began to talk rapidly.

'If this man Maurice insists on meeting me then he'd better, and as soon as possible. Ring him up and try to arrange it in your house in the evening. Next, I want you to find a small house in a quiet part of the town. It would be a good idea to get Ba to help you but in that case you'll have to tell him a bit more. What do you think his reaction would be if you told him you're trying to get Thai out of Vietnam?'

I said I didn't think he would object. Gruson looked at me sternly and asked if I was sure. I explained what I felt about Ba and how I thought he would let himself be swept along by events.

'I hope you're right,' Gruson said, 'because if this thing really starts moving I suspect you and he will have to make another trip together into the countryside.'

House-hunting, another journey out of Saigon – Gruson took it for granted I wouldn't object to either. He was right, but he couldn't have suspected that I agreed partly out of curiosity about the world of Thai and Maurice, so different from Gruson's and all the more intriguing to a naïve young Englishman for that reason.

It was just after four o'clock when I left the embassy and since Gruson had stressed the need to hurry I walked towards Tu Do and the café where I had first met Ba. I knew there was a good chance of finding him there. There was a crowd of schoolchildren outside the post office standing round an old man who was shaving bits of ice into dirty-looking glasses. The children chose between a bottle of vivid red or green syrup which the man poured over the shaven ice. One of the boys who was shouting at the others to stop pushing looked familiar but it was only because, in his anger, he had the same petulantly tough face as Colonel Dinh and the urchin who had guarded Maurice's car. It reminded me that I had forgotten to tell Gruson about Dinh.

Ba was in the café. He was sitting with a Vietnamese man dressed in a khaki-coloured safari suit. He had a wispy beard growing on the end of his chin and wore rimless spectacles.

'Aha! A banker!' he said when Ba introduced me. 'You are the people with the real power. Money makes armies fight. Money makes revolutions – aren't I right?' He took a pipe from his pocket and started sucking it. He looked very pleased with himself.

'Monsieur Liem is a very well known journalist,' Ba said. 'He knows all the plots in Saigon even before the plotters themselves. Isn't that so, Liem?'

The man took his pipe from his mouth and waved it deprecatingly but in transparently mock modesty. Soon after he left, shaking my hand and giving me a look that I did not find altogether friendly. Ba watched him knowingly as he went out of the door and leaned towards me. 'You have to watch out for him. He's very close to the police. Some people say that he reports directly to Colonel Dinh. You know who he is, don't you?'

I said I did and left it at that but in spite of myself I felt a shifting of my stomach at the mention of the name. He seemed to be cropping up everywhere and I wondered if as soon as I was out on the street again I would come across yet another child in a tantrum reproducing the Colonel's expression of fury.

Ba interrupted my thoughts by asking if I needed him to do anything. I had come with no idea about how best to put Gruson's plan to him so I told him straight out that Thai wanted to leave Vietnam; that a man in the British embassy was involved; and that we needed to find somewhere to keep Thai safely in Saigon until he could be smuggled abroad. Ba was even more tense than usual while I talked, like a dog that doesn't know which of several scents to follow. Then he burrowed inside his camera bag and came up with a packet of American cigarettes. He fumbled as he lit one and started puffing the smoke out without inhaling as I had seen him do the first time we met. He seemed confused, rather than shocked, by what I had told him. Perhaps it was difficult for him to fit this new information into the puzzle he was always trying to solve in his head. After a few moments' silence he looked at me, his jaw stuck forward, which I had learnt to recognise as a sign that he thought he had the answer.

'*Voyez-vous*, Monsieur Michael, I always told Thai that he shouldn't go over to the other side. I said that with his background they would never really trust him. It was different in the old days. When we were fighting the French it didn't matter so much about being a communist. I don't expect Thai's Uncle Bernard, the one who is now in Hanoi, was really a communist when he first joined the *maquis*. Maurice wasn't, that's certain. But the war is different now. It has gone on for so long and so many people have been killed. The other side is suspicious of people who go over to them now, particularly if they come from a well-off family like Thai's. I told him that if he wanted to help them he would do better to stay in Saigon and do what he could for them here.'

He paused and then nodded his head.

'Yes, yes, I'll help. When shall we look for the house?'

He would have been out of the chair if I hadn't leant forward and put my hand on his shoulder. I told him to scout round for something on his own. He jumped up as soon as I took my hand away and hurried out, giving an absent-minded wave as he disappeared through the door.

He turned up the next evening at my house to report success. He had found a place belonging to a woman who was a distant relative and proposed that he drive me on his motorbike to look at it. We set off towards Cholon, the Chinese city, past the market and the railway station and down a road parallel to the tracks where the people had built shelters out of cardboard and plastic sheets. Naked children were playing next to mounds of rubbish. Just after a cinema showing Kung Fu movies Ba turned down a narrow street and then into an alley barely wide enough for two cars to pass. On one side there were a dozen houses, most of only one storey, and on the other a high blank wall protecting the back of a large villa.

Ba stopped in front of a house with a small porch filled with crates of empty bottles. He rattled the wooden shutters. There was a shuffling sound and one of the shutters opened a little and an old woman peered out. She had grey hair drawn into a bun and the face of a mistrustful mouse. When she saw Ba she simpered and smiled and let us in. A weak electric light bulb hung from the ceiling. A large part of the floor was covered with crates of Coca-Cola and beer. Dusty glass jars containing what looked like very old biscuits stood on a small table and against the back wall was a large black cupboard inlaid with mother-of-pearl flowers. The old woman went over to a large Japanese calendar with a picture of a girl in a prim bathing suit and took a key from behind it.

She led us out of the house, putting a padlock on the wooden shutters, and shuffled to the house next door. This had a modern cement front and a heavy door of opaque glass covered by an iron grille. It screeched as Ba and I helped her push it aside.

The house was a long, narrow box, each room giving on to the next. The first two rooms were divided by a wall that went up only two thirds of the way to the ceiling. There was a sofa and two armchairs covered with green plastic in the first room and a bed in the second. The rest of the house was divided off by a proper wall. A wire screen window and door gave onto a tiled area where there was a large refrigerator, a tap, and a water tank partly enclosed in what looked like a cupboard. When the woman opened the cupboard door there was a crackling sound as two shiny brown cockroaches hurried out of the light. She pointed to a hole in the floor.

'*Voilà le cabinet, monsieur,*' she said proudly.

Another screen door led into a small kitchen that consisted of two rings connected to a cylinder of gas standing on a white tiled shelf. Something rustled on top of the corrugated iron roof and then dropped heavily onto the wall where the house ended. Ba said, 'It's nothing serious. It's a rat.'

The woman paid no attention and led us back through the house. I noticed that the side walls in the washing area beyond the bedroom did not go up all the way to the roof and that there was an open space into the back parts of the old woman's house and the one on the other side. She stopped at the front door and clasped her hands and in her heavily accented French began praising the house. It was not air-conditioned but it was cool. It was quiet. And it cost only forty dollars a month. Ba started to bargain with her but I thought it might be useful to have her good will. I said I would take it from the following week.

The house had a curious effect on me. Like all empty houses it seemed to be waiting for something to happen but I could not imagine that I was ever meant to be part of those tragedies and comedies for which it was fated to be the stage. The old woman, though, seemed to regard me as an ideal tenant and as we drove off she was standing among the crates on the veranda making little noises of gratitude.

'She's a greedy old woman,' Ba said as we turned the corner. 'But she has a pretty daughter.'

I asked where the husband was.

'Oh, she's never had a husband. She used to be housekeeper to a French priest and the girl is his child.'

Ba turned round to look at me and laughed.

'Ho! Ho! Ho!'

7

My attempt to get Maurice to meet Gruson was not so successful. When I telephoned to say that my 'British friend' was ready to meet him he insisted that we both be his guests at lunch the following Sunday and there was nothing I could say to budge him.

'To be quite honest with you,' Gruson said as we were waiting for Maurice to pick us up at my house, 'I don't trust this man. He's too close to the communists and he's too close to the French. It's when you come up against people like him that you realise how utterly buggered up this place is. And because he's buggered up he probably takes a lot of pleasure in buggering up other people.'

Gruson, nevertheless, did not look worried. In fact he was looking particularly glossy. His shoes were highly polished and he had put some lemon-scented dressing on his neatly parted hair so that it, too, shone. As usual he wore the sleeves of his cream silk shirt rolled down, and from the left one was visible the corner of a silk bandana.

It was obvious, too, that Maurice had dressed for the occasion. His shirt was in better condition than the one he had worn at our first meeting but it was his feet that both Gruson and I stared at. He was wearing a pair of heavy brown and white golf shoes and although they were so old that the leather was flaking away in places they signalled that their owner was a man who knew his way around the world.

Maurice announced that he was taking us to a special restaurant just outside the city and sat us in the Citroën. During the drive he and Gruson discussed Paris as though they had nothing more urgent to talk about. The restaurant was in a dusty little town that was almost part of the city suburbs and at first I thought Maurice had made a mistake for the place looked abandoned. There was a small swimming pool, quite empty except for dead leaves and old newspapers, and a row of what had once been changing rooms from which came a strong smell of urine. A large, ragged thatched roof in the shape of a tent sheltered some tables. Two unhealthy-looking dogs got up when they saw us, yawning apprehensively.

'It is not as smart as it once was,' said Maurice coolly, 'but they do some things here that you can't usually find in Saigon.'

When a girl appeared he asked Gruson to let him do the ordering and began a lively conversation with her in Vietnamese, several times nodding his head in satisfaction. First she brought us glasses with large roughly cut pieces of ice. Maurice put his hand over each of the glasses and tipped them upside down to let out the melted ice water.

'Have you ever noticed,' he asked, shaking the water from his hand, 'that almost the first industry a colonial power establishes is a brewery and ice-making plant, like our own dear Brasserie et Glacerie d'Indochine in Saigon? In poor little Laos I believe it was the only industry. But at least if it brought profits to the coloniser it brought comfort to the colonised.'

'The only trouble is that the French have never known how to make beer,' Gruson said. Maurice tilted his head, a sign that his politeness was inexhaustible.

'That may be true. But you can't blame us for it. The French chose us, not us them. I often try to imagine what this country would have been like if the British had colonised us but I can't, you know. It is like trying to imagine a motor car without wheels. It's a pointless exercise.'

The girl put some white eggs in plastic holders in front of us.

'This is one of the specialities of the place,' Maurice explained, picking up an egg and cutting off the top with an expert chop of his spoon to reveal a deep orange yolk. I tried to imitate him but it was harder than it seemed. The white part of the egg was almost as tough as rubber. When I did manage to push my spoon through to the yolk I felt something solid. I poked around a bit before I realised that it was a tiny embryo chicken, its head, feet and wings clearly formed. I looked at Gruson. He had just started his first egg and was examining what he had struck.

'Good God,' he said and put down his spoon.

'How do you find it?' Maurice asked, as though he had noticed nothing. 'The principle is simple. The eggs are allowed to fertilise and then you can eat them at various stages, after six days, twelve days, or even more. The yolk becomes very rich. In fact (he was still paying no attention to our reluctance to eat) this is already somewhat westernised for in the old days we used duck eggs which were of course far richer and had a stronger taste.'

He took a second egg, removed its top as deftly as he had the first, and plunged his spoon into the yolk. Gruson looked away. Only when he had eaten the second egg did Maurice look at our unfinished ones. I could have sworn that for a fraction of a second he smiled.

'Of course, not everyone likes them so please don't eat any more if you find it disagreeable.'

I put my spoon down. A tiny head hung over the top of the egg that Gruson had opened. The girl came with the next course. She giggled when she saw what we had left.

She replaced the eggs with small, stuffed pancakes that had been fried in oil till they were crisp, a plate of lettuce and other green leaves, and bowls of a clear brown sauce in which floated prettily cut slices of carrot. Maurice took a lettuce leaf and some of the smaller leaves and using chopsticks put a pancake in the middle and wrapped the leaves around it. He dipped this green tube into the brown liquid. Gruson and I followed him but with considerably less deftness.

Gruson, whom I knew to be fond of his food, was tucking into the pancakes with enthusiasm, but he did not let it distract him. He was a man who liked to be in control of the situation and the business of the eggs had been a point to Maurice. He went over into the counter-attack.

'Monsieur Tan' (he had not used the name Maurice once), 'If your nephew wants to get out we can help him. With Michael's assistance I can get him to Saigon and then to Europe. It should be perfectly safe but both you and he should understand that you will have to do what I say.'

Maurice did not object but also gave no sign of being impressed. He called for more beer and announced that the next course was particularly interesting. It would be a chicken roasted with spices to be eaten with a cake of sticky rice that was also cooked in the oven. I thought Gruson was going to lose his temper when Maurice started to explain in detail how the chicken and rice were prepared. Probably that was what Maurice wanted for he was obviously teasing him. Gruson puckered his lips as if to rein himself in but when the chicken and gold brown rice cake were brought they were so good that his humour improved in spite of himself. And it was only then that Maurice began to talk seriously.

'I have a question to ask you, Monsieur Gruson. Why are you so anxious to help my nephew? I am touched that you should be so sympathetic to his father's feelings. Of course he is very worried about his son. Thai could easily get killed or fall ill. The Viets have very few good medicines at the moment and I would not like to be operated on by one of their doctors in the jungle, would you? But as I already told Michael I can't see why the British government should go to such trouble for the sake of my family. I don't believe there is anything my brother in London can do for you in return. So I have to conclude that there is something you hope to get out of Thai. What is it?'

Gruson looked neither surprised nor put out. In fact no one

could have sounded more understanding. It really was true that London wanted to do Thai's father a favour. But Maurice was right that there was another reason. I looked at Gruson then with as much interest as Maurice. I hadn't been told of another reason. Gruson's manner became flatteringly confidential.

'It's a delicate matter because it has to do with our support for the Americans here, and for the Saigon government too, for that matter. The truth is we don't see anything wrong in helping people like your nephew who may not be happy with either side in this war. One day there may be a chance of a compromise and to make that work you'll need people who've shown they've a capacity as leaders and who aren't compromised themselves.'

Thai, he went on, was such a person. One day the Americans might thank London, but not yet. So a risk had to be taken. Of course there was no obligation on Thai. Once out of Vietnam he would just be in reserve. Anything more would be his decision.

Gruson glanced at me. I took this to mean that if I was surprised by what he said I was to say nothing in front of Maurice. But Maurice showed no astonishment. He had a chicken leg in his right hand and having carefully chewed off the cartilage was crunching the end to extract the last juices from inside the bone. He already had a pile of bones on his plate that looked like dry twigs.

He gave the chicken leg a final crunch and put it down.

'I'm flattered you think so highly of my nephew, but you are right to. Let me tell you about him. Towards the end of our war against the French Thai's father was working in the Delta as a civil servant. Thai, still not a teenager, stayed in Saigon with his mother's sister who had a big house and a large family of her own. She and her husband were pro-French but their children . . .' He stopped and laughed. 'I once went round there by chance on a May Day. The grown-ups were out and the children were putting on an anti-French show. They had made a stage and hung up blurred photos of Stalin and Mao and Uncle Ho, too, of course. The servants were the audience and Thai was squatting at the front. He was only ten, I think. They were all singing when I came in. It took a few minutes before I realised it was the *Internationale*. The little Thai's eyes were shining and he was singing at the top of his voice.

'I promised I wouldn't say a word to the parents. The next

year Thai's two eldest cousins, both girls, went off to the *maquis*. Their mother tried to stop them but in the end she went round all the Indian shops to find the best material possible for their black pyjamas. I'm sure the girls protested. "Communism means an equal share for everyone" was what they used to tell our servants.'

He looked at us, still laughing at his own story, and lit a cigarette.

'It was an intoxicating atmosphere for a child to grow up in. Those girls – they shouldn't have done it – used the little Thai to take messages for them when they were making their contacts in preparation for going to the *maquis*. They also used to take him when they went out to distribute anti-French leaflets. Who was going to suspect two pretty schoolgirls in Western frocks leading a neatly dressed little boy by the hand? The only time they tripped up was when they took him to the funeral of a student the French had shot during a demonstration. The resistance had ordered everyone to attend. Their *lycée* expelled them for that and soon after they went on hunger strike to make their parents let them join the guerillas.

'Of course Thai drank it all in. That big old house, with its family love and young idealism still protected from the real harshness of the world, allowed him to grow up with the best sort of faith, imitating good people whom he loved. That was why he was such a fine student leader. The others knew they could trust him, that he wouldn't use them. And that's why he was such a good catch for the communists. He made them look good. He has that knack.' He paused, sighed, and went on. 'Now it is my turn to make a confession. We are desperate to get Thai out. The communists, you see, want to test him. You know that he isn't a party member yet. They've no more work for him writing declarations to the Saigon intellectuals. The war isn't going well enough for the communists for that to work. You see, Thai had hoped that there was more to the Vietcong than just the communists. Others have thought so, too, though I didn't believe it. But he wouldn't listen to me. I suppose he had to find out for himself. Now it seems he's come to the conclusion that Hanoi does control the Vietcong. He thinks they are going to ask him to join one of the terrorist squads in Saigon. If he refuses they'll never trust him again. If he agrees, the way things are going these days the chances are that Colonel Dinh – I think you've both heard of him – will catch him. The Saigon police are doing rather well these days, at least when it comes to catching Vietcong.'

Gruson had entirely recovered himself. It was as though there had been no ghastly eggs, no Maurice goading him by seizing control of the lunch. He even seemed to take Maurice's last remark as a compliment to himself. At least I thought he made a slight bow in Maurice's direction. Over the coffee, which was served in the same metal contraptions that had so embarrassed me at my first dinner with Gruson, they discussed how Thai was to be extracted. Maurice had a plan which he outlined in a theatrically conspiratorial manner, holding his cigarette and holder so that they hid his mouth from some people who had come into the restaurant after us. The idea seemed simple enough. Thai was expecting in three days time to be near the house of an old cousin south-west of Saigon. He thought he could slip away. My job was to be to pick him up in my car, get him through the police checks on Saigon's outskirts – easy enough, for Westerners were seldom stopped – and bring him to the house I'd rented. Gruson too seemed satisfied. On the way back from the restaurant he even sang French songs with Maurice.

Maurice taught him one that went

Saigon I love you
But I love Paris more

But he changed as soon as Maurice had dropped us off.

'Christ,' he said, giving the disappearing black Citroën a look of fury. 'That man really is impossible. Fertilised eggs. He did it on purpose – you understand that, don't you? The old bugger.' He said nothing about the new reason he'd produced for wanting to help Thai, and although it puzzled me I did not press him.

He took his handkerchief from his shirt sleeve and gave his nose a trumpet-like blow as though it would help rid him of the abominable Maurice.

'I told you he was an old bugger, didn't I, and by God I was right. We're going to have to look out for him.'

8

It wasn't clear to me what Gruson meant by 'looking out' for Maurice for three days later I was up at dawn in order to carry out precisely the plan he had proposed. I was still shaving when Ba arrived. He was as eager to be off as a puppy waiting to be taken for a walk and while I finished in the bathroom I could hear him wandering impatiently round the sitting room. The early start was necessary because Maurice had insisted it would be dangerous for Thai to wait for long at the cousin's house. As soon as the Vietcong realised he had made a breakaway they would send out people to look for him so Ba and I were to be there in time to whisk him away the moment he arrived.

I tried to persuade Ba to have a cup of coffee because I wanted one but the idea of such an unnecessary delay horrified him. He said we could stop somewhere on the way. Stopping once the journey had already started apparently didn't worry him, perhaps because by then he would already have the delightful feeling of being in motion.

I was relieved he didn't comment on my clothes. On our first trip into the countryside I'd worn slacks and shirt that had seemed fine when I bought them in Regent Street. But among the Vietcong I'd felt distinctly uncomfortable in them. Most of my London clothes didn't even seem right for Saigon where the Cercle Sportif crowd dressed with more panache than I was used to. I'd even considered buying a gold identity bracelet – they were much favoured at the Cercle – until I remembered that Byrne wore one. But I did go down to a tailor on Tu Do to order what he called a 'four-pocket shirt', sand-coloured and to be worn outside a pair of matching trousers. The effect was faintly military and, I hoped, more dashing than anything else in my wardrobe. I was shy about wearing it but I don't suppose Ba even noticed the change.

It felt odd to be driving Ba, who made an uneasy passenger. He lent forward in his seat giving instructions about the road to take out of the city. Saigon's pretence to organisation and dignity, never very convincing, collapsed entirely as we got to the outskirts. There were a few houses, gaunt concrete boxes that looked as though their builders' money had run out before they could be finished, but mostly there were desperate shacks of wood and tin, cardboard and plastic, set along the edges of fields that had the sickly look of all land that is close to a big city. It was in these unpromising surroundings that Ba proposed we look for somewhere to have our breakfast. He pointed at some wooden kiosks down the road. People were squatting in front of them on stools and a little further on there was a line of buses.

'This is where people catch the buses to the Delta,' Ba said, 'and the main police check on traffic going in and out of Saigon is here too. So it's a good place for cafés.'

We found two empty stools and a boy with a gold Buddha on a chain that hung outside his dirty tee-shirt brought us glasses of coffee and a long French loaf. The coffee, which was thick and dark, had been poured onto a layer of condensed milk at the bottom of the glass. It was powerful and good and so was the bread which was still warm from the baker's.

Ba, who had been looking over the shoulder of the man next to us to look at his newspaper, tapped my arm.

'It says that there has been a plague of insects in the village where the president was born.' I asked him if that was significant and he replied that people would take it as an omen. Good or bad, I asked. Ba consulted with the man with the newspaper. Bad, he announced, and they both laughed.

I suppose I ought myself to have been looking for omens for the success of our trip but the truth is that I wasn't the least bit worried. Our first expedition at the New Year to make contact with Thai had gone so smoothly that I had no fears about this second one. The moments of apprehension during our night in the rubber plantation having proved groundless, I even felt a sort of invulnerability.

The drive was easy except for the little buses that we had seen drawn up by the coffee stalls. They drove at top speed with their conductors, young boys, leaning out of the back door and yelling and gesturing to slower traffic to get out of the way. Since they stopped every few miles the same buses would keep on overtaking us, but each time the conductor shouted with triumph as though they were leaving us behind for good.

We stopped outside My Tho to ask the way to the cousin's village. There were market gardens on both sides of the road and the fresh morning air carried the smell of young vegetables, the smell of any English garden on a summer day. The village was at first just as reassuring. It was only two miles off the main road and looked suburbanly prosperous. Small tiled houses stood between neat clumps of palm trees, well-tended flowers and bushes. But towards the end of the village the palm trees grew thicker and here we turned off down a track till we reached a clearing across which stood a house far larger than those we had just passed. It, too, had a tiled roof but it swept down in a noble curve to cover a veranda that ran the length of the house. The clearing itself had once been a garden. There were the outlines of ponds and paths and here and there large blue and white ceramic pots that had once been planted with flowers. A pig was penned into a space near the veranda and there were some unhealthy-looking chickens around the steps.

Ba got out and shouted something in Vietnamese. There was no answer except from the hens who raised a feeble cry of alarm. Ba hurried in front of me and disappeared inside the house. The veranda floor was covered in chicken droppings and feathers. There were two broken-down cane chairs and a table with a large ashtray that said PERNOD.

Ba came out followed by an old woman in shiny black trousers and a grey jacket.

'It's the right house. The old man's inside. This is the woman who looks after him. His wife is dead. There's no sign of Thai.'

The woman gestured to me to go in. The house was one great room, open to the roof which was supported by round pillars of dark polished wood. I'd never seen so much dust anywhere. The chairs, tables and wooden beds were covered with it and it lay thick enough on the floor to preserve layers of old footprints. The woman took us to the side of the room where a partition had been put up.

Inside an old man in pyjama trousers and vest was lying on a reed mat on top of a small wooden bed. He was looking at a newspaper. A boy, scarcely more than a baby, lay asleep by his side, his thumb stuck in his mouth. The man was very old. The pale skin was drawn tightly over the bones of his face and his wrists and arms were so thin I wondered how he managed to hold up his paper. He turned his head towards us.

'*Soyez le bienvenu, monsieur*, I've been waiting for you.'

He spoke French with a strong Vietnamese twang. The woman pushed forward a chair which she wiped with her hand and made me sit down.

'You have come to help our family and I am very grateful. You can see for yourself what a state we have come to.' He waved a fragile arm. 'You have seen the garden. It is a pigsty. In the old days, when the French were here, we lived properly. But now I daren't even go out. The Vietcong, you know. They are looking for people like me.'

He stopped and looked blank as though he had forgotten what he had said. Then he remembered.

'You see, I must take care,' he whispered.

His face went blank again. He looked at the sleeping child and then picked up the paper as though we did not exist.

As we went out Ba whispered to me, 'He's an old opium-smoker. He doesn't make much sense any more.' I asked him how he knew? '*Moi, je sais*' was the answer and he would not add any more.

There was nothing to do but wait. Ba went off to explore the village. I walked round the big room. There were three large cupboards against the back wall, each inlaid with fine mother-of-pearl flowers, far grander than the ones in the old woman's house: I found the mother-of-pearl's acid, underwater colours oddly threatening. Incense sticks and a bouquet of plastic flowers, their colour almost vanished beneath the dust, stood on the top of each cupboard. Photographs hung on the walls, showing people in both Vietnamese and Western clothes. In one of them some young men in flannels and shirts stood round a low, long-bonneted car. I tried to make out Maurice among them but the glass was too stained and their faces had become almost indistinguishable on the faded photographic paper. Perhaps they were Thai's father and his brothers, so alike then but now scattered by the years of war and transformed into fighters and non-combatants, sceptics and believers.

I was examining two pendulum clocks, neither of them working, that hung in fine wooden cases when I noticed an unpleasant sweet smell, like a mixture of burning sugar and rubber, coming from the partition behind which the old man lay. I went closer and saw the old woman kneeling on the floor and holding the end of a long pipe that the old man was drawing on. The child was awake and waving its arms and legs in the air.

Ba came in and sniffed the air.

'What did I tell you?' he said, pleased with himself, 'opium.'

We waited, but Thai did not come. At midday the old woman brought us rice, vegetables, and fish, and in two delicate blue and white china bowls a clear brown liquid: *nuoc mam*, the fish sauce which Ba, after tasting it carefully, declared to be particularly fine. When we had eaten Ba said he would take a siesta and lay down on a wooden bed. I couldn't see myself getting much rest on one of those so I went onto the veranda and sat in one of the broken chairs, pulling up the other for my feet. It was now very hot and the high sun had taken away all the delicate colours of early morning. The palm trees could have been made of metal, for all the freshness that was left in them, and the abandoned garden looked no more alive than those little artificial trees and shrubs that architects put around models of their buildings.

A monotonous chant, like the low groan of a bagpipe, came from the house behind me. The woman had put the child in a basket which she had slung on a crossbeam between the wooden pillars. She pushed it slowly backwards and forwards, chanting as she did so. Ba looked up when I came to the door.

'She's singing a lullaby' he said. I asked him what it was about.

'Oh, most of them are sad. This one says: "Can you gather all the dead leaves in the forest, can you catch the wind in the sky?" My mother used to sing it to me.'

The heat and the woman's insistent singing made me feel drowsy and I went back to my chair on the veranda. I slept and began to dream, what about I don't remember except that the dream ended in a shout. It was a moment before I realised that the shouting was real. It came from the far side of the garden. Where the palm trees ended and the clearing began a man was on his knees, struggling to get out of one of the dried-out and now overgrown ornamental ponds. He got on his feet and moved unsteadily towards the house, holding his arms straight and away from his body like a little boy playing aeroplanes. Until I realised that he had grey hair I thought it was Thai. The man was wearing old tennis shoes, grey trousers and a white shirt whose long sleeves flapped unbuttoned on his outstretched arms.

He tripped and almost fell again and when he managed to reach the bottom of the steps his eyes were wide and staring from the effort. I took his arm and guided him to my chair. He looked at me, a mixture of gratitude and surprise. *'Merci M'sieur. Merci M'sieur.'* He repeated the words each time he breathed out.

Roused by the noise Ba appeared, inquisitive and commanding. He at once started to interrogate the old man who waved his arms in a despairing way as he answered, stopping every now and then to throw an appealing glance towards me. Finally he leant back in the chair and pulled out a dirty handkerchief with which he mopped his face.

'The plan has gone wrong,' Ba said.

I wasn't surprised. When I saw the old man struggling across the garden I had had a presentiment that things were going to go wrong and that Maurice's plan might be less than foolproof.

Ba said that Thai had been in a village a three-mile walk away across the fields as had been agreed. He had been meaning to leave there early in the morning and had he managed to he would have been waiting for us at the house when we arrived. But the government had unexpectedly launched an operation that very morning and when Thai had struck out across the rice fields he had found his way blocked by the government forces preparing to sweep through the area. He might have tried to bluff his way through but the chances of his being arrested were too great so he had stayed put. The village where he was wasn't fully controlled by either side. The government troops hadn't tried to enter it yet but they probably would hoping to find Vietcong agents and sympathisers. The old man was called Do and was himself a distant relation of the old opium-smoker and therefore of Thai, too, which explained why he was helping. He told Ba that the Vietcong occasionally used him as a runner because his age and innocent appearance made it easy for him to pass through government checkpoints. He also, Ba added, had a plan for 'saving the situation.'

I looked at Mr Do who was lying back in his chair and staring about him as though he could not understand where he was. He did not look capable of producing a single thought, let alone a plan, but Ba would have none of it.

'I know his type,' he said firmly. 'He looks like a silly old man but underneath he is cunning.'

9

At first hearing, Do's plan sounded as simple as the one that had gone wrong. We would take my car and drive into the village where Thai was before the government troops got there. Thai had told Do that he would stay there unless the Saigon soldiers moved in. We would pick up Thai, hide him on the floor of the car and drive out with him. The police and soldiers wouldn't stop us because I was a Westerner and because we would take good care to show ourselves to them on our way to the village. They would see three people driving out and three people driving back.

I objected that we had to have a reason for going to the village in the first place. What would we say if we were stopped and asked why we wanted to go there? Wasn't there something special about the village that we could use as a pretext?

When Ba put this to Mr Do the latter nodded vigorously. He turned to me and started to speak in French slowly and in the same twangy accent as the opium-smoker. Yes, there was a tomb in the village belonging to a famous general, a great patriot who fought the French a hundred years before. It was a very important place, Do said, and even foreigners went to see it.

I looked at Ba for his reaction but he was already rummaging through his camera bag which I knew was a sign that he was preparing to move off.

'*On y va?*' he said, looking at me eagerly.

I could have said no. We could have turned down Mr Do and been back in Saigon in a couple of hours. In my gut that was what I wanted to do because I didn't believe in Do's judgement. But with the two of them standing and looking at me with all the innocent expectation of people about to set off on a picnic I couldn't say no. I didn't want to seem afraid. But I also felt I was being drawn along by invisible threads attached by Gruson, Maurice and Thai himself. Gruson's thread was fear of his scorn, Maurice's, fear of turning out the foolish young English man he seemed to believe that I was. Thai's thread I could not quite make out but I knew I would feel guilty if I broke it now.

It was after three o'clock when we got into the car. Do sat in the back but he leaned forward so that his head was in between Ba's and mine. The village was eight miles away by road. The rice had been harvested and the fields were brown with stubble and there was no one to be seen. Ba had noticed that too.

'I don't like it,' he said, 'it's too quiet.'

Mr Do protested from the back seat. It was all right. He knew the area well. We only had to trust him.

After ten minutes we passed the first soldiers. They were sitting beside the road and made no attempt to stop us. I waved at them and one or two waved back.

We drove on for another mile through still deserted countryside. The few houses we did pass seemed to be unoccupied. The second lot of soldiers we saw did stop us. A young man in black pyjamas and a camouflaged bush hat walked over to the car. I smiled at him but he didn't smile back. Ba lent across me and greeted the young man as though he were an old friend. The latter seemed bored by Ba's explanation of where we were going. He wore a gold identity bracelet on his wrist and had left uncut the nail on the little finger of his left hand. It was an inch long and ended in a nasty point. He looked at Ba as one might at a child telling a foolish story. When Ba finished he said nothing but shrugged and stepped back from the car.

'*On y va. On y va,*' Ba said urgently. 'I told him where we were going and he didn't try to stop us.'

'It's all right,' echoed Mr Do, 'I know these people. They're always like that.'

'You mustn't take such people too seriously,' Ba said. 'They just think they are very important. Did you see his fingernail? That's to show he doesn't have to work with his hands. He thinks he's a little mandarin.' He laughed.

'*C'est vrai. C'est vrai,*' Mr Do sang into my ear.

We went round a bend and saw the village. As Do leant

forward to point out the general's tomb there was a whirring noise above us, followed seconds later by an explosion, and then more whirring and another explosion. I stopped the car and looked at Ba. He sat very straight in his seat looking to the right and then left as though there had to be an explanation somewhere. He seemed more indignant than afraid.

'It's nothing unusual,' Mr Do said calmly. 'It's just the government artillery. But it's not falling near us. You can see the shells are landing beyond the village.'

He was right. Little brown clouds hung above the ground a good mile away from the houses in front of us. I drove on. The road surface, never good, began to vanish and soon it turned to dirt. Ba noticed this and began talking agitatedly to Do who waved his arms in grand unconcern.

'You must follow the tracks the other cars have left,' Ba said urgently. 'This is the kind of road the VC sometimes mine because they can dig it up so easily. But if we go where the other cars have been we should be all right.'

I asked what Do said about it.

'He says sometimes there are mines and sometimes there aren't. He usually walks to the village across the fields.'

I gave Ba a look of what I hoped was measured disapproval but he didn't notice. He was peering at the dusty tracks ahead, his forehead almost touching the windscreen. I decided I had better do the same. It kept my mind off the shells which still intermittently whirred above us.

The village, or that bit of it we could see, consisted of a line of houses stretching down the side of a canal until they disappeared under the cover of trees and, on the right of the road, a low concrete building with a corrugated iron roof that Do said was the school. There was a piece of worn grass in front of it and I turned the car round so that it pointed back down the road along which we had come. Its dirt surface, although safely negotiated once, looked as welcoming as a sea full of sharks.

The village was silent and apparently deserted. Neither Ba nor Do hurried to get out of the car till I reminded them that we had to get back while it was still light. Ba put his hand on Do's back and gave him a gentle push in the direction of the houses. The old man walked across the road with the delicacy of a cat trying not to get its feet wet and went down a path along the houses. He turned and waved to us and we waved back.

It was obvious that his confidence in his own plan was ebbing. I was already convinced that we were doing something very silly and so, I guessed, was Ba though I knew he would not admit it. He stood watching the disappearing Do, his chin stuck out, challenging fate to a fight.

The artillery shells were now falling on a line of trees and had started small fires. A small plane circled above. There was a crackling sound, like electric wires being rubbed together, from the direction of the path that Mr Do had taken. It was followed by a popping noise.

Ba ran towards the path and shouted, 'They're shooting down there.' We could not see far because the path veered to the right and bushes and banana trees blocked our view. That's what guns sound like, I thought to myself. It wasn't so frightening after all.

'I don't understand,' Ba said, 'nobody said anything about the government soldiers being here.'

I reminded him that the unpleasant young man in black hadn't said anything at all. We started to move down the path after Mr Do when something coughed and seconds afterwards came a great bang. Leaves and pieces of wood rose into the air about fifty yards in front of us. We both fell to the ground.

'Mortars,' shouted Ba.

I looked back at the car. I had a strong urge to run back to it, and drive off down the road as fast as I could, mines or no mines. But I just said 'fuck' out loud. There was another bang, but no closer than the first.

Ba grabbed my arm and pointed down the path. Two stooping figures were coming towards us. They wore camouflage uniforms and both carried rifles. One of them was also carrying a half-open tin of sardines and the other a black cooking pot full of rice. The two soldiers laughed then they saw us but didn't say anything. They went round the back of the house nearest to the road, took out spoons and squatted down to eat.

Ba went over to them. They answered him politely but without showing any interest in why we were there.

'I don't understand.' Ba turned to me. 'They say there's a VC company at the other end of the village and that the government is bringing up reinforcements. They say it could be quite a big battle.'

The soldiers hadn't seen Mr Do. Had he got hurt by the mortars? We looked at each other, knowing that we ought to go down the path to look for him. Do saved us the decision. A familiar cry turned our heads. He was running slowly towards us, arms away from his sides, dirt on his trousers, shirt and face. He was out of breath when he reached us. The two soldiers, showing curiosity for the first time, walked over.

Mr Do produced a giggle. He seemed quite unfrightened. He gestured at his clothes. *'Je suis tombé dans le nuoc mam,'* he said and giggled again.

'Where is Thai?' Ba hissed at him in French. Do shrugged. When the first mortar fell he had been only half way down the village. The villagers had left and there were government troops everywhere.

I said that we should leave at once. Ba, to my relief, agreed. After seeing Do and hearing us talk French the soldiers had become suspicious and I wanted to get away from them too. We walked back to the car without looking at them and had just got in when there was a roaring above our heads followed by a deafening sound as though a vast pile of bricks had been poured from a great height onto the ground.

We fell out of the car and into a shallow depression that ran along the side of the road. I was gratified to note that Mr Do at last looked scared. But across the road the two soldiers were laughing at us. They were still squatting, spoon in hand. They shouted at Ba.

'It was a helicopter,' Ba said. 'It came over low and we didn't see it. It was just above us when it fired its rockets into the village where the Vietcong are.'

He grinned and we helped Mr Do back into the car. I very much wished that the old man had never entered my life. As I got in the crackling started again and this time the two soldiers put away their spoons and lay down. They dragged their rifles towards them and began firing down the road in the opposite direction to the one we had come from. Little puffs of dirt shot up from the grass around us.

'The VC are shooting at us,' Ba said, sounding more surprised than frightened. God, I thought, don't flood the carburettor, but the engine started first time and I put my foot hard on the accelerator. We bounced down the dirt road.

'Don't worry about the mines,' Ba shouted. 'Keep driving.' We both bent forward as far as we could. There were silent explosions of dust from the road as bullets struck to our left but nothing hit us. I didn't slow up until we had reached the metalled surface and the village was out of sight. I turned round to see how Do was bearing up. He was lying back in his seat smiling. 'That was like a cowboy movie,' he said and closed his eyes.

10

I've never slept so uncomfortably as I did that night on one of the old man's wooden beds. A thin rush mat laid over its polished surface took away none of the hardness. I had to put the small pillow I had been given under my side to protect the point where my hip pressed on the mat and the black wooden planks beneath. Every now and then, sitting up to rub my sore bones, I looked enviously at Ba and Mr Do whose bodies seemed to be floating on feather mattresses. Eventually I managed to fall asleep by lying on my back but each time woke up when I turned on my side and a knee or an elbow hit the bed.

When this happened at dawn I gave up and went out onto the veranda. Soft colours were coming back to the overgrown garden and the palm trees beyond it. The air was fresh. It was a different country from that of the midday sun: gentle and hopeful where the other was harsh and despairing. But which was the real country? The search for Thai seemed to be taking me more and more deeply into the midday with its exhausted colours and pressing heat.

It had been getting dark when we got back to the old man's house: too late, Ba said, to drive on to Saigon. I was angrier with myself and Ba for having trusted Mr Do than I was with Do himself. How could I have thought that he would manage to lead us to Thai when the plan had already gone so badly wrong? I blamed Ba for not having given me a hint that Do might be erratic. Ba, in self-defence, still insisted that the old man wasn't the fool he looked. Hadn't he done errands for the Vietcong for years and never been caught? In the old days he had been a civil servant for the French in the provincial town of My Tho. 'I know his type,' he said again. 'He often pretends to be silly so that people shouldn't think he's *rusé*.'

As for Mr Do, he was not so much impenitent as unaware that he had done anything that might be criticised. He behaved as though what had happened in the village had, for him, been a quite ordinary afternoon. And when we were sitting on the veranda after dinner he announced off-handedly as though it should not surprise us in the least that he still had one more plan for getting at Thai.

Thai had told him that if anything went wrong and we were unable to extract him from the village he would set off on foot in the opposite direction towards another village some ten miles away. He knew a monk there who ran a pagoda and who would shelter him. This village was controlled by the government so he should be safe there, for a while at least, from any search parties the communists might send after him. The village with the pagoda was close to the main road to Saigon. It would be easy for us to stop there on our way back to the city.

Watching the dawn fill the garden I said to myself what I had thought many times the evening and night before. If there was this one last chance we had to take it. I could escape the feeling of obligation to Thai no more than I could the painful planks of the old opium-smoker's bed. Ever since I had seen Do struggling across the garden the previous midday I had been troubled by a feeling of no longer being in control of events but rather in their grip. Wasn't this what I had already felt about Ba, a man who appeared driven this way and that by events which he no longer even tried to influence but accepted and then dealt with as best he could? I wasn't surprised that Ba at once nodded approval to Mr Do's new plan but I was still surprised that I accepted it almost as easily.

Ba got up while I was standing looking out over the garden. He produced his damp flannel from its plastic bag and rubbed his face and then hurried over to the far side of the veranda, holding a small, thin piece of metal in the shape of a U. Holding it at both ends he used it to give his tongue a vigorous scrape, stopping once or twice to spit into the garden.

Do rose from his bed as easily as a curl of mist. He needed even less preparation to face the day than Ba. He smoothed his hair with his hands and spat into a spittoon by the door. The old woman brought us bowls of sticky rice mixed with peanuts and slices of sausage the colour of bright red lacquer, and a grimy pot of bitter, yellow tea. Ba and Do ate in quiet concentration. I just drank the tea.

The old opium-smoker was playing with the little boy when we went behind his partition to say goodbye. He didn't seem surprised that we were leaving and he did not ask about Thai.

'Come back and see me again, Monsieur, if the communists don't kill me first.'

He turned back to the child and tickled its stomach. There was a strong, sweet smell of opium.

'These old landlords,' Ba said as we walked to the car. 'Look at the money they once had and what's happened to them now.'

'Opium took some of it, the communists took some of it,' Mr Do put in, dreamily. 'But I've never had any money so it doesn't worry me.'

Do was at least right that we would get to the new village without difficulty. It was just off the main road back to Saigon. We went down a dirt road – this time, apparently, quite safe – and past little boys scrubbing the backs of water buffaloes as they lay in a shallow, muddy pond. The houses were scattered among the trees like mushrooms. Some had shiny ceramic tiles that ran along the top of the roof and ended in curly-tailed dragons.

The pagoda turned out to be a group of buildings none of which from the outside looked particularly religious. The main one was a large concrete box with a new roof of shiny corrugated tin. A girl in reddish-brown trousers and tunic and a towel wrapped round her head like a turban came up to us as we got out of the car and took us to one of the smaller buildings. She was obviously expecting us and asked no questions. The room she put us in was bare except for a table and some chairs and a Buddhist calendar hanging crookedly from a nail. She brought glasses and a padded wicker-basket that contained a teapot, poured us tea and disappeared.

Mr Do said that we had to wait for the monk but Ba, after sitting still for a few minutes, began to fidget and when there was a noise from a nearby room – a half moan, half chant – he announced he would investigate. He was back in a moment, signalling us to follow him. He led us to the next building and into a room where a woman was lying on her back on a canvas-covered trestle bed. She was covered up to the chin with a straw mat, and a yellow cloth decorated with red signs had been laid across her forehead. The shutters over the windows were closed and the room was lit by candles, one in an upturned teacup placed on the woman's chest and others on a low table at her head. A monk dressed in robes of the same red-brown as the girl who had welcomed us sat cross-legged behind the table.

It was the monk's chanting that we had heard when we were drinking tea. He held a small stick in each hand. With the left he struck an empty coconut shell, and with the right a brass bowl. He hit the shell rapidly, getting louder and then softer, while from the bowl he produced a steady, slow, bell-like chime. There were women in the room, standing and silently watching. Most wore baggy, black trousers and light-coloured blouses, but there were others in the red-brown robes of nuns.

'It's an exorcism,' Ba whispered. The monk repeated what sounded like the same chant again and again and gestured to an old nun who was standing by the prone woman's head and cooling her with a fan. She waved the fan over the candles to extinguish them, took another in her hand and lit it, and filled her mouth with a clear liquid from a bottle on the floor. She put her right hand on the woman's forehead and blew a spray of liquid into the flame of the candle she was holding. The liquid, some sort of alcohol, caught fire and a dramatic lick of flame briefly lit up the troubled woman's face.

After a moment she got up as though nothing unusual had happened and one of those watching took her place on the bed. The monk began to chant again.

Someone coughed behind us. A young monk, very straight and still, was standing by the door, his hands joined in front of his body in a gesture of tranquillity. On his head, just within the line of his shaven hair, were three round burn marks. Ba and Do hurried towards him. The monk held up his hand and spoke to them softly. Ba translated.

'He says Thai has arrived safely but that he is very tired and has a fever. He will take us to him.'

We walked across to the big building with the silver roof shining in the sun. It, too, was dim inside, for all the window shutters were closed. A line of beds stood on each side of the one large room. There was a clutter of cooking pots and dishes around each bed and bed-matting, too, on which people were sleeping. A middle-aged man and woman sat on a bed near the door. The woman had a long chain tied round her ankle, the other end of it attached to the bed. Her hair was tangled and the muscles of her face taut. She watched us come in and, still sitting, bowed low towards me.

'It's a hospital for mad people,' Ba whispered.

The woman pulled on the chain and gave a short cry. The young monk laughed and said something to Ba.

'He says that if they didn't put a chain on her she would try to run away. The last time she got free she climbed to the top of the roof and it took them half a day to get her down. The man with her is her husband.'

The middle-aged man, in a gesture of sharing his wife's affliction, picked up the chain and held it in both hands.

The monk looked at me. He seemed to be judging the effect the scene had on me. He spoke quietly to Ba.

'He says that everyone here needs help and that most of them are in some way victims of the war. So he thinks that perhaps Thai has come to the right place.'

The young monk smiled. He was extraordinarily calm and self-assured. For a moment he reminded me of the Vietcong officer with the elfin ears. Both men seemed equally unshakable. But the monk's smile was more questioning, less self-satisfied, than the communist soldier's had been. He turned to me. Ba translated.

'You are right to help Thai. I have talked to him in the past. He is restless but good. He is worth saving for he can help others.'

He looked me in the eyes for a moment and left without another word.

Thai, in grey pyjamas, was asleep on a narrow bed at the end of the room. His face and neck were shiny with sweat.

The only person to pay attention to us was an old peasant with a fine pointed beard. He began to explain to Ba what was wrong with the people around us and when he came to a young man who was squatting on a bed and turning his head agitatedly from side to side he called him over. He gave the young man a bamboo flute which he began to play. Within a few minutes he had become calm and even managed a brief, hesitant smile at us. He was a policeman, the old man said, who had been wounded by a grenade and was still suffering shock. He was only calm when he was playing the flute.

I asked Ba what was wrong with the old man.

'He says he is getting better. He says there are thousands of people who have the same illness as he had. It is because many have been killed in the war. The dead have left behind too many wandering souls. They have nowhere to go to for they died too soon. So they enter living people and possess them. The sufferers come to the pagoda to have these spirits driven out. The exorcist here can do this because he is a good man.'

The old man looked at Thai, put his hand on his forehead for a moment and walked away.

Ba looked around the room. He was impressed.

'*C'est formidable, uh?* The Catholics couldn't do anything like this. Perhaps we ought to leave Thai here.'

He laughed but he knew when he made the joke that there was a trace of seriousness in it.

Thai turned on the bed and opened his eyes.

'You've found me,' he said in English. He seemed to want to say something more but the effort was too great. In a couple of minutes he was asleep again.

11

We left the pagoda in the early afternoon. Do, saying he had important business elsewhere, did not come with us and neither Ba nor I tried to make him change his mind. We put Thai, in jeans and a white shirt that were pathetically big for him, into the back seat. He had a false identity card provided by the Vietcong and we agreed that if we were stopped he would do the interpreting. It would explain his presence. I also knew that the French I talked with Ba sometimes aroused suspicion. Thai's English would, I hoped, smooth our way.

I realised our mistake when we were a couple of miles away from the checkpoint on the city's outskirts. The plan had been to get there at midday when the soldiers wouldn't want to disturb their siesta but by now both traffic and soldiers were back to normal. I felt we would be stopped and I was right.

Thai wiped the sweat from his forehead. I lit one of Ba's American cigarettes from a packet he'd left on the dashboard.

The soldier was very young, with a round face and small snub nose. He was trying, with small success, to grow a moustache. He wore full combat dress, with helmet and a new pair of boots. Ba and Thai gave him their identity cards. He frowned when he saw my British passport.

'He asked if you were American,' Thai said. 'I think I ought to have answered yes.'

The boy soldier opened my passport at an empty page and frowned again. He walked round the car holding the documents, opened the boot and shut it again.

'He thinks something's wrong,' Ba hissed, taking a cigarette for himself. Thai was the calmest of the three of us. The soldier came to the window. He bent down so his head was level with mine, put two fingers to his lips and said urgently *'Thuoc la. Thuoc la.'*

There was a scrabbling in the seat beside me. Ba had seized the cigarette packet and thrust it past me through the driver's window. He spoke quickly, shaking the packet up and down in his hands as people did when making offerings at a pagoda. The soldier took it and, rewarding us with his first smile, waved us on.

After that getting Thai into the house unseen – a task I'd dreaded – seemed easy. The little alley outside was heavy with heat and all the houses had their shutters closed against it. The sound of the car did not arouse even the inquisitive old landlady, though we had a bad moment with the grille across the front door which screeched as we pulled it open.

I left Thai with Ba who promised to buy some medicines for him and I only returned in the late evening after attending a dinner at my boss's house that I could not get out of. I tapped three times on the glass front door as we had arranged but there was no answer so I unlocked the padlock on the grille – I had bought a new one to replace the landlady's – and went in. Thai was in the bedroom, asleep. He was wearing blue pyjamas that I guessed were Ba's for they only covered three quarters of his arm and leg.

I went back into the sitting room and lay down on the sofa. My legs hung over the end, and the arm rest on which I put my head was almost as unyielding as the wooden bed of the night before. My despairing contemplation of the prospect of another sleepless night was interrupted by a murmur of voices outside the window and the sound of something soft scraping along the dusty concrete of the alley.

To my surprise I felt frightened. I had been scared the day before when we went to look for Thai in the village and had got caught up in the battle, but that was a different sort of fear. In the village I hadn't supposed that anyone was meaning to harm me and my strongest feeling was that it would be ridiculous to die an accidental death in the middle of somebody else's carefully planned battle. But as I listened to the murmuring in the alley I was sure that someone outside was watching the house. They could be Vietcong – people were always saying how the communist agents managed to find out most of what went on in Saigon. But there were other possibilities, too. They could be Colonel Dinh's men or Gruson himself could be having a watch kept on us. Ever since I had heard him so adroitly give Maurice a new explanation for wanting to help Thai I doubted that he was taking me completely into his confidence.

This feeling that several different people had reason to spy on me scared me. The little house made it worse. It was so hot and airless and the strange city from which I was protected in my neat villa on Nguyen Du seemed here to press in on me and threaten me. Even the war, so remote from the villa and the day's work at the bank, seemed closer. Every now and then there was a crackle of rifle fire which I guessed to be from bored sentries amusing themselves. But just after I had lain down on the sofa the low rumble of a bombing raid rattled the glass in the front door. Although the bombs were dropping miles away their reverberation was like a warning finger shaken at the city.

The murmur outside stopped and then started again and the curious shuffling noise with it. I got up and went over to the window. The bottom was covered by opaque glass but the top was open and protected only by a wire mosquito screen. But it was covered with so much dust that I could see nothing through it and so I opened the door a little.

A man and a woman were standing a few yards to the left of the door. The man was wearing white undershorts and a tee-shirt and had his arm round the woman's waist. Both of them were short, stocky and middle-aged. They moved a little and I realised that the curious noise was made by their rubber sandals brushing along the dusty concrete of the alley. They went out of my sight and there was the sound of a door shutting several houses away.

I went back to the sofa not feeling proud of myself: I had been scared by a couple of loving neighbours. After several attempts to find a comfortable way of lying on the wretched sofa I had just managed to convince myself that I was feeling drowsy when there was a chilling cry from the back of the house. It was like the sobbing of a savage child, half-fury and half-despair. I ran through the bedroom where Thai slept undisturbed and into the bathing area under the tiled roof. There was a scratching sound on the tiles followed by a hissing and something heavy fell onto the corrugated iron over the kitchen. A few minutes later the sobbing began again, but from a distance.

God, I thought, can that only be a cat, and then I remembered seeing in the alley when we arrived with Thai two thin, scarred creatures, their bodies tense with suspicion, and to whom no one could ever have called out 'Kitty! Kitty!' in all their life.

I went back through the bedroom thinking Thai was still asleep until I heard him call my name. He had propped himself up on his elbows and his voice was so deep it was almost a growl.

'You think I'm a coward, don't you?'

His face was shiny with sweat and the dark eyes that stared at me so angrily seemed to have sunk far back into his skull. I asked him if he was feeling all right and he waved an impatient hand.

'You're still an English schoolboy, aren't you? You don't like to hear real things talked about. But that's what you think, isn't it? You thought you could get me away from the communists because I'm afraid to go on fighting with them.'

There was a scratching on the wall as two lizards chased after each other and then even they were still, their heads to one side, as though their attention too had been caught by the intense and angry figure on the bed. Thai slipped back onto the pillow and lay staring at the ceiling as he talked.

'I have been poisoned by you and your white world and the communists know that. Those peasant boys – the soldiers you saw the first time we met in the rubber plantation – even they understood it without knowing why. They could smell that there was something odd about me. They knew, without anyone telling them, that I had read your books and thought your thoughts and so couldn't be like them any more. They knew that part of their enemy was in me so how could they trust me? Because that's what they are fighting against, this huge weight of the West that presses down on their minds and has crushed the old ways and beliefs of their villages into paper-thin ghosts. It has made them feel ashamed and weak as though they are the eternal children in a world of white grown-ups.'

He stopped, his face contorted as though in pain, and he beat his fist on the bed.

'I wanted to be like them. I knew how little they knew, how small their world was. But I wanted to be as small as they were, as obsessed as they were. But I couldn't do it. I couldn't do it. I am a half-caste now. Inside here I am just a little *métis*.'

The voice was shrill now and the fist, at the word 'inside', beat hard against his sweating temple. I didn't know what to say and stood at the end of the bed. I had never felt so uncomfortable in my life for I felt as though I were eavesdropping on one of those fights that go on inside a man's head and which should never be observed by others. I was sure he would never have talked to me in this way had it not been for the fever that was driving his thoughts so hard that he had to speak them aloud. I gave him a glass of water, hoping that it would remind him that I was listening and prompt him to end the confession that I had neither expected nor wanted to hear. He looked at me as he took the glass but he went on talking, though his voice was quieter and he seemed more calm.

'Do you remember those songs the Vietcong soldiers sang when they were having their Tet party? They have lots of songs, you know. The day I was running away from the village where you went to pick me up the words of one of them kept going round and round in my head. Perhaps the fever had already begun then, but I kept on muttering it to the rhythm of my feet as they hit the ground. It was about those rubber sandals that they all wear and that I was wearing too. "Their heels are thin," it goes, "and their straps supple and lasting as love."

'That's what they're like, mixing the war and their feelings together, and the more they suffer the more they feel free. I used to look at them and think what masochists they were but they were wiser than me because that's the only way they could go on fighting.'

His voice became shrill again and his eyes were fixed and staring like those of a medium in a trance. I said that he ought to rest and to my surprise he heard me.

'How can we rest?' He sounded puzzled. 'We don't know how to rest.'

He closed his eyes and I thought he was going to sleep, but as I turned to leave the room he called out.

'I met an American once. Let me tell you about it. It was when I first started thinking about going over to the communists. He started to make jokes about the Chinese and Mao's little red book. He said it was childish, grown men going around looking for answers to everything in a little book of quotations.

'I tried to explain to him that everything that you take for granted in the West we have to make new for ourselves. I said our past was no good for us any more. The proof was that it didn't help protect us when you came to conquer us. It didn't give us the right answers. And so why shouldn't there be some new answers for us in Mao's little red book, or someone else's little book. Why shouldn't a Chinese doctor be guided by it. Your doctors have been guided by the ideas in your bible and no one laughs at that.'

He turned towards me and looked at me searchingly. 'Don't you understand? We have to make something of our own but the only thing we have been able to make is this war.'

He closed his eyes again. The fever-driven speech had come to an end. I took the sheet from the end of the bed and covered him, for the midnight air had cooled, and I went back to the front room.

The city was silent at last, as though its insects and animals, soldiers and guns were all gathering strength for the next day's battles. I realised how foolish I had been to suppose that I could ever have helped anyone in such a country. And yet it had all seemed so easy when Gruson had suggested that we might help Thai. I now knew that there was nothing I could do to help him because even if we did smuggle him abroad we could never spirit him away from the battles that were raging inside his own head. I wondered if I should talk to Gruson about it but at once realised that it would be pointless. He wouldn't care, I was sure. But worse was my suspicion that he knew already, that he knew the shape of Thai's mind and guessed at the anguish there and that he still did not care.

12

'Well,' said Gruson, twisting his signet ring on his left hand and a look of real curiosity on his face that his smile did not disguise, 'how does it feel to be back in civilisation again?'

Thai had seemed pleased when, the next evening, I had told him that Gruson was coming to see him. He insisted on getting up and dressing even though he had still not shaken off his fever. Ba had brought him some new clothes during the day – a white shirt, grey trousers and a blue cravat which he tied carefully round his neck. He slicked his hair back with water. Had it not been for his cheap rubber sandals, the Saigon sort, not those he had worn in the jungle, he could have passed as a public schoolboy dressed cautiously for leisure.

Gruson came to the house on his own. I'd drawn him a map of how to get there and he had turned up exactly on time, appearing at the front door as from nowhere for there was no warning sound of his feet in the alley. Used to his usual self-assertive stride I hadn't realised that he could move so quietly when he wanted to.

'Perhaps I shouldn't have said civilisation,' he said as he sat down in one of the armchairs, poking its plastic covering as though he had never seen anything like it before. 'I'm afraid we haven't been able to fix you up with any great comforts.'

Thai answered Gruson's questions quietly, calling him Sir. This at first surprised Gruson and then seemed to please him. He watched Thai closely as a man might look over a prize animal he had bought, trying to make up his mind if the deal had been worth it. They talked about nothing very serious and Gruson asked no questions about Thai's time with the communists. I, too, watched Thai with some amazement. I could not connect this quiet, deferential man with the anguished figure of the night before. I was glad about that. When I'd arrived that evening Thai had made no mention of his outburst and I, for my part, was happy to act as though it had never been for I was not sure how to deal with a man who had revealed so much of himself to me.

The only question Thai asked was how long it would be before he could leave.

'A few days at most, I hope,' Gruson replied. 'A Royal Air Force plane is due here on a routine run and we'll be able to slip you onto that without anyone being the wiser. It'll take you to Singapore and from there you'll be put on a commercial flight to London. But as long as you have to stay here Michael and his Mr Ba will do their best to look after you.'

Thai began to thank Gruson for helping him but he was cut short.

'Look here, my dear chap, I just want to make it plain that you don't owe us anything and we don't expect anything from you. Your dad has been a good friend to us and we're happy to do him a good turn. When you get to London you'll be free to do as you like. With your British education there shouldn't be any problem about getting a job. Above all, you mustn't think we're going to make you sing for your supper in any way.'

Gruson paused as though to give himself time to judge Thai's reaction but there was nothing to read on the politely inexpressive Vietnamese face. This lack of response seemed to irritate him and there was an edge to his voice when he continued.

'Of course, one day you might feel that someone like yourself could do something for Vietnam. Well, if the war stopped and there was some sort of deal between the two sides. People like yourself might be useful then – I mentioned this to your uncle Maurice and he agreed. But that would be up to you of course.'

He obviously didn't want to say any more. He got up, looking at his watch, and as though he had just thought of it asked if he could see the rest of the house. Judging by the care with which he examined each room he had been meaning to do it all along. He was particularly interested in the open space between the walls and the roof in the bathing area that gave onto the houses on each side. We could hear the old woman, our neighbour and landlady, muttering to herself as she prepared her evening meal.

'Not very private back there, is it?' Gruson said when we returned to the sitting room. 'I'd keep your voices down if I were you.'

Thai glanced at me. Was he wondering if anyone had overheard his shouts of the night before? It hadn't occurred to me before. I felt my stomach jump. The little house that was meant to be a refuge seemed to be becoming once again more like a trap.

Gruson was at the front door when Thai quietly said that he wanted to see his wife and son before he left Saigon.

'Better not, old chap.' Gruson sounded understanding but firm. 'I know how you feel but it really isn't worth the risk. Moving them to you or you to them just increases the risk that someone will recognise you. Colonel Dinh's men may be watching them, you know. Wait a few weeks and you'll see them in London.'

Thai was about to object. There was a flicker of stubbornness across his face, but he glanced at Gruson and said nothing. Although neither man had moved I felt they had almost come to blows. Thai, though, was polite enough when he shook hands and he even managed a few more words of thanks.

I left with Gruson for I had promised to take Jeannette out to a late dinner. Gruson said nothing till we were out of the alley and had reached the main street where he stopped and looked at me.

'It's not a bad little hideaway, even if it could be more private. But I'm not so sure about the hider. He's presentable enough but underneath those schoolboy manners and English accent he's Vietnamese through and through, you can count on that. What's more I expect he's bloody proud of it. He probably thinks we're every bit as barbarian as his old horror of an uncle does. Well, anyway he needs us now.'

That thought seemed to comfort him and he grinned at me.

'You've done a splendid job, Michael, no doubt about that. I'm most grateful.'

This was the Gruson I first knew, the friend whom it was fun to be with. But was it the real Gruson? I didn't know any more. I already knew more about Gruson than I dared to tell Thai, about how his reasons for this whole operation changed according to whom he was talking to. And after last night I knew more about Thai than I wanted to tell Gruson. I didn't want to expose Thai to that cold eye.

'Is there anything else you want to tell me?'

I shook my head.

'I'll be off then. By the way, when you come here, take a taxi rather than bring your car. And I'll let you know when the plane's coming. From then on I'll take over.'

He shouted at a cyclo that was going by, its driver a stringy old man in ragged shorts. Gruson jumped in and waved his arm as though he was directing a cavalry charge. The old driver stood on the pedals to get the cyclo moving, clicking the brake handle in time with Gruson's cries of '*On y va*'. He too had fallen under the spell of the Englishman's enthusiasm.

I drove back to the villa on Nguyen Du to change before meeting Jeannette at Au Maréchal, a restaurant on Nguyen Hue not far from the nightclub Maurice had taken me to.

It was owned by a Vietnamese general who had been on the losing side in a coup. He was said to be Francophile and so stood no chance of edging back to power in the new days of American influence. He left the running of the restaurant to a French manager, a man with a lined, dog-like face and unquenchable desire for young Vietnamese girls. Whenever Jeannette and I went there he would bring us a free drink so that he could sit with us for a while and squeeze his knee against Jeannette's thigh.

Jeannette, I suspected, rather liked this. There was enough of the uncertain Vietnamese girl in her to be flattered by the attention of almost any European. She also liked the food. She ate huge amounts, far more than I did, without it having any effect on her body whose shape, half-girl, half-woman, never changed. I was late getting to the restaurant and she was already there, at a table at the back, wearing a simple silk dress, her brown-black hair drawn back and caught in a knot at her neck.

The old Frenchman was standing over her, his hand on her shoulder. He took it away when he saw me come in and gave me a pacifying smile that showed his long yellow teeth. Jeannette didn't smile. She had ordered a glass of Coke that she had already half drunk. She looked at her watch and told me I was late.

She seemed more agreeable when we started ordering our meal. Half-way through I tried to make her laugh by remarking that I'd noticed the old Frenchman had had his hands on her again.

'What's wrong if he likes me?' she said, and launched into an attack on me for not liking her enough. I was taking her for granted. I was secretive because I had gone away on trips and told her nothing about what I'd done and even now in Saigon I was behaving in a strange way. Why had I been late coming to the restaurant? There were plenty of men in Saigon and I shouldn't think myself so wonderful that she couldn't do without me.

I was silly enough to ask if she meant Byrne.

Her face screwed up in anger so that it looked like the statues of fierce warriors that I had seen at the entrance to pagodas. It was the same expression that Colonel Dinh had worn when I had seen him displaying mock anger in the nightclub. The corners of her mouth were drawn down and the eyes enlarged so that they seemed to be coming out of her head.

It was a battle to persuade her to come back to the villa after dinner. She was unusually greedy when we made love. Her face in orgasm was that night indistinguishable from her face in anger. As I held her in my arms all I could imagine was Colonel Dinh as a warrior-guardian, his features screwed up in a rage that was meant to terrify, but which perhaps also meant that he, too, was frightened.

13

I got to the bank early the next morning so I could catch up on the work that had accumulated while I was away, but I found it hard to concentrate on the papers on my desk. I kept on thinking of the contrast between Jeannette's body, smooth and firm like a new fruit, and her face which when ill-tempered had looked as old as rage itself. I studied the Vietnamese secretaries working near me. Most of them wore the *ao dai* but with a cardigan over it because they found the air-conditioning uncomfortably cold. To my surprise I found I could easily also imagine their demure faces screwed up in anger as Jeannette's had been.

The bank had not been open for long when there was a tapping on the counter which ran across the centre of the main hall. The girls near me started to giggle and I looked up to see Ba, only his head and shoulders visible above the counter, tapping on it with the stem of his pipe. He caught my eye and waved the pipe at me. The old Sikh who guarded the front door was looking at Ba suspiciously and so were some of the customers. My boss came out of his office. He looked first at Ba and then at me and his eyebrows shot up. He leaned over to talk to a secretary but he still kept his eyes on us.

I walked to the counter as calmly as I could. Ba leant across it and whispered 'Something's happened.'

His manner was obviously conspiratorial. The girls had stopped giggling and were trying to hear what we were saying. I told him that I'd meet him outside and he scurried off like a clockwork toy that had run up against an obstacle and then been turned round and pointed in a different direction. I went over to my boss. He watched my approach with evident disapproval. He was wearing the sort of cream silk shirt that Gruson sometimes wore.

I told him that Ba was connected with the work I had been doing for Gruson and that I needed to go outside for a few minutes to talk with him. He nodded towards his office. We went in and he shut the door behind us.

'Tell Gruson that I don't expect him to send his funny men to disturb the bank's work. On second thoughts I'll tell him myself.'

He put his hand on the telephone.

'Hop it outside, then. But don't forget I expect you to catch up sharpish on your backlog of work.'

He waved me out and was dialling a number as I closed the door behind me.

Ba was waiting for me on the pavement and we walked into Ham Nghi. He talked very fast. He had stayed the night with Thai and in the morning, about ten o'clock, when he was getting ready to leave, the doorbell rang. He didn't know whether to open it or not but when the bell went on ringing he thought it better to open the door than let the noise attract the neighbours' attention.

It was a man who said he'd heard the house was for rent and

asked to look round it. Ba told him it wasn't for rent any longer but the man began asking questions. Who had rented it? Since when and for how long? Ba said he didn't know and shut the door in his face.

I said it didn't sound suspicious to me.

'But listen,' Ba said. 'That man was a policeman.'

I must have looked disbelieving for he put on his most knowing expression.

'Moi, je connais le type. He had a moustache and wore dark glasses and one of those American caps with a big peak. That's the type Dinh uses. And when he went away I talked to the old lady next door. She said the man had already been round to her and she had told him the house was taken by an Englishman.'

I felt sick. For a moment I had the sensation of falling and I involuntarily stamped my foot on the pavement as though to stop myself. I suppose I panicked. I told Ba to wait for me and I dashed back into the bank to my telephone.

I rang the embassy and asked to speak to Gruson. The girl whom I'd met when I'd gone to that first Sunday lunch with him answered. Gruson wasn't in Saigon. He had gone to the Delta with the ambassador to present English books to a teachers' training college. They wouldn't be back till the evening. She must have guessed something from my voice because she asked if I was all right. I said yes but I knew it sounded unconvincing and hung up.

Next I tried to find Byrne. I don't know what I expected him to do and I certainly didn't look forward to admitting to him that I was in a jam. I could imagine the sneer on his face. But the desk clerk at the Caravelle said he, too, had gone out of Saigon and didn't know when he would return.

I was sure of only one thing: Thai had to be moved. Without Gruson's help the only place I could think of was my villa. It was eleven o'clock. At noon the city would begin to quieten down for lunch and siesta. It would be a chance to move Thai without too many people seeing.

I rushed out of the bank, pointedly not looking in the direction of the boss's office. Ba was talking to one of the women who squatted all day on the pavement over a pile of black market American army goods. He was holding a khaki-green aerosol and jabbing at it with a finger. He was back in his cocky schoolboy mood.

I touched him on the shoulder and he spun round.

'*Voyez-vous, Monsieur Michael.* She wants five hundred piastres for this insect spray. I told her it's no good. The mosquitoes like it. It makes them fat.' He gave his deep Ho! Ho! laugh.

The woman unwound the check scarf she wore as protection against the sun and scratched her head. She smiled at me, sensing she had found an easier customer. Ba put the can on the pavement and laughed again. The woman gave an angry wail.

Ba seemed to have forgotten why we were there. It took a few seconds before he understood that I was talking about Thai. I told him the first lie that came to my mind. I said I had talked to Gruson and that he would extract Thai from the house at once and move him somewhere safer. I said nothing about my going to the house at noon. All I knew was that it would be wrong to involve Ba in whatever was going to happen next.

He looked disappointed but he was also worried about something. He was silent for a moment and then he took my arm.

'*Monsieur Michael*, I must tell you this. I went to see Thai's wife. He asked me to take a letter to her last night and she came to the house very early this morning with the baby. They only stayed for half an hour. But I'm sure no one saw her.'

It was the first time I had seen him look apologetic, and it disarmed my anger. I told him it would be better for us not to meet for a while and that when I needed to see him I would stop by in the afternoon at Givral, the café where we had first met. We could seem to be meeting there by chance. He was disappointed but he did not object. His admission of his errand to Thai's wife had for the time being at least weakened his usual stubbornness.

I left the bank about half an hour after midday. The noon rush of people going back to their homes for lunch had almost ended and the sun shone harshly on the empty streets. I left the car on the main road, beyond the alley that led to the little house. Walking back towards it I discovered that there was another and smaller alley, no wider than a footpath, that would allow me to get to the front door without passing the old woman's veranda.

The alley had blank walls except where half way down I could see an open door. There was the smell of charcoal smoke and the sound of wooden chopsticks beating against china bowls. As I passed in front of it I saw a young girl in loose black trousers and a blue and white check shirt swinging in a hammock, but her head was turned away from the door and she could not see me. The eaters were out of sight. I had just gone past the door when I heard a loud, shrill shout.

'*Ong My! Ong My!*' A child of about four, the top half of its body covered by a short smock, had crawled onto the doorstep and was pointing at me with a dirty finger.

It went on shouting 'Mr American! Mr American!' and the girl in the hammock turned round and looked at me. I panicked and ran round the corner. When I got to the house I didn't knock but unlocked the grille and got inside as quickly as I could. My heart was beating hard. If a baby and a curious young girl could put me in such a state, what would one of the colonel's men do? I tried not to think about it.

Thai was lying on the bed reading a newspaper. I told him that Ba had been to see me and that I'd decided he ought to move to my villa. It couldn't have been easy for him waiting there after the 'policeman's visit in the morning but he seemed quite calm. Later I thought it was probably more because of fatigue than good nerves. He no longer had the strength to worry. But he had enough spirit to turn down my idea. I must have looked startled for he smiled and said: 'Don't you understand? They'll probably track you down thanks to the old woman. Or someone might remember seeing your car. That would be enough for Dinh and his men to find you. They're not stupid, you know. I don't think Gruson could help you much if they found me in your house. And if someone did see my wife coming or going this morning they'll put a lot of men on the job. I would be a nice catch for them.'

He didn't explain why he had taken the risk of summoning his wife and I wasn't in the mood to ask him. Thai was getting dressed slowly when he turned to me and asked, as though it was a most ordinary question, 'Do you trust Gruson?'

I said it was a funny thing to ask.

'I'm sorry. I didn't mean to offend you. But I trust you, you see. Uncle Maurice trusts you too. But Gruson – well, he could be working with Dinh, couldn't he? I don't quite know how. But even if it's partly true doesn't that mean that I'm running away from him too?'

Whatever my doubts about Gruson I'd never supposed he could have been working with Dinh. The whole business of putting Thai in the supposedly secret house would have been only a façade, and what would have been the point of it? Thai smiled at my evident astonishment.

'Don't worry about Gruson,' he said. 'I've decided where I have to go now. It's close to here. It would be better if I went alone but I'm feeling so weak I'm going to have to ask you to help me.'

He sat down on the bed. He was sweating and looked very pale.

'Do you understand why I did it? Do you understand why I joined the Vietcong and then left them?' The tone was more accusing than questioning. I suggested he should not tire himself further but he only shook his head bad-temperedly.

'Sometimes I wish I were ten years older. It was much easier to be with the Vietminh against the French. They were nationalists. Perhaps the communists controlled them even then but most of them were nationalists. I'd hoped the Vietcong would still be a bit like that, more open than the real communists are. The people I talked to before I went over gave me reason to hope that. And, you see, I had no choice but to work with the Vietcong. The government here is rotten. Everyone knows that. The Americans – the Americans are foreigners and it is in our blood to be against foreigners. Even my ancestors who became French citizens couldn't forget that, though they might have wanted to. We cannot use foreigners to fight our own people and keep a peaceful conscience.'

I tried again to quiet him but there was another angry gesture.

'Even what I learned in your country pushed me that way. A duty to help others, to care for society and not as so many of us have done for generations to put our private family concerns above everything else. You see, I thought there could be a middle way, not Saigon's, not Hanoi's. Perhaps there might have been if so many of the Southern guerillas had not been killed. But the Vietcong are now a Northern army. Whatever their propaganda says they are run by the communists. They don't need to listen to people like me. And I have too much pride to let them make use of me as they wish.'

He looked at me as though hoping for some sign that I had understood him. Then he got up and walked slowly to the door. He turned to me before opening it.

'After this you must forget about me. It isn't your war, you know. We must decide it among ourselves.'

The midday heat fell on us when we went out, like a great hand pressing us into the ground. Thai swayed and I took him by the arm and we went slowly down the alley, this time past the old woman's door. No one was about, though. At least I had been right about that. Thai held a folded newspaper over his head to keep off the sun but it also served to hide his face. We walked very slowly, stopping under trees for him to catch his breath.

We walked for almost ten minutes, past the cinema that showed the Kung Fu films and then, in the shadow of a Gothic church, Thai turned into a small yard. A dog with a long open sore on its back was sitting in the shade of some empty crates. It looked at us nervously. Thai opened a door on the far side of the yard and we went into a room so dark that we both stumbled. The air was thick with a sweet, sickening smell that I could not place but knew I had smelt before.

We felt our way past two small beds draped with mosquito nets. On each there was a sleeping child, lying on its back, fists clenched, mouth open. A picture of the Virgin Mary torn out of a magazine had been stuck to the wall above one of the beds, a picture of the child Jesus over the other.

We walked slowly up some stairs. I was half carrying Thai by the time we reached the top. I asked him where we were.

'The French call it a *fumerie* but in English I think you say opium den.'

14

That was the smell, of course. Here it was stronger than in the old opium-smoker's house: like sausages fried to burning point but much sweeter.

I was about to move into the room when Thai pulled at my arm. He pointed to two figures lying by the far wall. The light was dim here, too, but I could make out the skinny figure of a man in singlet and shorts lying on his side on a low platform under the wall. In front of him, on the floor, was an even smaller, thinner man, naked to the waist. He was lying on his right side, his left leg bent and his right foot curled back to support it just below the knee. His head was resting on what looked like a small shoebox.

The man on the floor poured a treaclish liquid from a small bottle into a minute saucer. Then he took an instrument like a dentist's probe and dipped the end into the saucer. He held the end of it over the flame of a spirit lamp and the liquid on the point of the instrument bubbled and expanded. Without shifting his legs from their contorted position he kept on adding liquid from the saucer and heating it in the flame until he had a ball the size of a spent piece of chewing gum. He took what looked like the earpiece of an old-fashioned telephone receiver which was attached to a mouthpiece by a long rubber tube. He kneaded the ball against the earpiece which was the pipe's bowl and shaped a bit of it into a plug which he fitted into a hole in the middle of the bowl.

He studied it and, satisfied, held it out to the man on the platform and nodded.

The man took the mouthpiece between his lips and when the other held the bowl over the flame and the opium began to crackle and smoke he took a long unbroken breath until the plug was burnt out. He blew the smoke out slowly, giggled and handed the mouthpiece back to the man on the floor who began to prepare another plug from the rest of the opium ball that he had left sticking to the bowl of the pipe. He repeated exactly the same movements, his head never moving from its uncomfortable-looking resting place.

Neither of them paid any attention to us, and Thai took my arm and we moved into a corridor beside the platform. The wall behind it turned out to be no more than a wooden partition beyond which lay another room with another low platform. It had a window which was shuttered and also a table and chairs. Most of the light came from a single yellow bulb fixed on a damp-stained wall. A man in dirty pale blue pyjamas was sitting at the table reading a newspaper. A small schoolboy in white shirt and blue shorts sat at his feet, studying a comic book. Thai called out to the man in Vietnamese and he looked up, surprised, and then smiled.

'*Tiens*,' he said, '*c'est le petit Thai*.'

He came towards us and taking Thai by the hand looked carefully into his face. He had grey hair, brushed straight back, and a small moustache. In different surroundings I might have taken him for one of the lawyers or doctors who gathered every evening at the Cercle Sportif to exchange rumours and gossip.

'*Vous êtes venus pour prendre une pipe?*' he said to both of us, but then put his hand on Thai's forehead.

'*Mais non, tu es malade!*' He made Thai sit down and took a teapot from a wicker basket. He poured a little tea into two smudged glasses, swirled it around and tipped it onto the wooden floor. Then he filled the glasses. The tea was lukewarm, urine-yellow and acrid, but Thai drank his down at once in greedy sips.

The grey-haired man looked at me and Thai said something in Vietnamese.

'I've told him you're a friend of Uncle Maurice. Maurice brought me here a few times and this old man knows him well. I can stay here till I get a message to Maurice.'

The schoolboy tugged at the man's sleeve. Thai spoke to the boy.

'He wants some money so he can go and see one of those Kung Fu movies.'

The old man got up to look for his purse. 'Did you like films as a child?' Thai asked me but didn't wait for an answer. 'When I was that boy's age my cousins took me to the movies a lot. They were patriotic and anti-French but they loved American movies. Ingrid Bergman in *Joan of Arc* was a great favourite. We all had pictures of her in our scrapbooks. But the one I liked best was *A Song to Remember* – Cornel Wilde with curly hair playing the part of Chopin. I saw it at the Bonard Cinema next to Saigon Hospital. It's the Vinh Loi now. I cried a lot, especially when Chopin is driven into exile and his girlfriend gives him a handful of Polish soil so he shouldn't forget his country. That movie made more impression on me than the Russian books my cousins read to me. And now they're all crazy about Kung Fu . . .'

The grey-haired man came back and said something to Thai in Vietnamese.

'He wonders if you'd like to smoke a pipe.'

I was shocked and Thai saw it at once. He grinned.

'Come on, this is the exotic East. Don't you want to be able to tell your grandchildren that you once smoked opium? One pipe won't make you an addict, Uncle Maurice comes here once or twice a month and he's not an addict.'

It seemed such a crazy thing to do but all I could say was that it wasn't the right time. After all Thai was hiding from the police and the police surely often raided places like this.

'Don't be so naïve,' Thai said. 'Who do you think he gets his opium from? Dinh's men, of course. You're in no man's land here. That's why I thought of coming here.'

The *patron* took my hand.

'Don't worry, Monsieur, everyone comes here. The government comes here. The other gentlemen come here. But they come here for tranquillity. Why should they hurt the only place that gives them tranquillity? Thai will be safe here and you will be safe here too.'

He got up and went to the other side of the partition. I asked Thai what he meant by the 'other gentlemen.'

'That's his way of talking about the communists. He wouldn't be so polite about them if he didn't see them quite so often.'

I said I still didn't see how it could be a safe place for him.

'He's got another room upstairs. Uncle Maurice will get me out by tomorrow night. He might even get me out tonight.'

I asked how I was going to be able to tell Gruson where he was.

'Oh yes, Gruson. Well, Maurice can get in touch with you and then you can tell Gruson.'

I was relieved that there was no more talk of not trusting Gruson though I noticed that Thai didn't seem to think that keeping him informed was very important. I asked if he had told the *patron* why he had come to him.

'I just told him I was in trouble. Of course he knew I went over to the Vietcong and I've let him think I'm still with them. But the outside world isn't very real to him. This room is his reality, as it is for the men who come here to smoke. Perhaps you'll understand that when you've smoked a pipe.'

The *patron* came back with the smoking equipment and pointed towards the platform. I hesitated, for it seemed a wildly silly thing to do, but Thai smiled again and pushed me towards it. It was dark there and to my surprise I saw that someone was already lying on it.

'It was an old man, a European. His head was resting on two dirty pillows and his small black eyes were staring at the ceiling. He had the face of a lizard, all lines and creases, and every few minutes his lips pouted out and then sucked inwards as though they were catching insects. He wore a white shirt and black trousers and a shiny, narrow black tie with a knot so tiny that it could never have been properly untied but just slipped on and off over his head.

He seemed not to see me when I lay down on the opposite end of the platform. The *patron* lay on the floor. Like the half-naked man he put his head on a small block but he did not manage the same contortion of the legs. The sweet burning smell had already begun to make me feel sick when he handed me the mouthpiece.

'You must try to inhale it all at once,' he said.

I drew on the mouthpiece and the opium ball spat and crackled in the bowl of the pipe. But after a few seconds I could draw in no more and I choked. The *patron* looked up and nodded his head encouragingly. He had made enough for three pipes but I did not manage to finish any of them in a single inhalation as I had seen the Vietnamese do.

I sat up on the platform, my back to the wall. The opium seemed to have had no effect on me except that I still felt a little sick. The *patron* folded up his equipment as methodically as a doctor putting away his stethoscope. Something touched my arm and I turned to see the old European leaning forward, his hand outstretched. His mouth made its insect-catching movement.

'*Vous êtes dans l'état, Monsieur?*'

The tone, deeply polite, was matched by the look of concern on his face. I felt I had to say yes and this satisfied him for he settled back onto the pillows with what I took to be a sigh of content that we had become brothers in a mutual pleasure.

Thai left the room and I was just about to go and look for him when the Vietnamese smoker came in from behind the partition and poured himself some tea from the pot on the table.

'*Salut, Ton-Ton,*' he said to the old European. He took a chair and brought it up to our platform.

'Ah Ton-Ton,' he went on, 'You are my guiding light. That's what I always say to the *patron*. Monsieur Franchini is my guiding light.'

The old European made a slow gesture of infinite modesty with his hands. The Vietnamese introduced himself to me as a schoolteacher and began a monologue on justice and why he deserved to be paid more money than his colleagues. Then he sighed.

'Viet Nam! Viet Nam! Why should anyone expect justice here?'

I felt the old man's hand on my arm again.

'Monsieur, this country used to be a paradise, an earthly paradise. Why cannot men learn to live in the paradise that the world offers them?'

'A paradise for you, perhaps, but not for us,' said the schoolteacher, though without ill-feeling.

The old man shrugged.

'There is a paradise around us,' he went on calmly, as though he had not heard the interruption, his eyes fixed on the stained wall, 'and we can see it if we want to.'

He moved his head on the pillows and for the first time closed his eyes.

'Of course he is right,' said the schoolteacher. 'I must go back to my paradise.' He got up and went into the next room shouting, '*Encore une pipe.*' The tiny half-naked man came out of the shadows and followed him.

I closed my eyes and it was as though I were in the room behind the partition with them, watching the gnome settle down on the floor, his head on the brick pillow, his eyes fixed on the opium treacle in the saucer and the eyes of the schoolteacher watching these unhurried, unchanging preparations for paradise. I fell asleep and woke to find Thai shaking me. He was smiling but he looked very tired.

'There's no reason for you to stay any longer. I'll be all right here. All you have to do now is wait for Maurice.'

The opium must have stilled my fear for Thai's safety for I got up without resisting. Monsieur Franchini was still lying on the platform and the *patron*, a pair of rimless glasses on the end of his nose, was reading his newspaper and picking his teeth with the long nail on the little finger of his left hand. I said goodbye to him and shook hands with Thai. In the outer room the schoolmaster was asleep or day-dreaming but the gnome was still on the floor at his feet watching him. Downstairs the children, too, still slept.

I must have been asleep for over an hour for it was almost four o'clock when I came out onto the street. It was busy with people but I felt far away. The buzzing of the motorbikes and the chatter of a crowd of schoolchildren in bright white shirts outside the Kung Fu cinema were somehow muffled. Everything seemed as it ought to be because it could be no different. Even Thai's flight to the *fumerie* was necessary and right.

I had almost reached the car when I realised that the people on the pavement round me had stopped and were staring in the direction from which I had come. A large van had drawn up just between the two alleys leading down to the house where we had hidden Thai. Its back dropped down and about a dozen men came out of it.

They were the strangest, ugliest Vietnamese I had ever seen. They wore a mixture of civilian and military clothes and carried an equally odd selection of weapons – American rifles and the AK47s that the Vietcong used, shotguns, submachine guns and pistols. Some were fat, others thin, but the faces of all of them were mean to the point of being misshapen. They were commanded by a small man in a bright green Hawaiian shirt and tennis shoes. His hair was crew-cut and he had a thin moustache. He had almost no chin, and was directing the men with a revolver in his right hand. His speech was abrupt and yapping but the thugs were silent. When they were all out of the truck they divided into two groups. Each moved off quickly down an alley.

I knew at once that they were Colonel Dinh's men and that they thought they had cornered Thai. My fear proved stronger than the opium and I began sweating. I could feel panic building up inside my stomach again. I walked quickly to the car and drove off to my villa. As I drove I had a sensation of pins and needles throughout all my body but whether that was from the opium or the fear I did not know. Paradise was over.

15

The next two days were horrible. The sensation of pins and needles kept on coming back and I had bouts of nausea, whether from fear or the opium I did not know. I went to the bank and somehow managed to do my work. The fear, I soon realised, had several components. I was frightened for Thai, no longer knowing where he was, and also for myself. I could not forget those men of Colonel Dinh's, springing out from the van like anarchic spirits of the underworld. I had supposed that as a white man, an Englishman, I was beyond danger. Even Dinh himself, I thought, would not risk the scandal of maltreating me. But those men, the incarnation of Dinh's own worst passions and fears, might be beyond control. Sitting at my desk in the bank I imagined the van drawing up in front of my villa and the yapping commands from the chinless man in the Hawaiian shirt and shuddered.

I was not surprised that I was also frightened about what Gruson's reaction would be. I had helped destroy the plan he prized so much. I could not make up my mind what to tell him but I knew it would not be the truth, because I wanted to protect Thai but at the same time myself from Gruson's wrath.

An adventure that had at first promised to win applause all round now condemned me to wriggling my way as best I could to avoid blame. I knew I would wriggle for I still did not want to lose Gruson's respect and friendship. But he did not get in touch with me and I was scared to seek him out.

On the second evening after Thai had escaped to the *fumerie* Ba turned up at my villa. I recognised the sound of his motor-bike and the usual seconds of hesitation before he quietly rattled the grille on the front door. I should have been angry and from the expression on his face he expected me to be. I had told him not to come to my house. I was more convinced than ever that it was wrong to involve him any further. But the truth was I was glad to see him for I felt I could talk almost openly to him. I was now as puzzled as he usually seemed to be. Like a child playing blind man's bluff, eyes covered and spun this way and that, neither of us knew which way to move. We needed each other.

Ba broke into a rapid explanation of why he had disobeyed my order not to get in touch. The evening before he had gone to Maurice's house only to find a frightened maid, a stupid country girl, who said that Maurice had disappeared two days before. He had left the house in the afternoon saying he was going to play billiards at the Cercle Sportif and would be back for dinner. That was the last time she saw him. There was little food or money left in the house. She started crying and Ba could get no more out of her.

I told him what had happened to Thai, of our escape to the *fumerie*, and of the raid by Dinh's men, though I tried to keep my horror about the latter incident as well concealed as I could. We looked at each other with the same thought. Maurice had vanished before Thai had made his escape. Thai would not have been able to contact him and might still be trapped with the *patron*, Monsieur Franchini and the other inhabitants of the den. Whatever Thai might have said about it being a safe place, a no-man's-land, it seemed crazy to let him stay there longer. And if Maurice had disappeared who else was there to look after him?

I didn't know what to do except that we had once more to make contact with Thai. Ba, without my saying a word, suggested that he go to the den. Somewhat to my surprise he said he knew where it was. He waved his hand impatiently. '*Tout le monde le connait.*' He would arouse less suspicion there than me. However polite the *patron* had been on my first visit he would very likely not appreciate my turning up again.

I had no arguments against that and Ba set off, promising to report back within an hour. I sat on the terrace and waited. The nights now brought little relief from the heat which each day grew more pressing. Ba had said the rains would come bringing intervals of coolness with them. The geckoes darted up and down on the wall behind me, clucking at each other like scolding nannies. I could not make out if they were playing or fighting but their cry and their abrupt movements suggested they were every bit as irritable as the city around them.

Ba was back within an hour, as puzzled as I had ever seen him. Thai was not there. The *patron* had been hostile and suspicious and had at first denied that he even knew Thai. Perhaps he was just testing Ba for from what he said later it seemed that Thai had spoken of him. But he either would not or could not say where Thai had gone. The only clue he gave was the name of a pagoda in the same part of the city. He also gave the name of a monk. Was Thai there? He had looked blank and offered to make Ba a pipe. Ba refused the offer and was told to leave.

Ba made a joke of it.

'Perhaps I should have smoked a pipe together with him. It might have made him more talkative.'

I smiled for I couldn't imagine what Ba would be like under the spell of opium. It was hard to believe that it would calm him down. His would still be an agitated paradise.

Whatever we decided to do we would have to wait till the morning for it was getting near to curfew. I was glad about that because I hoped that in the morning I would feel a little braver.

The Pagoda of True Enlightenment was on Cao Thang Street. There was nothing obviously religious about it from the outside. The stained concrete façade, separated from the pavement by a small courtyard, was bigger than those of the workshops on either side but, apart from some Chinese characters in moulded, crumbling cement, was indistinguishable from them. There was a small flagpole in the courtyard but it carried no flag.

Ba had decided that it would be better for us to go there together. There was nothing unusual about a foreigner poking round pagodas and Ba could pass for my guide. We went on his motorbike and attracted no attention as we wheeled it in off the busy street.

The heavy wooden door was ajar and gave onto a small, dark vestibule. Ba looked around like a dog hoping to pick up a scent. He took my arm and pulled me towards a large notice, covered by dusty glass, hanging on a side wall. The pagoda's name had been traced in large, chinoiserie letters in Vietnamese, French and English and underneath were two photographs. I pushed the door open to see better.

The left-hand photo showed a European in Edwardian dress. He wore a winged collar and a closely buttoned suit. His left hand rested on a table on which there was a sword and a large oriental-looking jar. The other picture was of a Vietnamese in a robe down to his feet and a small round hat on his head. In his hands he held a piece of paper. Both men had moustaches, the European's luxuriant, the Vietnamese one neatly clipped. Both wore an expression that was self-confident and commanding.

The inscription under the European's picture read: 'M. Albert Bonhomme functionary of Nancy, France. 1916.' The Vietnamese was described as 'The Superior Au Minh Phuong our founder, 1923.' There was more to be read, close-typed lines but so faded and hidden behind the dirty glass that they were hard to make out. I managed to distinguish the word 'PNEUMATOGRAPHY' printed in capital letters but Ba was impatient and pulled me on towards an inner door. We pushed it open slowly and hesitated before passing through.

The room we entered appeared to be the main hall of the pagoda. At the back was an altar, but without any figure of Buddha. There were incense-burners on it and a plate holding perfumed bananas, the bunches little bigger than a man's fist. Two photographs stood in the middle of the altar. M. Bonhomme and the Superior Au Minh Phuong, greatly enlarged, stared down at us as though we were most unwelcome intruders.

A table covered with a red cloth stood in the middle of the room. At its centre was an incense-burner flanked by two large candles, and in front of them a vase of dusty plastic flowers and an old, unsheathed sword. Ba fingered the blade.

'It's not very sharp,' he said and gave his laugh. His curiosity had got the better of his nervousness. He took me over to a wall, where inscriptions had been painted in Vietnamese and French but not, this time, in English, and pointed to the names of Confucius, Lao Tzu and Buddha. There was a sweet smell in the room from the offering of bananas and old incense whose burnt remains lay crumbled on the table like fly droppings. The windows which were set high in the wall above our heads were closed. Apart from the flies that circled the bright yellow bananas there was no sign of life.

The *patron* had given Ba the name of a Buddhist monk, but what sort of religion was being – or had been – celebrated here? Ba shrugged and said that it certainly wasn't Catholic. He himself, he once told me, was a Catholic though he did not approve of going to confession. 'Some of those priests should be confessing to me.' His attitude towards other religions was enquiring but a little condescending.

I had just suggested that we had either been given the name of the wrong pagoda or the wrong monk when there was a loud shout from behind the altar. Ba set off at a trot and fumbled his way through curtains at the back of the room. We went into a small passage that led into a room little bigger than a cell. An iron bedstead stood in the corner, covered by a bare mattress and a mosquito net that had turned brown with age. A Toyota calendar showing a neat, smiling Japanese family getting into a shiny red car hung on the wall. Beneath it was a plain wooden table at which sat a large man in a monk's brown-red robe. He had a heavy, shaven head and fat hands which as we entered were breaking a piece off a long French loaf. He put the bread down beside a box of processed cheese decorated with a picture of a red cow showing its teeth in a grin. The label on the box read '*La vache qui rit.*' He gestured us to sit down on two chairs which were the only other furniture in the room, picked up a mug of what appeared to be cocoa and drank deeply.

'Please forgive me,' he said in French. 'This is the hour of my breakfast. Even men of religion must attend to the needs of the body.'

He wiped the chocolate from his lips with the back of his hand

and displayed two rows of broken teeth in a smile that was distinctly less friendly than the red cow's. Ba started to say something but the monk waved his hand at him. Ba, taken aback, fell silent. The monk turned towards me.

'You have come to enquire about our pagoda. Many foreigners do though not as many as in the old days. This is not a time for religion. Religion, and in particular our religion, requires tranquillity and where in our time is a man to find tranquillity?'

He stared over my head and his hand moved towards the box with the picture of the grinning cow. The thick fingers took out a portion of cheese and started to unwrap the silver paper. He looked at the cheese before putting it whole into his mouth. He tilted his head back and chewed slowly. When he spoke again he kept his eyes on the ceiling.

'Our Founder, whose portrait you saw in our hall of devotions, was a great man. Already as a youth he understood that the human race was wilfully divided in its search for truth. Some followed Buddha whose truth was brought to us from across the Himalayas. Others followed Confucius or Lao Tzu, the geographer of the Way. The French came and brought us their sage, Jesus Christ, and we were more divided than ever before.

'But' – he lowered his head to look at me – 'here was the miracle. It was from France that there came the final impulse that our Founder was waiting for.' He grinned, a conjuror who had extracted a rabbit from the most unexpected place. 'Monsieur Bonhomme of Nancy, a school inspector and a person of great spiritual achievements, revealed to our Founder the way in which man may receive guidance from the spirits that preside over the destinies of the world.'

He pulled back a drawer in the table and took out an old cardboard folder from which he slowly extracted two sheets of paper.

'Here, Monsieur, is the very letter in which our French – I may almost say co-founder, explained the rules of pneumatography by means of which we were able to establish the principles of our religion which embraces all religions. It is true that there are some spirits with whom we have not had contact, Mahomet, for example.'

Ba began to fidget. I felt that I was unable to interrupt the flow of ponderous French and hoped that he would manage to. But in spite of his obvious impatience he too kept quiet.

'Monsieur Bonhomme was a Christian and we take it as a sign that a man of this faith should thus have joined hands with those of Eastern faiths.'

At this point Ba did manage to break in but to my surprise his question had nothing to do with Thai.

'And what,' he asked, 'is pneumatography?'

The monk smiled and held up a fleshy hand.

'Exactly. Exactly. I shall explain. You have heard of psychography in which a medium, holding a pencil, having put his spirit into a state of serenity, may capture the fluids from on high and transform them into writing on a piece of paper? Or in which a beaked basket, a pen fixed in its Phoenix-shaped head, is held by two mediums and traces the movements determined by the spirits?'

Ba nodded his head eagerly. I realised that there was no point in my intervening for I discerned a pattern that had repeated itself in my search for Thai and my attempts to protect him. Helping him to escape from the colonel's men I had found myself introduced to the world of opium-smokers. Trying to make contact with him among the Vietcong I had been drawn into a lecture on revolution and authorised to send messages to Bertrand Russell. Now I had to submit to a lecture about some crazy spiritualist sect though it was delivered with the same seriousness that had marked the words of the Vietcong commissar and old Franchini's praise of an opium paradise. It was, I thought, a game of snakes and ladders in which most of the ladders could be counted on to turn into snakes. Having resigned myself to that I found it easier to summon up patience for the fat monk's lecture which he obviously had no intention of breaking short.

Pneumatography, he explained, was more pure than these other methods of contacting the spirit world. It demanded the utmost serenity and purity of its practitioner who, having carried out the preparations outlined by M. Bonhomme in his letter – here he waved the sheets of thin paper in my direction – had merely to place in an envelope a piece of plain paper, to which were attached two symbols cut out of red paper and shaped like the handle and sheath of a dagger (the Frenchman had thoughtfully supplied their design). The envelope was suspended on a cord just below the ceiling whereupon an invocation was made at each corner of the red-cloth covered table which bore the incense-burner and sword (all the equipment and its exact positioning had been indicated by the careful M. Bonhomme). The invocation was simple. The monk's face, so very much of this earth and with a crumb of French bread still at the corner of his mouth, here took on the expression of someone calling for a lost pet. His voice became high and entreating.

'In the middle of the flowers and incense of this invocation . . . In the middle of the flowers and incense of this invocation . . .'

He repeated the phrase four times, indicating with his hands the movement of the officiant around the table.

Ba could not contain his curiosity.

'And what happens? Is there writing on the paper?'

'Of course,' the monk answered sharply. 'It was in this way that we received the written rules and principles of our cult. They are in verse, naturally.'

He looked at the empty mug of cocoa and sighed. 'Our last communication with the spirits was in 1941 but our contact with them had been growing weaker. They were no longer completing their poems. The writing turned into meaningless lines. At first we thought we were hurrying them too much, taking the envelope down from the ceiling too quickly. Then we tried the beaked basket, though less pure of course, and it produced some more instructions for us but then it, too, fell silent. Our medium disincarnated soon afterwards.'

He looked sad and puzzled. He was silent for a while, and then went on.

'I am not surprised. For many years this country has been in no condition to commune with the spirits. We have had the French and the Japanese and the Chinese and the English, and the Blacks the French brought with them and the Indians who came with the English. Strangely, one hardly notices the Americans. They are noisy but very obsessed with themselves. They do not know how to sting us like the French. And then we have fought among ourselves. Communists against nationalists. Buddhists against Catholics. Soldiers against civilians.

Countryside against town. There has been no harmony, no harmony. Both our Founder and M. Bonhomme were insistent that nothing could be achieved without a state of harmony.'

He stood up, gesturing to us to remain where we were. He was tall for a Vietnamese with almost a wrestler's body. He went out of the room and there was the noise of bolts being slammed shut on a door. Within two minutes he was back, holding a small piece of paper. He sat down at the table and put on a pair of round metal-rimmed spectacles.

'You,' he said to me, reading from the paper, 'are Monsieur Michael and this', turning to Ba, 'is Monsieur Ba. You see, I know all about you.' He laughed, pleased as a child at our surprise.

'I thought that was who you were. Forgive my lecture but you were interested, I hope, in the history of the pagoda. I'm afraid very few people come here now and it is my duty to explain our belief. I am the venerable Phap Long, a Buddhist monk who grew tired of my own pagoda. It was not a quiet place, not a quiet place at all. Too much boasting and too much politics. It is much more peaceful here.'

He seemed about to start on another long speech but he glanced at the scrap of paper in his hand and waved it at us.

'Thai wrote your names down for me. He said you would come. He came here yesterday but it was not sensible for him to hide here. You see, I am his uncle – on his mother's side. Very different from his Uncle Maurice whom I think you have met.'

He laughed again.

'Poor Maurice. He has never been very spiritual. Clever, yes, but not spiritual. He has always had a weakness for nightclubs and whisky. This time he has let Thai down. And Thai's father, a more serious type, was at heart just a little Frenchman. Our side of the family is more simple and much more strong.'

I wanted to ask him where Thai was now but he went on: 'And poor Thai. When will he ever find tranquillity? I would have liked to give him refuge here but everyone knows that I am his uncle and this is an obvious place for the police to come to look for him.'

He looked sad but I was not sure that he would have welcomed such an intrusion into the calm little world he had created for himself. We pressed him to tell us where Thai was but he either would not say or truly did not know. All he said was that he was safe and if it was necessary would somehow get in touch with me.

As Ba and I got up to go – Phap Long's face had gone blank as though we no longer existed for him – there was a loud banging on the front door and a rough voice shouted *'Canh sat! Canh sat!'* Phap Long and Ba looked at each other and both, as in unison, said: 'It's the police.'

16

For a man who professed to be devoted to the service of superior spirits Phap Long reacted with unexpected and rapid good sense. Ba had jumped off his chair. I was too scared to move. But the monk put a thick finger to his lips and gestured calmingly with his other hand. It was as though he was expecting this interruption. He had, after all, gone out to lock the front door before starting to talk about Thai.

'Keep quiet and follow me,' he said.

He led us out of the room, into the passage and round a corner where he drew back a dirty red silk hanging decorated with gold Chinese characters to reveal an opening in the wall.

'Go up the steps.'

I had to bend almost double to pass inside. It was dark and I stumbled on what was little more than a wooden ladder. We climbed it, Ba following close behind me, and found ourselves in a small room smelling of incense and dust. Light came from a little square ventilation grille half way up the wall through which I found I could look down into Phap Long's room. Ba found another opening. It was little more than a crack and covered on the other side of the wall by another red silk hanging. Someone had cut a slit in it and Ba pulled the cloth apart a little. We were looking down into the main hall of the pagoda, over the red table with the sword.

We were in time to see Phap Long emerge from the vestibule followed by Colonel Dinh who was swinging in his hand a plastic bag that contained something red and round. Dinh was shouting. The monk turned back to him and made a placatory gesture. Dinh banged the plastic bag down on the table beside the sword and they passed out of sight towards the passage that led to Phap Long's room.

I moved over towards the grille that looked down into the monk's room and saw Dinh, his cap off and the scalp shining through his close-cropped hair, pacing up and down. The monk was sitting at the table where we had found him eating breakfast. His left hand was fingering the box of processed cheese. Perhaps he regarded it as a good luck talisman. His expression was penitent but watchful.

Ba pulled at my sleeve and gestured warningly and I realised that if Dinh looked up at the ventilation holes above his head he might notice us moving behind it. There were two chairs in the room, not the simple wooden kind that were in Phap Long's cell but far grander ones with carved backs. They were thick with dust and when I rubbed the seat I saw the faint luminescence of mother-of-pearl.

We must have sat there for almost half an hour. Ba was bent forward on his chair, listening to the conversation below. Dinh's shouts soon died away but his words still sounded harsh and threatening. Phap Long might have been speaking a different language altogether. It was a liquid, half-sung chant and I imagined that this was how he might sound if he was making an invocation to the spirits to send their pneumatographic messages. I felt sorry for the monk who, by his own account, had come to the temple when the spirits had already been silent for so many years. Had he tried to re-make contact with them? He had said nothing about that.

Unable to understand the conversation going on below and scared to ask Ba to translate for me, I examined the little room. As my eyes became accustomed to the gloom I realised that it was not the abandoned store-room that I had first taken it to be. Someone sitting here could, through the slit looking into the main hall, observe almost everything taking place there. The location of the slit, parallel with the centre of the table above which, in the envelope suspended from the ceiling, the mysteries of pneumatography took place, was perhaps not haphazard. There were some metal fittings at the top of the slit and what looked like the wheel of a small pulley. Might an assistant, hidden here, have managed to draw in the envelope from above the table and substitute a written message for the blank piece of paper? It was hard to see how the mechanics of such an operation could have worked without being spotted by those in the hall, but if the ceremony was conducted in the evening, and the hall lit dimly by candles, it might have been possible.

But if that was how it was done why did the spirit messages cease all those years ago? That seemed as great a mystery as pneumatography itself. Then I remembered Phap Long's complaint that the temple's message of harmony, a harmony that was to embrace all the struggling forces and ideas that the country contained, could only fade away when so few were ready to appreciate it. The last message that had been received, he'd said, had been that the followers of the cult were to continue on their own, relying on their own belief and the invisible encouragement of the spirits. Even if that message had been written by someone secreted in the little room above the hall it was a wise piece of trickery.

Phap Long, now demonstrating all his monkish innocence for the benefit of the colonel, was holding the fort till better days arrived. Perhaps he saw himself as a hermit in the middle of the squabbling city who one day would emerge to find an exhausted, chastened population ready at last to receive the true enlightenment the temple promised. He had said all he needed to us. He had given Thai fleeting protection, but what more could he have offered a man who knew no tranquillity and whose flight over the last few weeks had proved as pointless as the darting of a fish that tries to escape into the watery world it imagines beyond the walls of its glass tank? With Colonel Dinh he was behaving as though their two worlds had no point of contact. If ever a man was unready for the monk's message it was the colonel. They were scissors and stone and to judge by the quiet chanting which was Phap Long's part of the conversation, the stone expected to win.

Ba, I noticed, was becoming more relaxed and even once or twice laughed at what he picked up from the conversation going on below us. My own panic had subsided. The dusty little room, with its mysteries I could only guess at, proved to be oddly comforting and it also seemed clear that Dinh, for what reason I could not understand, did not mean to carry out a search of the building.

Ba held up his hand and whispered that Dinh was leaving. We heard his army boots on the stone floor of the hall. He stopped for a moment in the middle of the hall, said something to the monk and gave a half-laugh, half-giggle. The boots continued their noisy march to the door. Phap Long locked it behind him and came back to the stairs leading to our refuge to call to us.

Ba was grinning as we climbed down.

'He's clever, that monk. Dinh got nothing out of him.'

Phap Long didn't look like a man who felt he had been clever. He was sitting at his table, scratching his shaven head.

'Colonel Dinh does not understand what is going on,' he announced, 'and that is why he was so cautious. I think he wants to catch Thai very badly but he suspects that someone important is helping Thai and that is worrying him.'

He looked at me enquiringly.

'Perhaps you know who is helping Thai but perhaps even you do not know the whole truth. Dinh, you see, wants to understand everything before he makes a move. He could have arrested me. He could have had his men search the pagoda. But he doesn't want to find Thai until he knows all the people who are involved. He suspects that someone is playing a trick on him and that frightens him and makes him angry.'

It was as though he was thinking aloud. I asked him if he thought Dinh knew that Thai had been in the pagoda. The monk shrugged.

'It's not important. He knows that Thai would never try to hide here for long just as he wouldn't try to hide with Maurice or any other member of the family. What worries Dinh is that someone may help Thai hide somewhere where he cannot reach him.'

He looked at me as though I might give him an answer. I protested that Dinh had tried to catch Thai. He had sent his men to raid the house where he had first stayed in Saigon – I did not explain my part in that episode. The monk was not impressed.

'But they didn't catch him, did they? Perhaps Dinh knew it was too late. Perhaps he just wanted to send a signal to someone that he was on Thai's trail. You are a European and rather young. You may not understand that we approach things in – how shall I say – a more oblique way. We are good conspirators. Your friend here understands that.'

'It's true, it's true,' Ba said, nodding happy agreement.

Phap Long stood up as though he had no more to say to us, but he changed his mind and held his hand up, a sign that he wanted our serious attention.

'I am not frightened of Colonel Dinh. He is a cruel man but it is the cruelty of a child. He may hurt you one day and forget you the next. You see, there is no real plan behind his cruelty. He lives in a world that is changing all the time. How can he have a plan? But you must remember that the Vietcong are different. They are serious about their cruelty because they do have a plan. As a man of the spirit it pains me to say it but they even have their conception of harmony. It is true that they must break up everything first. Then they believe that they will be able to create harmony. It is not the way of the great sages but it gives them a strength that Colonel Dinh can never have.'

That was his last speech to us. It was obvious that he did not mean to impart any more of his wisdom. As if to make that plain he again took on the appearance of a shabby monk, the unconvincing apostle of a religion that had run out of steam and which might never have been more than a conspiracy in the first place. After all, it was he who had said 'We are good conspirators.'

We followed him out into the big hall. His big sandals flapped against the floor.

The hall seemed to be in a different world, untouched by the events of the morning. I could imagine Phap Long standing here, letting the calm envelop him and persuading himself that the spirits would come back or at least that the time was ripe for a little holy subterfuge which was also, in its way, a form of worship. But I was wrong about the hall. Something had changed. Ba noticed it first and touched my arm. He pointed at the red-covered table.

Lying next to the sword was a pig's head. It was bright red and must have been cut off one of the roasted and lacquered pigs that the Chinese restaurants in Cholon prepared for banquets. This was what Dinh had been carrying in the plastic bag. One of the animal's ears flopped forward giving it a roguish look. Behind the other someone – presumably the colonel – had stuck a plastic flower taken from the vase on the table.

We looked at Phap Long and he gestured dismissively with his hand.

'It's sacrilege to put something like that in a pagoda,' Ba whispered. The monk overheard him.

'It was a childish trick. It is of no importance.' But he did not look as though he believed what he said.

It was only when we went out into the courtyard and the monk had locked the door behind us that we realised Ba's motorbike had all the time been standing there for Dinh and his men to see. Ba behaved as though it did not matter. He started the machine and called out '*On y va*' in his usual impatient way.

All the way back to the villa I could not forget the animal's head. I could imagine Phap Long hesitating before he removed it from the sacred table. Perhaps it was just a childish trick and perhaps Dinh was capable only of childish cruelty, but the object of that cruelty would suffer all the same. Ba's thin body, tense as he drove through the heavy noon-time traffic, seemed entirely vulnerable and I wondered if the pig's message was not meant as much for him and me as for the keeper of the Temple of True Enlightenment.

17

When I got home I sat on the veranda and forced myself to think. My first conclusion, and it surprised me greatly, was that I envied Thai. He was ill and on the run but I envied him. I couldn't forget that ridiculous story about how a little Asian boy had found revolutionary inspiration in an old Hollywood tearjerker. I envied him that passionate childhood which was so much more important to him than his later years at an English school. I envied him his flight to the communists and his escape from them. He was only two years older than me but I was a child by comparison, ignorant and spoiled. Gruson had been right to treat me as a child, telling me no more than was necessary to make me fall in with his plan.

He was right, but I resented it. I knew I had to talk to Gruson again for I needed his intervention to protect Ba from Colonel Dinh. This time I would try to do the manipulating. I waited till lunchtime and then took a cyclo to his house. I tried to see if anyone was watching my villa or if anyone followed me but soon realised that a platoon of men could be pursuing me in the crowded streets and I would have little chance of identifying them or remembering their faces if I did. There was usually a small boy at the street corner nearest my house who mended bicycle tyres. He wore torn, greasy shorts and shirt and squatted over the few instruments he needed for his work. Sometimes he withdrew to lean against a treetrunk where there was shade. He was there from early morning to late evening. I had heard stories of how the Vietcong had used such boys as spies and lookouts when they were preparing their invasion of the city in 1968. Why shouldn't Dinh use them too? The boy could see everyone who came to the villa.

I looked at him as I went by in the cyclo. His hair had a brownish-red tint to it and his features were unusually angular for a child of his age. The cyclo driver noticed him, too, and turned round to me.

'Métis.'

He gave the French word an exaggerated twang and laughed unkindly. If the boy was a half-caste that explained his odd look. Perhaps it would make him all the more willing to work for the police for he would not have many other friends to count on.

By the time we got to Gruson's house I had begun to feel that there was nowhere I could go in the city without being spied on. I could not understand how careless I had been in my movements before. I had behaved as though I was almost invisible. Now I felt myself growing taller and fairer. It was as though I were accompanied by a spotlight wherever I moved. Everyone who saw me would remember me. I might just as well have rung the colonel up each morning and told him what I planned to do.

I don't know what I would have done if Gruson had not been in. The maid showed me into the room with the bar. He was eating lunch and reading a copy of *Newsweek* that was propped against a bottle of white wine.

'You've caught me at my bachelor's feast. Not much to offer you I'm afraid but what about a glass of wine? I can promise you it's better than that Chinese plonk that they cook up in Cholon out of buffalo piss and God knows what else.'

He went over to the bar to get me a glass and as he was pouring the wine asked me if anything was the matter. The question and the change of tone that accompanied it put me off my stride. I had promised myself that I would be careful about what I told him but instead I started to describe everything that had happened from the morning that Ba had appeared in the bank tapping on the counter with his pipe. I told him how I had taken Thai to the opium den, about the raid by Dinh's men on our supposed refuge, and the morning I had just spent with Phap Long at the pagoda. I told him that Dinh must have the number of Ba's motorbike and that I was worried about what might happen to him. I explained that I had tried to find both him and Byrne before taking Thai away from the house. The only thing I did not tell him was that Thai no longer seemed to trust him or want anything more to do with him.

None of it appeared to surprise Gruson. He kept his eyes on me as I talked and tweaked his nose between forefinger and thumb a few times and when I'd finished said, almost as though he thought it funny, 'You have got us into a pickle, haven't you?'

He picked up his glass and walked about the room for a

minute, holding the glass up to the window and admiring the colour of the wine. I was relieved that he didn't seem angry but I couldn't fathom what he was thinking. He drank some wine and then perched himself on one of the red bar stools. He crossed his legs to reveal a bright suspender holding up a sock. My father had worn suspenders like that when I was a child but I hadn't seen them since. They would have seemed ridiculous on anyone else but they didn't on Gruson. This is a man, they seemed to say, who keeps everything under careful control, even his socks. I looked at the strip of yellow elastic around the white hairless shin and, in spite of myself, felt reassured.

'We've got two problems here, haven't we?' Gruson spoke in the calming manner of an officer explaining something to not very bright soldiers.

'Problem one is what to do about Thai. Problem two is what the police may do about you and your Mr Ba. Let's start with problem two. I can make sure that Dinh keeps his men away from you though the odds are that he'll still want to keep a watch on you. It might be a bit more difficult with Ba. Mr Ba may be in for a fright.'

I was going to protest but he waved the wine glass at me.

'Sorry, old chap, but you have to realise the rules of the Vietnamese game. I said "a fright" and I expect we can make sure it's no more than that. But the good colonel may feel he has to do something to restore his dignity and show that he is in control again. He can't have every grubby little conspirator from the Saigon cafés going around making contact with the Vietcong and thinking he can get away with it scot-free.

'But the real problem is Thai, isn't it? And that's where you have still got some work to do. That young man needs friends and you're the only person he knows who hasn't been dipped in the Vietnamese poison. His family will help him all right if they know how, which judging by Maurice and that other monk uncle you've just met I rather doubt. Thai won't get in touch with me, that much is certain.'

I must have looked surprised but I hoped not guilty. The conversation was getting close to the one thing I was determined not to reveal to him.

'Perhaps you didn't notice it but he saw through me that evening I came round to meet him. I knew it was a risk but there wasn't any choice. It might have been all right if he wasn't such an arrogant little sod.'

I asked him what he meant by Thai seeing through him. He looked at me, his head on one side, as though weighing up in his mind whether this was the right moment for what he had to say. Never had he seemed so calculating, so concerned that words and events be arranged in exactly their right order.

Instead of answering me he checked his watch.

'I think we've got time for a practical lesson in life and politics.'

He finished his wine in his glass, picked up his car keys from the table and waved them at me.

'Come on, we're going for a little drive.'

I followed him down the stairs and into the garage. We got into the car which he reversed expertly into the narrow front yard and drove out onto the street with a blare of the horn. Cyclos braked hard to avoid us and a little Lambretta bus crammed with passengers swerved onto the wrong side of the road. Its driver shouted at Gruson but the passengers, hanging onto the sides of the swinging vehicle, laughed.

He drove fast in the direction of the embassy but turned to the right after the Cercle Sportif. We passed in front of the presidential palace and he parked the car at the side of the avenue that led up to its front gates. There were few people to be seen. Two soldiers, in sharply creased battle dress and shiny American helmets, stood in front of the gates which were obstructed by barbed wire barricades. The palace stood far back from the tall iron railings, a red and yellow flag hanging still in the heavy afternoon heat. It was surrounded by a park of bright green grass and fine trees, an unexpected oasis of tidiness and calm in a city that had lost the knack for either.

I sensed that Gruson felt unsure of me and would now try to win me over once and for all. But I couldn't figure out how he would set about it. We walked across to the palace railings.

'What do you think of the building?' Gruson asked, but didn't wait for my answer. 'It makes me think of the console of a giant organ constructed by some manic organist.'

I could see what he meant. The concrete rectangle of the façade was broken by a balcony on which I could imagine someone sitting down, his back to the avenue, to strike the notes of a vast keyboard.

'That's how the little president sees himself, you know,' Gruson went on. 'The trouble is that only he can hear the music. He thinks that other people can't because they are wicked or stupid. But the real trouble is that there's no power to plug the damned machine into. The result is, of course, that the man is suffering from a terminal case of paranoia.'

He set off along the road that led up the side of the palace. We came to another gate, also guarded by soldiers. There was a courtyard beyond it in which military vehicles were parked and a building, obviously a barracks.

'The place is crammed with weapons. Tanks, anti-aircraft guns. You name it, they've got it. But you only have to see the little man's shifty eyes to know that he doesn't believe in any of it. It's the organ with no power again. All those guns aren't worth a damn if one day the poor buggers holding them can't be bothered to pull the trigger.'

He pointed at a tall building on the other side of the street.

'When the Vietcong came and attacked the city in 1968 a squad of them got into that building. They sat there and fired rockets over the palace wall. The army was running round like frightened rabbits so Dinh collected a team of goons like the ones you came across the other day and brought them here. You're right, they're about the nastiest lot of characters you can imagine, but they went in there and cleared the commies out. I watched them do it. Afterwards they dragged the corpses into the street and left them there like a lot of dummies from Madame Tussaud's.

'The VC got their sums wrong then. They believed their own propaganda and thought that the people would rise up and drive the Yanks into the sea. It was crazy but they really believed it. The truth is that most people in this awful country are fed up with both sides. If they've got any *nous* they're scared of the Vietcong because they're the most frightful know-alls as well as being bullies. And they know what to expect from the little man in the palace – bullying, too, though of a much more inefficient kind, but also robbery and lousy government. Which of course all adds up to a sort of freedom.'

We started walking back to the car.

'What I'm trying to explain is where people like Dinh and myself come in. If you've got a country like this which has been falling apart for years you can patch it up, for a time anyhow. You patch it up by bribing some people, tricking others, but a lot of the time just by hitting them on the head. It's much easier than trying to make yourself popular. The little president doesn't have the power for that but he has got enough power for patching up. That's what he uses Dinh for and it's my business too.

'The trouble where Thai is concerned is that Dinh is keen on head-hitting while I want to make use of him. That young man is still too much of a prig to understand that he's got to get his fingers dirty if he ever wants to stop those commie friends of his that he's now disillusioned with. Okay. Let's wait a while, but one day we might be able to propel him back here with his halo of honesty and put him to good use. Once I get him out of here we'll be able to work on him. I dare say a little flattery and a little pressure will do the trick. In any case we've a better chance of succeeding with him than the Yanks have.'

We stopped at the car but he didn't unlock the door. A cyclo went by slowly, the driver clicking the brake handle to attract our attention. The two sentries at the palace gate stood with their American rifles balanced against their thighs. I wondered what they had done when the palace was attacked.

Gruson looked at me for a moment.

'Am I shocking you?' he asked. I shrugged.

'My dear Michael,' he began, 'you are quite an intelligent person but you suffer dreadfully like most English men of your class from your upbringing. You see, you expect the world to proceed according to rules without having the foggiest idea of how those rules ever came to be made. You think it quite natural that laws should be obeyed, taxes paid and motorists stop at pedestrian crossings. This makes you in many ways an admirable person. And in a country like this where only the suicidal or the very stupid obey the rules it gives you an aura of reliability that someone like Thai finds very reassuring. That, by the way, is one of the reasons I picked you to make contact with him.

'Look, don't you understand?' His tone was irritated, a schoolmaster addressing a wilfully stubborn pupil.

'Let me tell you something about myself. When I started out

in this business they sent me down to an old barracks near Portsmouth. I was just out of university and so were the other chaps who were there. You know what they taught us? Kim's game, looking at a jumble of oddments on a tray and then trying to remember them all. I learned how to write messages on paper that dissolved if you had to swallow it, the best way to set fire to a building, how to put a microphone in a wall.

'It sounds pretty low level James Bond stuff, doesn't it? I thought so at the time. In fact I thought it was pretty stupid. I'd been told I was going to help defend the English way of life against the wicked reds and there I was choking on bits of paper. They tasted foul, by the way. I didn't understand the first thing about microphones and still don't. The bloody things usually conk out after the first day anyhow.

'But now I realise that the point of it all was to teach me the lesson I've been trying to drum into your skull. Life doesn't come easily, not even for such a bloody lucky country as England. There are all sorts of ugly nuts and bolts in there that most people don't know about and would be shocked if they did.

'And let me tell you – the little men in Hanoi understand that very well. Don't you believe all that stuff about the inevitable march of history and people rising up as one man. History doesn't go anywhere unless you give it a bloody good shove. That's what's happening here. The commies are shoving at one end and people like me are shoving at the other. I think it's your job to help me because if you don't you'll only have yourself to blame if one day the bloody thing runs you over.'

He had become unusually excited. He knew that I was an unwilling listener and he was annoyed by his inability to make me submit. But it wasn't me that he could not overcome. It was the thin band of loyalty which I felt binding me to Thai.

I promised him that I would let him know if Thai sent me a message, hoping he wouldn't realise it was a lie. I couldn't see any reason why I could not convince him that Thai had just disappeared. Meanwhile I could still count on Gruson to do his best for Ba. That was important enough to make me feel quite easy about the lie.

Gruson drove me back to my villa in silence. But he stuck his head out of the window and shouted after me. 'Don't forget.

You're not in lucky little England now.'

His face was red and it sounded more like a threat than a joke. I wondered if he would really keep his word about intervening with Colonel Dinh.

18

When my boss saw me the next morning he called me over.

'Your friend Gruson's won a reprieve for you. I just hope that whatever it is isn't going to go on too long. After all, we do pay you.'

The tone was grudging but not too protesting. I wondered if he had put up any resistance to Gruson and decided probably not. He was a mixture of pompousness and vulnerability. Gruson would have enjoyed launching one of his verbal assaults on him.

It was hard to bring my mind back to the work on my desk. When I'd said goodbye to Ba after our morning at the pagoda we'd arranged to meet at Givral, as if by chance, in two days' time. I hoped in this way to keep an eye on him and also to give him what reassurance I could, though I didn't put much store by my ability to do that. The thought of him riding round the city like a fragile jockey on his motorbike scared me. It would be the easiest thing in the world to contrive an 'accident' for him, but perhaps Dinh wouldn't even bother to be as subtle as that if he had made his mind up to punish him. I was relieved that Gruson had spoken to my boss so soon for that gave me hope that he had also lost no time in getting in touch with the colonel.

I could not bear the thought of an evening on my own in the villa watching the squabbling lizards and listening to the cyclos rattle by on the street. When Jeannette rang up and said she wanted to see me I told her to come round for dinner. I knew she would tell me that I had been neglecting her and that I was keeping something hidden from her and that we would quarrel again but I didn't care about that. I could at least hold on to her body and stop for a while the sense of falling.

When I got back from the bank I had a long lukewarm shower to try to drive away the heat. The Frenchman who had built the villa had done his best to make a refuge of it with thick walls and eaves that protected the windows from the sun. But it gave little relief in those April days. The heat followed you everywhere, nagging without cease, and the more you resisted the more it nagged back. I poured myself a whisky, took that morning's *Saigon Post* into the bedroom where there was a noisy American air-conditioner and turned it on.

The newspaper looked as though it had been printed none too expertly on a child's printing set. The type did not sit straight in the columns and the smudged picture on the front page – the president inspecting a troop of boy scouts – appeared to have been taken in the dusk. I turned to the horoscope and found that the day had been good for my business but that I needed to show understanding in personal relations. Ba had once suggested that we pay a visit to an astrologer who was reputed to cast horoscopes for generals close to the president and perhaps even for the great man himself. I wondered if they would offer advice more suited to the world I had been drawn into.

Jeannette said she would come at eight o'clock but about half an hour before that someone started to beat at the door and a thin, male voice called out softly, '*Ong oi! Ong oi!*' For a moment I thought it was Ba but I had not heard his motorbike and his tone was always assertive, while this was a tentative, almost conspiratorial cry.

At first I did not recognise the man at the door. He had wispy white hair and his clothes, too, were white though the trousers were stained and his old-fashioned gymshoes had never been smartened up with blanco. The sleeves of his shirt flapped unbuttoned around his wrists. At school there had been an old cricket professional who sometimes coached the youngest boys. He had dressed like that and had the same air of apologetic decay. We called him Old Calico Bags. I don't believe I ever knew his real name for he was treated not as a person but as part of the school furniture. Even the boys who were most inexpert at cricket and hated going to the nets didn't mind when Old Calico Bags was there.

The old man, sensing my confusion, stared pleadingly at me. He had a broad, high forehead which gave him the look of a clever child until you noticed the eyes which were in perpetual retreat.

'You remember me, Monsieur?' he asked in French. 'I came with you to the Delta. I was the man who helped you find Thai.'

It was Do, the old man I had first seen stumbling across the garden of the opium-smoker's house and who had nearly got us killed with his foolish plan to go and look for Thai in the middle of a battle. He obviously had a knack for the unexpected entrance. I knew instinctively that whatever news he brought it could not be good.

Do, who had been so impenitent over our earlier misadventures with him, now at least seemed more sensitive to my unwelcoming look. He was sorry for bothering me but it was a serious matter. He had by chance been that evening to call on Ba – '*C'est un vieux ami, voyez-vous,*' he explained, as though he felt an explanation was needed – and had found everything in uproar. A grenade had been thrown and Ba's house damaged. A lot of people were there. Ba was all right but he didn't know if anyone else had been hurt.

My first reaction was anger with Gruson. He hadn't got hold of Dinh or, if he had, he had not talked to him properly. Perhaps he had never meant to. To my surprise I saw that Do was almost smiling. It was a wisp of a smile, a little sly flicker on a face that no longer seemed puzzled.

'Perhaps it was the Vietcong,' he said and looked at me expectantly.

I asked him why he should think that. The question and the little smile irritated me and I must have sounded abrupt for he at once became a lost old man again, a pointless target for anyone's anger.

I asked him if he could guide me to Ba's house and he nodded. I wrote a note for Jeannette and pinned it on the front door, hiding the key where she could find it to let herself in. Do had come on a bicycle and I told him to leave it and come with me in my car. Ba had only told me that he lived in Gia Dinh, a town that had become part of Saigon as the city became swollen with years of war.

Do, sitting on the edge of his seat and his head almost touching the windscreen as if it helped him see better, directed me past the embassy. We went over a bridge. The street was wide but dimly lit and the buildings on either side were no more than brick and concrete boxes, some of them unfinished and with twisted metal rods sticking like insects' legs from the tops of walls. Do prodded my arm and pointed to a large building with a roof of heavy tiles. Even in the gloom it seemed as out of place as a prince surrounded by guttersnipes. The old man nodded his head meaningfully.

'*C'est le temple d'un grand maréchal.*' He paused and then, with the trace of a sneer, '*pas comme les maréchaux d'aujourd'hui.*'

He said no more but directed me in silence down a side street which might have been a village lane. There were thick hedges on either side. The air was cooler. I could understand why Ba had chosen to live here. It was a refuge. After a night here he could return refreshed to the next day's adventures in the city.

I parked the car as best I could and Do led me through a gap in the hedge. We were in a little village of small one-storey houses set haphazardly under trees. Hens attacked the baked black earth and there was a strong smell of pigs. Someone was playing a radio. A woman's voice, yearning but not at all innocent, rose and fell slowly, accompanied by instruments making the same half-eastern, half-western sounds that I had heard when Maurice had taken me to the nightclub.

It was obvious where Ba's house was. The life of the little community had tipped in its direction like water collecting at the side of a bowl that has been rocked to one side. Children looking about them for something to tease or fight and ugly dogs whose curiosity had got the better of their usual caution marked the edge of a crowd of women carrying babies and men in pyjamas or trousers and vests. At its centre were Ba and a plump, brown-faced policeman. He was a big man, the sort of officer I had seen sitting at pavement cafés, face growing redder with each glass of beer but with eyes that never stopped moving and checking everything about him.

The two men were shouting at each other but as Do led me through the crowd the policeman turned round and walked off leaving Ba to address his final protest to his neighbours. Some of the men laughed.

Ba wasn't hurt but when he saw us and came hurrying over he looked grim.

'That fat *flic*,' he said angrily. 'He won't do anything. He said someone probably dropped the grenade by mistake.'

He looked as puzzled as he was angry and it was only when he took us over to his house that I understood he was in a state of shock. The grenade had exploded at the front of the house but sufficiently to the side for only part of the blast to catch the veranda. The wall was pockmarked and there was blood on the tile floor. There was blood, too, on a plastic toy gun made in one of the little workshops in Cholon. A hammock hung between two of the posts holding up the veranda roof.

We stood looking at the bloodstains while Ba explained what had happened. He had been lying in the hammock watching his four-year-old son playing. After a while he went into the house to look for his pipe. That was when he heard the explosion. He rushed out to find the boy screaming, the right side of his body torn by fragments of the grenade. Ba's wife had rushed the child to hospital.

Ba insisted we go into the house. There was very little furniture in the front room: a table, a cupboard in the corner, on top of it a colour photograph of a baby. A large but elderly refrigerator stood in the corridor leading to the back of the house. It was almost monastic.

I could hear sobbing and whispering in the next room. Ba called out and a strange little troupe appeared in the corridor, led by a teenage boy who could only have been Ba's son, short and with a stubborn chin. He was holding a whimpering baby. There was a girl and two younger children in pale-green pyjamas. They stood in a line and after a sharp word from Ba bowed to us like grave little mandarins, for all the fear that was in their eyes. Ba made us sit down and the girl was sent out for tea.

I had never seen Ba at a loss before. He did not know in which direction to move next and this was a kind of torture for him. We tried to work out who might have thrown the grenade. I explained why I didn't think Dinh was responsible. I told him I had spoken to a friend at the British embassy and that he had promised to speak to the colonel. I didn't offer any explanation as to why my diplomat friend should have access to Dinh or expect that he could influence him but Ba did not find that strange. But Do, I noticed, pricked up his ears. He asked if my friend was 'an important man.' I didn't reply and his face relapsed into its usual look of fecklessness.

I remembered that Do, at my house, had suggested that the Vietcong might have thrown the grenade. Ba hadn't thought of that but the more we discussed it the more plausible it seemed to me. After all, we had not just been treading on the colonel's toes. Arguably our offence against the communists was even graver. We had snatched away a man who might have outlived his usefulness to them but who could perhaps be turned damagingly against them.

Up till then I had given little thought to the communists. At our encounter with them in the plantation there had been something ghostly about the way they'd appeared and in their almost equally magical disappearance the following morning. I could not connect the officer with elfin ears and his young, serious-faced soldiers with anything I knew in the city. Saigon was Dinh's world: irritable, undisciplined, and selfish. This was the real jungle. It was not a place for those boy scouts with their toothbrushes neatly wrapped up in plastic and sentimental songs about love and war.

Ba said it couldn't have been the Vietcong. He knew them, he said, and they knew him.

'*Voyez-vous, Monsieur Michael*, what could they have against me? I am a poor man. If one day they win I shan't leave, not like the bourgeois who will all run off to France and America. We don't need very much to live.'

He waved his arm around the room.

'What have I got that they could take away from me? I am a patriot, too. They will need people like me. They can't drive everyone out. Then who would they have left? They'll have to use the Khmers.'

In spite of his wretchedness he found that very funny and laughed. Mr Do laughed too and repeated Ba's words – '*les Khmers, les Khmers*' – as though the very sound of it was ridiculous.

I could not budge him. The grenade had been thrown either by Dinh's men or by a drunken soldier or some other hooligan. It happened, he said, all the time, especially at night. The city was full of weapons. Only the other evening two of the home guard, teenagers who were meant to man checkpoints in the evening, had had a quarrel and shot at each other, wounding an old woman who was passing by.

I felt helpless. When I had set off in the car with Do I had supposed that the business was reaching a climax. Dinh had given his warning. Ba could be left safely to get on with his life. Thai had disappeared, probably for ever. I could look forward to a few boring months before I left the wretched place for good. But once again everything was dissolving into uncertainty. Perhaps the Vietcong did want something from us. If the grenade carried no meaning, perhaps Dinh was still planning to frighten Ba.

Before I left I tried to make Ba realise that he had to be careful and that he was to have no more part in the affair if it did, against my hope, revive. There was to be no more talk of even 'chance' encounters with him in a café. He looked disappointed but did not protest.

Do and I left the way we had come. The people had gone back to their houses. Through one window I saw a couple, in shorts and tee-shirts, lying on a bed of plain wood, arms around each other and quietly talking. Someone was listening to the singer with the smoky voice. I noticed that the hedge by which we had parked the car was full of small white flowers that smelled of jasmine. A figure moved away from the car but it was only a small boy, as wretchedly dressed as the little tyre-repair urchin who sat all day by my villa. As we drove off I heard the 'put-put' of someone starting a Mobylette, the old French moped that was still occasionally to be seen among the Hondas and Suzukis that had taken over the city.

19

There was little traffic apart from the occasional blue and cream taxi, its lights so weak that they burned a brownish yellow. Do sat slumped back in his seat, lifeless as a scarecrow. I took the road past the big embassies. The French, a handsome old building set back from the street, was an aristocratic reproach to the prison-like mass of the American with its high white protective walls. Some cyclos were driving through the cathedral square and down into Tu Do to look for customers coming from the bars. Once or twice I caught a glimpse in the mirror of a small figure on a moped and wondered if it was the same one I had heard starting up outside Ba's house, but I forgot about it when Mr Do came to life as we passed the cathedral, and asked me if I was Catholic. He seemed disappointed when I shook my head.

'I know many priests,' he said. 'I can introduce Monsieur to some interesting priests.' He paused and looked at me. I shook my head again. I couldn't understand why he should think I might want to talk to a priest, above all one picked by him. 'They are much more interesting than the monks,' he persisted. 'The monks are not men of education, not like the fathers. I know some very clever priests. They know everything.'

I wondered what he meant by that. Had Ba told him that we had been to see Phap Long? But why should he want to put down Phap Long and offer instead a priest who knew everything? What was I supposed to want to ask him? When Ba had introduced me to Do he had said that he wasn't as silly as he looked. The old man made me feel uneasy. It occurred to me that he was, in an indirect way, offering to help me find Thai but I could not for the life of me understand why. Perhaps I would have puzzled over it more if I had not been so determined not to let myself get entangled with him any further. I said nothing and we ended the drive in silence.

I had forgotten that Jeannette might be waiting for me. As we got out of the car she opened the front door and came out. I guessed that she had prepared herself to be angry with me for standing her up but the sight of Do put her off her stride. She looked at him disbelievingly as he flapped his way across the drive and got onto his bicycle. He rode off slowly and unsteadily, waving an arm as he turned into the street.

'Who on earth was that?'

Her curiosity had got the better of her anger. I didn't have an answer ready and I cursed myself for it. The last thing I wanted was to get drawn into an explanation of where I had been. I put my arm around her and moved her back into the house. She pulled herself free.

'Leave me alone. You've got another guest.'

Byrne was in an armchair in the sitting room. My last bottle of Black Label Scotch had been opened and a good third of it drunk. He didn't get up but waved his glass at me in welcome as though he were in his own house. He was wearing a sickly yellow shirt outside a pair of dark-green slacks. As usual the shirt was unbuttoned to show the bush of black hair on his chest through which there was the glint of a gold chain. He wasn't drunk but he had had enough to turn his usual surliness into a more expansive sort of ill-humour.

'Do you always stand your girlfriend up like this?' was the first thing he said, making it sound more accusation than question.

Jeannette gave me a victorious look.

'When I saw your note I rang him up and asked him to come round for a drink. I didn't want to be alone all evening and he was very nice and said he'd keep me company.'

Byrne showed his teeth in a smile and waved his glass at me again.

'Nice Scotch, old chap. Glad to see you've got good taste.'

It was obvious that both of them expected me to explain where I had been. I had no intention of telling them what had happened to Ba or that I had even seen him that evening so I produced a story about one of the senior Vietnamese staff at the bank being ill. I said I'd been to see him about some work he was doing and which couldn't wait until he got better.

'But who was that terrible old man who came back with you?' Byrne pricked up his ears at Jeannette's question.

'You've been keeping strange company, have you? Wouldn't have thought it of you.'

I said he was a relation of the sick man who had come to guide me to his house. The answer seemed to satisfy them. At least they didn't ask any more questions. I poured myself a strong whisky but didn't offer Byrne any. Jeannette, whom I'd never seen drinking anything stronger than wine, asked me to give her one too. We sat down and no one said anything. Eventually Byrne broke the silence.

'I hear you've been having some adventures. I hope you don't get yourself into trouble, old man.'

He looked as though nothing would please him more. Jeannette gave me an accusing stare.

'What sort of adventures? Why didn't you tell me?'

She was angry again. The whisky had already given her face the beginning of a brick-red tint and it didn't become her. Perhaps that was why usually she was so careful about what she drank. I was sure Byrne's remark was meant only to cause trouble between me and Jeannette.

He succeeded. She said she had known all along I was hiding something from her. I didn't trust her. I was treating her as a child and it was just because she wasn't a European.

'You whites are all like that. You never really treat us like human beings. You think you can smile at us and pat us on the head and we'll be grateful. You think you're so big and important. I think you're just a big shit.'

She started to cry. She thumped her glass down, got up and walked noisily out to the bathroom. Byrne laughed.

'You really are an innocent, aren't you? We've got to learn how to treat the ladies, you know. A sexy girl like that needs to be looked after but it doesn't look as though you've done a very good job of it.'

I'd learned one thing, at least, which was never to let Byrne see me get angry. I smiled back and said I didn't think it was very clever of him to make in front of Jeannette even guarded references to what I'd been doing for Gruson.

'From what I hear you aren't doing anything for Gruson. From what I hear you've gone and ballsed the whole thing up. Where the hell is this little pinko that you were supposed to be looking after? As far as I can see the whole thing's over now and you certainly don't deserve any medals for your part in it. I told Gruson that it was crazy to ask you to do it in the first place. I've been waiting for you to prove that I was right and thank you very much that's exactly what you've done.'

He gave himself some more Scotch.

'You don't mind, do you? I think I deserve something for coming to hold your little girl's hand while you're out on your precious bank's business – if that's what you were really doing.'

He looked at me inquisitively.

'I hope you're playing straight with us, Michael. People like you sometimes get silly ideas.'

I said I couldn't imagine what he was getting at. This made him angry, and I was pleased.

'Come off it. You're not quite as simple as you look. You know what I mean. You thought that you were doing some boy scout's good turn when you said you'd help Gruson. You thought it sounded like a nice clean adventure, didn't you? That's because you're ignorant. Nothing out here is a nice clean adventure and no one here fits into the sort of adventure stories you're capable of imagining. I suspect that you've started to feel sorry for that silly bugger Thai. Poor little chap, the reds were so beastly to him too. It's something like that, isn't it? Well, I only hope you're telling the truth about him having vanished.'

The bathroom door slammed and Jeannette came back into the room. Byrne gave her a lecherous smile.

'Better now?' he said to her and then, quickly, to me, 'Just a friendly warning. I'd hate to see you get into trouble. We all would, wouldn't we, Jeannette?'

She didn't pay any attention.

'I've got a headache. I'm going home.'

I said I would drive her but she shook her head as though that was the last thing in the world she wanted. Byrne got up.

'All right. Party's over. I'll be going too. I'll see she doesn't get lost.'

To my annoyance she didn't object to his offer. They walked together across the courtyard to the street but instead of turning right, the way to Jeannette's house, they turned left towards Tu Do and Byrne's hotel.

20

It rained the following afternoon, the first rain since I had arrived in the city. But it was no more than a thin shower and the hot streets swallowed it up like a thirsty man presented with a few, taunting drops of water. Ba had said that this was how the rains began. These showers were called the mango rains. It was hard to believe that the sky, so long dry, would ever be able to squeeze out more than this pitiful amount of moisture that made no difference to the heat.

I realised then that I was more tired than I knew. I did understand, though, that I was waiting for more than the rain. I wanted a resolution of the problems in which I had become tangled. I wanted to pull Jeannette away from Byrne or anyone else for that matter, but I knew I could not give her what she wanted. I imagined taking her to see my parents – in Gloucestershire, of all places – and the politeness masking their horror at the thought of a half-caste daughter-in-law. I had never talked to her of marriage, never thought of it myself, but even that was playing a trick on her. I had never told her the idea was impossible.

And hadn't I played a trick on Gruson, and on the communists too for that matter? I could justify that to myself but it was painful to remember the enthusiasm with which I had begun my part in the Thai affair. I had tricked Ba – at least, not told him the whole truth. I had tricked old Do. The only person I wasn't tricking any more was Thai. This wasn't how I'd been brought up to behave. It wasn't what I'd been taught to expect from life. And though I longed for a resolution of the tension I must have known that it would not come. I had left the world of games played according to rules, of family propriety and honourable business without realising what was happening and there was no easy escape back to it. The memory of Thai, wretched and cold on an English football pitch, came back to me and I wondered if even then he hadn't understood what I was just learning. Games and rules weren't to be much use to him.

After work that day I went to swim at the Cercle and drove myself as many times as I could up and down the long pool, bumping into the frog-like children and scarcely noticing them. I wanted to unwind myself and I planned, when I got home, to drink enough Scotch to ensure that at least I would sleep soundly.

But it did not turn out that way. I found a folded piece of paper stuck into the side of the front door. It was in English, in carefully printed capital letters.

'DEAR MR MICHAEL. I WANT GREATLY TO SEE YOU THIS EVENING. PLEASE GO TO THE MARKET BY THE RAILWAY STATION AT 8. KINDLY GO TO TAXI WAITING AT VINH LOI CINEMA. THE CHAUFFEUR WAITS FOR YOU. HE WILL BRING YOU TO ME. I AM YOU FRIEND. PLEASE COME.'

My first reaction was to tear the note up and give myself the stiff drink I had promised myself. I had no idea whom the message was from. It could be a trap – Ba had once delivered me a long lecture on the art of provocation and how the Vietnamese, with their fondness for the indirect, excelled at it. He had several times read out from the newspaper stories of strange incidents – an unexplained fire at a pagoda or an explosion at some little Chinese factory – and exclaimed, not without pleasure, *'C'est une provocation, Monsieur.'* Many of his afternoons at Givral were apparently given over to wrangling about who stood to gain most from incidents like these. Judging by his account of these sessions the prize went to whoever could produce the most devious theory.

But if it was a trap I could not see that it would do me much harm. The note was so vague that I could convincingly protest innocence. And the chance to do something, now that it had been presented to me, seemed more attractive than an evening with the whisky bottle.

I was, though, still nervous enough to take some precautions. About seven o'clock I set out on foot in the direction of Tu Do and spent some time there walking up and down in front of the shops. A crowd came out here every evening before the dusk fell almost as quickly as a dark gauze dropping across a stage. This was middle-class Saigon – the people Gruson despised for not being aristocrats – and their evening promenade allowed them to behave for a short while as though life was normal and its small everyday pleasures quite secure.

They ignored the bars that made money from the Americans and went to finger the latest material in the tailors' shops that had pictures of out-of-date French fashions in the window. They stopped to look at the craftsmen's boutiques that sold ivory and lacquer ware and objects glinting with mother-of-pearl inlay. A family stood as though entranced by dark brown lacquer boxes decorated with plump red-gold fish, their tails and fins trailing behind them like Chinese robes. I wondered how many times they must have stared at them, for nothing in the street could be new to them any more.

There was a Chinese grocer at one corner. His shop smelled of coffee and French cheese and was a storehouse of shining, neatly stacked tins of ham, *marrons glacés* and goose liver pâté. The grocer sent his pale, graceful children to the smartest ex-French lycées, but in the late afternoon they stood at the cashdesk, smiling distantly as they took in the money. Their father, it was said, had promised to send them all to France. He was a rich man and could afford to buy them passports. Ba always spoke dismissively about the children. 'Poor little Chinese' he called them, as though their Chinese blood was a curse. The children seemed not to care. Perhaps they were already dreaming of Paris and that was why they smiled as they arranged the creased piastre notes tidily in the till.

I walked back up to the Assembly building and at Givral turned down into Le Loi. As far as I could tell no one was following me. The life here was much less decorous. A crowd of teenagers were fooling around outside the Rex cinema and there was a party going on at the top of the American officers' club next to it. A band was playing jazz and white faces looked down onto the street below. The pavement was crowded with women squatting over piles of cigarettes, toothpaste and soap. They waved their arms at the passers-by to attract their attention and bickered among themselves. There were beggars, too, but few people paid them any notice.

There was a crowd outside the Vinh Loi where the little Thai had shed tears over Chopin *alias* Cornel Wilde. That night the cinema was showing a Bardot movie. Little encouragement there, I thought, for young revolutionaries. I waited no more than two minutes before I heard a shout and spotted a taxi-driver in a plastic topee beckoning me to get in beside him. He was very small but with an exceptionally muscular body. He was wearing shorts and the few hairs on his legs stood up as though they were made of black wire.

He grinned and said questioningly, '*Ong Mickle? Ong Mickle?*'

I nodded and got in, folding my legs tightly to fit into the seat next to him. He drove off, thumping the tiny twig of a gear lever hard to make it stay in position. The little car sounded as though it might expire at any moment but the driver seemed unaware of the struggling noises coming from the engine and the rattle each time we struck a hole. We went in the direction of the airport. Every now and then he turned to grin at me. It was a peasant's face, round and snub-nosed. When we stopped at a traffic light he stretched across to pull the hairs on my forearm as the children had done the day we drove to the rubber plantation for Thai.

He seemed to speak not a word of English or French but when we were close to the airport he pointed to the road and said '*Evêque frongçais.*' All I could see was a stone construction like an elephant's howdah in the middle of the road. '*Evêque frongçais*' he repeated urgently. '*Très grand évêque. Mort. Très mort.*'

The thought of the very great French bishop who was now very dead – presumably this was his tomb – excited him very much. He nodded at me again and I noticed that he was wearing a small gold crucifix round his neck.

I remembered the remark of the infuriating Mr Do about Catholic priests and his attempt to interest me in an introduction to one. Was this the meeting to which I was now being driven? I tried to ask the driver if we were going to a church but he seemed to have exhausted his knowledge of French. We turned down a dirt track between shacks made of odd pieces of wood and covered with corrugated iron. Women stood at doorways holding babies in their arms. Children played in the dust. There were few men to be seen. The track ended in an open space surrounded by larger buildings, but no more solidly built than the little huts we had passed. One of them was topped by a small wooden cross.

The moment I got out of the taxi a crowd of children

appeared but to my surprise they did not shout out like the usual Saigon urchins. They seemed to know the driver who patted one or two of them on the head. They came closer but stayed silent, watching me. One of the smallest started to cry and the child next to it pulled reprovingly at its arm. Then without anyone saying a word they drew apart to make way for a tall man in a black soutane. He stopped to take the hand of the crying child and called to me in French.

'I am Father Quan. Welcome to my parish in exile. I am very pleased that you answered my message.'

I followed him into a hut next to the building with the cross. Its sparse furnishing reminded me of Ba's house. There was a wooden table and chair and two deckchairs covered with stained canvas. A typewriter stood on a filing cabinet in the corner. It was little bigger than a potting shed but very clean. He sat down with the child on his knee.

'This one is often sad. She has not had a happy life. I would like to tell her that everything will be all right but I think it is better that she learns to live with sadness.'

He was, I judged, in his forties though his thick hair had turned almost completely grey. It was brushed neatly and cut short at the neck and above the ears. He had a broad face, with strong cheekbones, and gave a feeling of solidity that I had come across in few Vietnamese men. Even his wrists were solid, quite different from the fragile sticks of Maurice and Thai. His soutane was frayed and in places shone almost green, one of the mysterious glowing colours of mother-of-pearl. He wore cheap rubber sandals on his bare, wide feet.

He put the child down and she ran out of the door.

'Will you excuse me while I get my pipe. Like many Vietnamese priests I am sinfully fond of my pipe.'

He went over to the table and came back with a small dome-shaped pot from which protruded a long reed mouthpiece. He grinned.

'I call this firing my cannon salute.'

He put some tobacco in a little hole in the lid, lit it, and sucked on the reed. The tobacco crackled and there was a bubbling, purring sound from the water in the pot. Three quick inhalations and the tobacco was spent. The priest's calmness was striking and soothed me. This adventure, at least, seemed unlikely to end in confusion or panic.

'Was the English in my note correct?'

He smiled with pleasure when I nodded.

'When the Americans came I tried to learn English but it was no good. I can write it, using a dictionary, but it is a painful business. But you know, it really wasn't necessary to speak English. The American Catholics – so many of them had learned Vietnamese. Not at all like the French who thought we were lucky to have the chance to speak their language. And perhaps we were. Perhaps we were.'

He grinned again. He was talking to give himself time to size me up. He was asking himself a question about me but I could not fathom what it was.

'Please allow me to tell you a little about myself. Then I shall explain why I asked you to come here. I am, as you see, a priest and a poor priest as priests should be. I am from the North, but I left there with my parish after the war against the French had ended. We built a village close to Saigon but then the new war caught up with us. Now we are refugees here in the city. My people's life is wretched, as you can see. I often ask myself: why did we ever leave our home in the North? Couldn't we have lived with the communists? After all, they are Vietnamese too.

'I always say to people that the Church of course can live in the North. The Church can live anywhere. I tell them that the Church has many masters but in the end she cuckolds them all.'

He sucked at the empty pipe and looked at me to see what effect his words were having.

'I am not afraid for the Church – or myself. But I am afraid for my parishioners. They are simple people. They are not always very clever or very strong. Their faith, and their children's faith, would be at peril in the North. Of course some of them would be happy to become martyrs. We Vietnamese have a talent for martyrdom. Do you know that there are many martyrs in the Vietnamese Church but not one saint? I often think about that. The communists – they have plenty of martyrs, too. Poor Vietnam. So many martyrs when what she needs is just one or two saints.'

I heard a rustle behind my back. The doorway was dark with the heads of watching children. One of the smallest had fallen down. The others picked him up and continued their silent, serious watch. I remembered the young soldiers who gathered to listen to my talk with the Vietcong officer in the plantation village. I had the same feeling of having been brought, against my will, onto a stage and being coached to play a part I was not ready for.

'You see,' Father Quan went on, 'the communists are, how shall I put it, so particular. They want everything to be just so. And as Vietnamese, arrogance comes easily to them. Do you by any chance know what the first poem ever written in our language was? It was a command to the crocodiles to leave the Red River and go back to their proper home in the ocean.'

He laughed, and then closed his eyes and began to say the Vietnamese words whose tones rose and fell as though they were set to music. There was a fluttering sound from the doorway when the children recognised the sound of their own language.

'The poet says to the crocodiles – go away home. Don't you know that this river is part of the holy territory of Vietnam and that the Vietnamese are famous fishermen who tattoo their bodies and even frighten the dragons?

'Arrogance, you see. The crocodiles paid no attention but we still recite this poem to show ourselves what powerful people we are. And then we look at our history and see all those battles against the Mongols and the Chinese and the French and now the Americans and it seems proof that we are indeed great people. But I look at it and just see so many martyrs, so much – so much glory in suffering. I think the word is masochism. Perhaps we had no choice. I do not know much about history but I think that some countries, like some people, seem to be lucky. We belong to the unlucky ones and it has shaped our characters till it has become quite uncomfortable to others and to ourselves.'

He got up and went over to the tin of tobacco on the table and refilled his pipe. His movements were slow and sure. The children watched excitedly and murmured with pleasure when he lit the pipe and let out another big cloud of smoke. He made a mock gesture as though to scare them and then turned to me.

'I asked you to come here because of our mutual friend Thai. Perhaps you suspected that?'

I nodded.

'Thai is with us here. Of course none of my people knows who he is. But they are used to giving refuge to runaways. They did it in the North and they have done it often enough here in the South too. A community like this easily believes that all the world is against it and finds it very easy to help anyone who is in trouble with that world. I like to think that we are showing the virtue of charity but really, I'm afraid, it is just another symptom of the illness of this country. The only people we will lift a finger for are our enemies' enemies. And we are more interested in spiting the former than helping the latter.'

He still seemed to be hesitating. He suggested we drink some beer and two of the larger boys at the door dashed across the yard and came back with tall bottles decorated with yellow tigers and large glasses that were half-filled with crudely cut ice. Father Quan carefully tipped out the melted ice water at the bottom of each glass onto the floor and poured the beer. It was weak and only faintly bitter. The two boys who had brought it laughed as we drank, as though it was the strangest sight.

'I asked you to come here because I want you to help. I do not know why you first went out to look for Thai. But now I am asking you to help him just for himself. It may cause you trouble and it may even be dangerous, but not very, I think. But you must help him as one man helps another, without asking questions about the purpose and who will benefit from it. Perhaps no one will, perhaps not even Thai. But I know that he cannot stay in this country.

'You see, it is very easy for me. I have my God. It is my only commitment. I can stay faithful to it anywhere, in the North, in the South, with the communists or against them. I sometimes think it is unfair that it should be so easy for me. But everyone can't be a priest. Think of this country full of priests. It would be more than faith could bear.'

He roared with laughter, but it was a diversion. He did not want to press me too hard or too directly.

'Thai is young. He wants to do something for this country. But he has seen both sides and he knows that neither is whole. So he must go away and one day he may come back when things are better or when he has learned to live with just a bit of what he wants and be satisfied with that.'

When I heard the priest say 'I want you to help,' I remembered the night Gruson had taken me out to the old French *colon*'s restaurant and after we had eaten our *couscous* he, too, had asked me to help. It had been easy to say yes then and it was easy for me now to say the same to Father Quan. But I knew that my two answers were very different. I was not the same person who had been embarrassed by the strange French coffee filter and who had blushed when Gruson had laughed at my clumsiness with it.

Helping Father Quan would be neither a game to be won nor a rescue mission. How did you rescue anyone in this country? How did you rescue Thai from the battles that were going on in him as much as around him? This helping could only be patching up, the roughest battlefield bandaging. At least I had grown up enough to understand that.

The priest seemed relieved when I said that I would help but when I asked him in what way he gave no clear answer. He said that I would have to wait and that he or someone else would get in touch with me. He shook his head when I asked if I could see Thai.

'It would not be wise just now. My people are very good but they are inquisitive. They would wonder why a European should want to see him and one of them might talk about it and be overheard. You must understand that both sides will be looking for him.'

He led me out to the gate where the taxi and its little driver were waiting. The children followed us at a respectful distance.

'Minh will take you home. He knows where it is. He left my note for you there.'

The driver grinned when he heard his name and opened the door for me. Father Quan stood and watched us leave. When he waved all the children waved too.

When we were close to home and passing the cathedral Minh touched my arm and pointed to it.

'*Ma maison*,' he said, '*grong maison*.' The words delighted him and he chuckled.

21

At the end of that week an American bank that had just opened an office in the city threw a big party in the Caravelle. My boss didn't like it at all. Our bank had been in the country for years and though we couldn't rival the French we had carved a decent corner for ourselves.

'You wait and see,' he said, 'that bloody hotel's going to be stuffed full of government ministers in their shiny silk suits. They can smell dollars a mile off.'

When I got to the restaurant at the top of the hotel shortly after seven o'clock it was already full of people. I had never seen a gathering in Saigon like it. The Vietnamese men had the same smooth, well-fed look as some of the members of the Cercle Sportif. But it was enhanced by their suits – my boss was right, there was a lot of silk around – and by the sleek heads of carefully combed back hair that reminded me of Maurice, but a Maurice in his prime. Many had brought their wives, large women whom it was impossible to imagine ever having been young slim girls. Most of them wore richly patterned *ao dai* and so many rings that they seemed to be carrying diamond-studded knuckledusters. There were several generals in beautifully ironed battledress and glittering black boots. One of them had added touches of a mountain tribesman's costume to his uniform.

The foreign diplomats and a large contingent of American officials moved deferentially among the Vietnamese as though trying to remind themselves that these, after all, were the country's owners. Most of the conversations were in English though some of the Americans were painstakingly speaking Vietnamese, making it sound a special language for dealing with sensitive and unpredictable adolescents. Gruson was there and I wasn't surprised to see that his attempts at deference were at best half-hearted. He was in a white suit with a blue shirt and bright yellow tie that gave him the look of an insect in search of particularly delectable deposits of pollen. When he caught sight of me he gave me a wave that seemed friendly enough.

The Americans had put on a good show. There were a lot of waiters and a lot of food and a central table had been decorated with an extravagant amount of flowers. From the restaurant's windows you could look down onto the Assembly building and across to the old Continental whose lack of air-conditioning ruled it out for this sort of occasion. The city, seen through the large, sealed windows, looked pretty and quite unthreatening. There was an occasional flash of light in the sky which at first I supposed were flares dropped from a plane but then realised was distant lightning. When I had walked down to the hotel from the villa it had still been light enough to see black clouds building up in the sky and the bats had been flying agitatedly around their nesting places under the roofs at the back of the buildings off Tu Do. The girls at the bank had said the real rains were at last about to start.

I was talking to one of the French bankers who was pretending not to be impressed by this American assault on an old French colony when I sensed someone standing next to me. I turned to look and at first sight did not recognise the man. He was in a white suit of dated cut but excellent material and his hair had a rich gleam to it.

'*Mon cher ami,*' he began. It was Maurice. He saw my surprise and smiled. When I looked at him more closely I realised that he was not quite so splendidly got up as I had first supposed. His shirt was frayed round the collar and the tie had almost the same look of exhaustion as the one worn by the old French opium-smoker. But the suit was magnificent and Maurice noticed me staring at it.

'Sharkskin,' he said. 'In the old days, under the old president that is, everyone wore it.'

He nodded disapprovingly towards one of the generals who was standing close by.

'None of this nonsense about military uniforms then.'

I introduced Maurice to the Frenchman but the latter, after studying him for a few minutes, made an excuse and moved off. Maurice took my arm and moved me towards a corner.

'I expect you're surprised to see me,' he began.

I interrupted him and with some heat asked where he had disappeared to. Although it seemed to me crazy for us to be talking in the middle of this of all gatherings, with Gruson around and Dinh, I was sure, not far away, I couldn't stop myself from showing my anger at the way he had not been there when Thai had needed him most.

He held his hand up in a gesture of pacification, sighed and, unless it was the whisky already doing its work, even seemed to blush.

'I heard that Monsieur Ba came looking for me. I'm very sorry about that.' He paused as though he didn't know what to say next. 'The truth is that I fell into some disreputable company and quite against my wish, let alone my better judgement, I found myself on the tiles. You know, Michael, I have never pretended to you that I was a saint but I do realise that at my age such behaviour is, well, undignified.'

He gave a defeated smile and I found it hard to sustain my anger. He appeared at that moment very vulnerable, not least because of the resemblance, in spite of the difference in their years, to Thai as I had seen him fighting against fever that evening in the little house. My mood changed quickly, though, for just then Gruson walked by. He turned towards us and gave a look that was clearly inquisitive. He raised his glass in mock salute but did not stop to talk.

I interrupted Maurice to say that this wasn't a good place for us to be talking. Even if Dinh himself didn't show up the room would be thick with informers. Maurice was not the least impressed.

'Quite the reverse, my dear Michael,' he replied. 'Meeting here looks far less suspicious than meeting in private.'

He stopped a waiter and took another glass of Scotch and water. He had lost his pitiful look and was perking up again.

'In fact I think we have been quite clever. This will throw people off our tracks.'

He looked about him and then moved me further back so that we were standing against the wall. It was such an obviously conspiratorial thing to do that anyone watching us would have had his curiosity aroused. Maurice, completely unaware of this, went on talking.

'I gather that you have met the holy father, who has turned up as the answer to all our prayers. I think I've told you before that I don't care very much for priests, especially our Vietnamese priests. Have you noticed that smug expression on their faces as though they've been invited to a party that none of the rest of us can go to? But this one is better than most, I'll say that for him. For the moment we don't have to worry about Thai. He's safe with the priest. The thing is, how to get him out? And at last we have the answer.'

His face was darkening as it had the evening he had taken me to the nightclub. I wanted him to get to the point quickly so that I could leave for in spite of what he said I felt uncomfortable standing there with him. But he was in no hurry. He took out a packet of Gitanes and fitted a cigarette into his holder.

'Do you know the lesson we have been taught? It's family and money.'

He repeated the words, making them sound like a spell.

'How could I have ever forgotten that? They are our only real ammunition and they fit so neatly together, don't you think? Both of them destroy the great world of the state. They make ideas ridiculous. In the old days we thought that the family supported the government – the son obeying his father and all men obeying the prince. But I wonder if that was ever true. You see, I have invented an aphorism. All families are subversive and the Vietnamese family is the most subversive of all.'

He laughed.

'What terrible things you are learning in this country. Come along. I shall prove to you that I am right.'

He set off across the restaurant. He seemed to know many of the people there but he did not stop until he came to a small woman who was talking to my boss. She was middle-aged – it was hard to judge her age more precisely than that – and very slight compared to most of the other Vietnamese women at the party. She was wearing an *ao dai* of dark green and there were large pearls in the neat lobes of her ears. Her hair, partly grey, was worn short and curled in European style.

I did not catch her name when Maurice introduced us but she smiled at me as though she knew who I was.

'I was just telling this gentleman about the horse races in Saigon,' she said. 'Do you like racing? I like to make the horses work for me but here it is rather unpredictable, because our poor jockeys are so dishonest. I do much better when I am in France. There the horses really work for me.'

My boss lifted his eyebrows and made an excuse to leave us. She looked inquisitively at me. She had clever eyes and they were enjoying my uncertainty. I still had no idea who she was or why Maurice had introduced us. 'You should have got in touch with me earlier. It was so silly of my son to imagine that he didn't need my help any more. And just because he thinks that I am a wicked woman who amuses herself by making all sorts of interesting deals with the generals. But now he needs me and I am going to help him. But I need you to help, too, Monsieur Bishop.'

It was Thai's mother, about whom both he and Maurice had said so little. I remembered Ba talking about her skill in business and her passion for diamonds. I had assumed that Thai had cut himself off from that world for ever. Perhaps he had. But this was not a woman to be impressed by gestures like that. If Thai and Maurice seemed at times to be floating over the surface of the country, reluctant to risk their feet on its treacherous soil, here was someone who revelled in her world. She thought that, like the horses, she could make it work for her.

She smiled and put her hand up to correct the fall of the hair round her neck.

'I don't know exactly where my son is and I shan't see him before he leaves. But I know how to arrange for him to get out. It was so silly of him and Maurice not to ask me earlier. I don't blame you, of course, Monsieur Bishop, for how were you to know? But I blame them.'

She put her hand on my arm and the rings sparkled at me. The hand was beautifully shaped, and the fingernails painted a dark red.

'You see, they ought to understand how things are done here but they just don't want to. Thai's father is like that. He wouldn't care if we starved to death. But look at the people in this room.'

She took my arm again and her face was alive with the excitement of the game she was about to play. She must have been very pretty as a girl.

'There – do you see that lady in the red *ao dai* talking to the big American? That is General Trinh's wife. He is the commander in the Delta – so much rice and so many rich Chinese merchants. Mrs Trinh is very happy. And have you heard of General Van – he was the chief of staff? Such a good man everyone said, almost a monk he was so good.'

She looked at me and giggled.

'That's his wife over there, in that yellow and blue dress. I think it is rather vulgar, don't you? She had some big shops in Saigon and when the fighting came here in 1968 they were all looted. Not by the Vietcong but by her husband's soldiers. She was so angry. You see, everyone has his business. Poor Thai used to get so angry with me when I said that. He said that the communists were different. You wait, I said, they have wives too, don't they? They're not all bachelors like that *méchant* Uncle Ho.'

She laughed again.

'Do you think I am very wicked? I'm not at all, you know. I am just a woman with common sense.'

She beckoned imperiously to a waiter and took a glass of coca-cola from his tray. She wrapped a paper tissue round the glass to cover the moisture that had gathered on it.

'You see, it is so easy to get out of this country if you have enough money and know the right people. There is a colonel at the Cambodian embassy – a big black Khmer' – she opened her eyes wide in mock horror – 'but a nice man. He speaks such good French and some of his children are already in Paris. He can smuggle Thai onto one of the Cambodian military planes and take him to Phnom-Penh. Thai will stay with the colonel's brother who will help him get a passport. Then he gets a French visa and off he flies on Air France to Paris.'

Her eyes were shining with pleasure, but as much, I thought, because of the neatness of the plan as because it would be the saving of her son. I said it sounded suspiciously simple.

'Oh, the colonel has done it several times before and that is why we trust him. If anything were to go wrong no one would use him any more, would they? But we need your help for one thing. The colonel has to be paid in dollars to his son's bank account in Paris. It will be four thousand, including the air ticket to France. We have no one in the family to work through in Paris – so I thought you could make the transfer in Paris and I would give you the same amount here in notes.'

The coolness with which she described her plan reminded me

of how Gruson had proposed I help him find Thai. Neither expected to be turned down. The difference was I was no longer a pawn. I was learning to be a player and had chosen sides.

She smiled – a signal of thanks for my agreement though I had not managed to say a word.

'Good. Now all you need to know is how to find our dear Khmer colonel. I have thought it all out for you. You can go to the embassy to ask about getting a visa to go to see Angkor. Everyone wants to see Angkor. And when you are there you just ask for the colonel. *Voilà*! It's so simple, you see.'

She clapped her hands together like a child. There was a tap on my shoulder and I turned to see Gruson.

'Nice to see you here, Michael,' he began as though he hadn't noticed me till then. He paused, expecting me to introduce Thai's mother. She noticed my hesitation and at once began talking to Gruson.

'I was just telling this nice young man what Vietnamese women feed to their husbands when, how shall I say, their interest is falling. The placenta of a cow! Can you believe it? It is quite true. Don't you think that is interesting?'

She smiled coquettishly at us both, shook my hand and walked off.

'My God!' he said, 'who on earth was that? Placenta. I mean I quite believe it. These people are absolutely capable of it. But what a thing to talk about at a cocktail party.'

My admiration for Thai's mother went up. To have thrown Gruson so expertly off his stride and to have escaped without submitting herself to his interrogation was no mean feat. Beside her Maurice seemed a mere apprentice at intrigue. I told Gruson that she was the wife of one of the bank's customers and he seemed to believe it. He was interested in something else.

'What was that old snake Maurice up to? Did he have anything new to say about Thai?'

I said that Maurice insisted he hadn't heard anything from Thai, that the trail was dead as far as he was concerned.

'Do you think he was telling the truth? I simply don't believe that Thai is going to disappear in this city and not get in touch with someone. If it was only Dinh's men who were looking for him it might be all right. But the other little buggers will be after him, too, and he can't stay hidden from both of them indefinitely. He's going to have to get out and that's why he needs to make contact.'

I tried to look blank and avoided his eyes.

'I still think he's going to contact you. And when he does for Christ's sake get in touch with me at once. It'll be best for him in the long run.'

For a moment I felt as though he could read my thoughts but told myself that it was ridiculous. To hide my embarrassment I remarked, as offhandedly as I could manage, that I was thinking of taking a short holiday in Cambodia.

'Really? Angkor and so on? I didn't know you were interested in that sort of thing? What gave you the idea?'

I mumbled something about it being a pity not to go and see the place when it was so close. Gruson put his head on one side and studied me for a moment.

'I hope you're playing straight with me, Michael. Don't forget what I said. Thai hasn't got a chance if he stays here. If he lets us help him then he may have a chance. Just remember that.'

He finished his drink and looked at his watch, nodded and turned round without saying another word.

The party was coming to an end. I couldn't see either Maurice or Thai's mother and my boss had left too. I walked over to the windows that gave onto the square to take a last look at the city below. There was a reverberant crack, as though a huge pane of glass had been snapped, followed by a long grumbling noise in the sky. The trees in the square swayed precipitously from side to side and the rain began to fall, rain that I had never seen the like of before, it was so thick and heavy. Several people rushed to the window to look.

'What a country,' someone said in American English behind me, 'what a goddammed country. Nothing here happens by halves. It's either dry or it's pissing down.'

He was an unusual-looking American. Although only in early middle-age he had almost white hair and a red, petulant face. The voice was precise to the point of being prissy. He didn't appear to be talking to anyone in particular but he saw me looking in his direction and nodded at me.

'I'll tell you one thing. This country has a curse on it. It is be-witched' – he stretched out the two syllables – 'and anyone who's silly enough to get muddled up with it has only himself to blame if he gets hurt.'

He watched the rain, which had already begun to form a thick sheet of water on the street below.

'Goddam rain,' he said and walked away.

22

The rain held me up. There was no point in walking home while it was pouring down so I found a young American banker and we sat drinking together. When I left the hotel I heard someone hurrying after me down the steps.

'Hi there. Think the rain's really stopped?'

It was the red-faced American with whom I'd watched the storm begin up in the restaurant. He had taken off his jacket and tie. He wore a short-sleeve shirt and his forearms were mottled pink and brown from the sun. He introduced himself as Harry Wynant. He seemed to know who I was.

'I'm just off to the Continental to have a drink with some friends. That Caravelle slays me. The air-conditioning's only fit for a morgue. It beats me why they don't build places like the Continental any more: solid walls, plenty of air and ceiling fans. The French did get some things right, you know.'

The voice was high and affected. It matched the complaints he was making. We reached the corner of the Continental terrace and he suggested that I join him. It was only nine o'clock. Jeannette had telephoned that morning – the first time I'd heard from her since the evening she'd walked off with Byrne – and she was to come round after ten. I had an hour to kill so I accepted the offer.

The old Chinese manager, crew-cut and in his usual white suit, was pacing the lobby like some heavy animal protecting its territory. He bowed when he saw Wynant and looked curiously at me. I spotted two military jeeps parked outside but didn't give them a second thought.

'We'll go to the little inner garden.'

Wynant took me by the arm. A few couples were finishing dinner in the restaurant. The waiters, white uniforms unbuttoned at the neck, rested against the thick pillars, staring ahead as though mesmerised by the slow-turning blades of the ceiling fans. We passed a young Vietnamese, his shirt over his trousers and a walkie-talkie in his hand. He smiled at Wynant but not at me. The table lights were out but I could see two men sitting at the back of the courtyard. They were the only people there. One of them got up and came towards us, his hand outstretched to Wynant.

'Glad to see you! Glad to see you!' he called out in English but it was a shrill Vietnamese voice and a familiar one. When he was a few paces from us I realised it was Colonel Dinh. He wasn't in uniform. I'd have recognised him sooner if he had been. He wore a red shirt with a pattern of white palm trees and on his wrist a heavy gold watch. After giving Wynant's hand an energetic shake he turned to me, arms held up in a gesture of surprise and pleasure.

'And Mr Bishop too! We haven't met but I already know you, yes, I already know you.'

He giggled as he repeated the words as though meeting me was the best thing that had happened to him all week. The man he'd been sitting with when we came in didn't join us. He was leaning back in his chair, tossing a ball from hand to hand. He seemed not the least bit interested in Wynant and me.

The old manager had followed us and when Dinh called for Scotch he clapped his hands at a waiter who vanished and quickly reappeared with a tray. He bent low as he put the glasses on the table and did not once look at Dinh.

'This is a friendly meeting,' Dinh announced, peering at me over his glass. 'Just a friendly meeting.' He giggled again as he repeated the phrase. The laughter this time sounded more nervous, making me think of Maurice's description of him as a man trying to keep afloat on a small raft and doubting his ability to do so.

'I don't like what you've done, do I?' He turned to Wynant but got no response from the American. 'Everyone tells me you're not to blame so this is just a friendly talk, see?' Wynant nodded.

Dinh had made it easy for me. There was to be no interrogation. Nothing would have to be denied. I was relieved but it seemed too good to be true. I looked at Wynant and started to get up. Dinh pushed me back into my chair. I could feel his strength.

'One minute. You meet my friend first.'

He called out in Vietnamese to the obscure figure that was still throwing the ball from hand to hand. The man got up and half-walked, half-shuffled towards us. A beam of light from the restaurant lit up a familiar luminous green shirt. The chinless man I had seen lead the raid on Thai's hiding place stood at Dinh's shoulder, upper lip lifted in a knowing smile. His front teeth were crooked. He threw the ball higher in the air to catch my attention and I saw it wasn't a ball. It was a hand grenade. He threw it in the air again and pretended to drop it.

'Boooom!' he screamed. I flinched and the colonel gave his first real laugh of the evening. He wiped the tears from his eyes with the back of his forearm. 'You shake hands with my friend,' he said in the sincere tones of someone introducing a new member at a Rotarian meeting.

The chinless man slipped the grenade into his trouser pocket. He took my right hand and then, catching me unawares, seized my left arm with his left hand. He was as strong as Dinh and almost pulled me off my balance.

'Your watch number ten.' He released my arm and thrust his in my face. He wore a gold Omega, bigger than Colonel Dinh's. 'My watch number one.' He wasn't laughing any more. He had proved my inferiority.

I tried to say something but realised that my stammer had returned. I looked helplessly at the ugly little man but then mercifully Wynant touched me on the shoulder and we left. 'Bye-bye,' the colonel called out after us.

I stopped on the pavement outside the terrace. I was trembling.

'Not a nice guy, that.' Wynant was staring at the sky, 'and he's got a name to match. Tam Heo, Tam the Pig. Tam means eight, so he's probably the last child of a peasant family. He's making good now, though.'

Wynant sighed.

'I'm sorry about that. Dinh didn't tell me he was going to

bring that goon along with him. But since he did I'd seriously recommend that you don't do anything to annoy the Tam Heos of Saigon. Not nice people. Not nice people at all.'

He waved his hand and walked off across the square in the direction of the Caravelle. I could only think of getting back to my villa as quickly as possible. I crossed to the other side of Tu Do and walked fast towards the cathedral. I told myself I had to stay calm. Dinh hadn't accused me of anything. He'd just said stay out of trouble. I probably had Gruson to thank for that. So what was there to worry about? Nothing – if I forgot about Thai and the Cambodian colonel who was his only chance of escape. But if I did forget, Thai would stay in the city and sooner or later Dinh's men would find him.

I'd forgotten about Jeannette. The door was unlocked and she was sitting, back very straight, on the edge of the sofa. She was so obviously primed to explode that for a few minutes I thought no more about Dinh and Tam Heo. She got up when I came in and I couldn't get her to sit down again. She was wearing a white cotton dress and her hair was loose over her shoulders. I couldn't remember her looking more beautiful. She walked about the room picking up old magazines and altering the position of the wicker-work furniture that she thought was old and dirty and said I ought to replace. She asked for a second glass of whisky and then burst into tears. She just stood there crying, not even bothering to wipe her face and letting herself sink further and further into misery.

I put my arm round her. I felt a great pity for her as though her wretchedly tearful face was the face of the many people needing comfort I had met since I began the search for Thai. Perhaps she sensed there was something smug in the gesture for she pulled away from me.

'You are so stupid, Michael. Why are you so stupid?'

She wasn't so much angry as puzzled though she did become irritated when she looked at me and saw I had no inkling of what she meant.

'You see I am right. You're so stupid you don't even know what I mean.'

The hit she had scored consoled her. She stopped crying and started to dab at her face with a handkerchief.

'Don't you understand what I've been doing? I've been spying on you. They want to know who you see and what you do and they asked me to report it all to them.'

I asked who had told her to spy on me and what she thought I was doing wrong to make it necessary.

'Dinh, of course. You know Colonel Dinh. Everyone knows him, everyone that counts, that is. He didn't say what you were doing. He just asked me, that's all.'

She looked at me as though to challenge me to say she had done something wrong, but my curiosity was stronger than my anger and I asked her when Dinh had put his request to her.

'Oh, I don't know. It was a long time ago. You remember when you went out of Saigon at Tet and you never really explained to me where you had been? It wasn't long after that.'

That surprised me. I'd supposed that Dinh's suspicion had been aroused when Thai was hiding in the little house. I'd assumed, as Ba had, that it was the visit there by Thai's wife that had tipped off the police. I couldn't understand how Dinh had come to notice me after our first and fruitless journey into the countryside. I tried to think of anything that could have made him suspicious. Could it have been the meetings with Maurice? Or even with Gruson? I remembered how Maurice had taken such pleasure in pointing Dinh out to me the evening he had taken me to the nightclub. Perhaps he had been marking me out for the colonel. But that made no sense at all. Surely Maurice wouldn't work with Dinh against his own nephew. I wondered about Ba. It had been Gruson's idea to use Ba as go-between. I'd never thought he might be playing a double game. It could be for Gruson. Or it could be for Dinh against both Gruson and me and the whole Thai operation. In that case, though, Dinh would have had plenty of chances to seize Thai if that was what he was really interested in. But that might be too simple. Dinh might still just want to watch Thai and see what happened to him, all the time knowing that he could pull him in whenever he wished. The thought that I couldn't trust Ba horrified me. It had been easy, easier than I'd expected, to slip into my new guarded relationship with Gruson. Maurice's move onto the other side of the boundary of trust I could also take, if necessary. He had always been elusive. Gruson, no mean judge of duplicity, had always said he wasn't to be trusted.

But Ba, the only one of them apart from Thai I considered a true friend? Yet if Ba was the informer and I was being led by the nose, why the scene in the Continental and Tam Heo's attempt to scare me? It didn't make sense. Nor did the grenade that had maimed Ba's child, unless the Vietcong threw it. I was damned if I was going to suspect Ba. Wynant, at the party in the Caravelle, had said the country had a curse on it. Suspicion was part of the curse. It could paralyse me as effectively as any fear of Tam the Pig. I knew I had to resist both. Ba for me would remain a comic hero, Thai a tragic one, and I had to play my part in their drama to the end.

The next few minutes with Jeannette hardened my new-found resolution.

'Don't you want to know why I did it?'

She didn't know how to take my reaction. She had probably expected that I would lose my temper. Instead I'd stood thinking my own thoughts, almost forgetting she was there. I did want to know, but not for the reason she supposed. She wanted to make a confession and probably hoped that a reconciliation might follow. But I was greedy for any clues that might help me with the problem she had unknowingly presented me with.

She took a mirror out of her bag and looked at herself before lighting a cigarette.

'You've understood so little. You didn't understand when we first met and why my mother was so keen that we should get to know each other. All she wants is to get me married to a foreigner so we can both get out of the country. I want to get out of this awful place too but from the start I knew you weren't going to be any help. You've been decent to me but you were never going to marry me, were you?'

I shrugged and said something about never having known that was what she was interested in.

'You won't help me, but Dinh might. Don't frown in that stuffy British way, Michael, you know what I mean.'

Eventually I got the whole story out of her. After Dinh began to be interested in me for the reason I still did not know – and over which Jeannette's confession didn't help at all – he'd made her an offer. She said the conversation had taken place on the terrace of the Cercle. He had been playing tennis and the meeting seemed quite by chance. He bought her a drink and while they sat watching others play he asked her if she knew me. Jeannette was of course perfectly aware of who Dinh was. He'd said that he would be grateful if she could make reports on what I did and said. And she had agreed. It was as simple as that.

When I asked her why she had agreed so readily her mouth turned down in irritation.

'There you go again. What do you think I should have done? Kicked him in the balls and told him to mind his own business? Don't you know who I am, Michael? I am a little *métisse*. I mean nothing here. None of the well-off Vietnamese would touch me. But I want to get out. I want to have a decent life like ordinary people do. I want a house and a car and nice things and not to feel all the time that everything is going to collapse and take me with it. There's nothing wrong in wanting that, Michael. You know there's nothing wrong in wanting that.'

Dinh knew that that was what she wanted and told her he would help her get it if she cooperated. He promised her a passport for herself and her mother, French visas and air tickets. It seemed an awful lot in exchange for information about me. I wondered if he'd slept with her.

She wasn't angry with me any more. She was looking at me, dog-like, in search of approval. I had never expected to see her like that. I remembered Maurice talking of a sense of coming horror – the guillotine in the sky – and how it seized a man like Dinh. The same fear possessed Jeannette. Perhaps it explained her greed. All I knew was that I could not judge her. I put my arm around her and this time she didn't pull away.

We talked for about an hour after that. The coolness the rain had brought began to go and we moved into the garden where there was a slight breeze. I didn't ask her why she had made her confession to me. I didn't want to give her any chance to express any emotion, true or false, about me. I told her that she should go on reporting to Dinh and that she wasn't to tell him about this evening. I said that Dinh was wrong about me but that she shouldn't risk angering him. I didn't offer any explanation for my absences and she didn't press me to give one. At the very end I said that if she did leave Vietnam I would help her and her mother with some money.

She would have stayed the night if I had asked her to but making love to her then would have seemed too much like rape.

Tomorrow, I thought, she would start to recover. The remorse would be over. Her search for a way to escape the country she had only half belonged to would be resumed, and that would make her untrustworthy again. When this happened I could make love to her again, both of us knowing it was only a moment of truce in an endless war of skirmishing.

I drove her back to her house. I had never been invited in for it was small and inside, I suspected, too threadbare to be shown to judging European eyes. When I got home I sat in the garden drinking a whisky. A fat moon hung over the frangipani tree, its bare, sinuous branches motionless like a dancer frozen by a spell. It was the same tranquil beauty I remembered in the dawn garden of the dilapidated house where we waited for Thai. There was a rustle in a clump of canna lilies and a little frog jumped onto the lawn. It looked at me and jumped again, coming to rest beside a white and yellow ceramic elephant that supported a bowl of cacti. After the rain the scent of flowers was strong. Jeannette did not belong in this peaceful night garden. I could not bring myself to apply the grand word treachery to what she had done. She was caught in her own trap and was destined to struggle out of it as best she could. But remembering Dinh and Tam Heo I could not believe the peacefulness was meant for me either. It was a tropical illusion, no more lasting than the effects of Ton-Ton's opium. The frog, having sized me up, seemed to agree. With two fine jumps it disappeared under an oleander bush. I did not want to disturb the innocent creature so I went to bed.

23

I drove to the Cambodian embassy the next morning doing my best not to think about the possible consequences of what I was doing. I didn't even look to see if I was being followed on the principle that it's better to dive straight into cold water than test it first. I also told myself that I had a legitimate reason to go there – my supposed interest in visting Angkor.

Colonel Yem Sambaur was not black, as Thai's mother had said, but a rich brown beside which the Vietnamese skin certainly seemed almost white. He was also very big, with a wide, flattened face. His thick black wavy hair was slightly greasy and he wore a large gold ring set with a ruby on his left hand. He wore a French sports shirt and well-cut grey trousers.

I was puzzled because there seemed something familiar about him and only afterwards realised what it was. I had gone into the visa section when I arrived at the embassy and asked the clerk there to call Yem Sambaur. The clerk, slow-moving and suspicious, took his time and I had walked round the room looking at the photographs on the wall. Most were of the temples at Angkor, fantastic piles of stone stained by centuries of tropical rain into diseased-looking patterns that some Saigon buildings had managed to acquire in just a handful of years. Was it, I wondered, a hint that this city too would suffer Angkor's fate and vanish from the world's map only to be rediscovered many years later? Some pictures showed the great temples' sculptures and it was there that the Cambodian colonel belonged. Broad-shouldered, narrow-waisted, with thick lips in a face that seemed at once profoundly calm but capable of great violence, Yem Sambaur might have walked out of Angkor.

He was extremely polite but cautious. When we were alone in his office he asked to see some proof of my identity. I gave him my passport, which I had taken with me for the charade of my visa application. He looked at it very carefully before giving it back and took a piece of paper from his pocket which he put on his desk in front of me. Typewritten, it gave the name of a Paris bank, a Cambodian-looking name that was quite unlike the colonel's and an account number.

'As soon as the four thousand dollars are paid into that account we shall begin at this end.'

It seemed too easy. I desperately wanted to get the money to Paris and finish with the whole business. But I could not make myself forget that if it didn't work Thai would be stuck in Saigon and eventually either Dinh's men or the communists would track him down even if he never moved out of Father Quan's sanctuary. I apologised and said that I had to know more about how the escape would be conducted.

Yem Sambaur smiled. He had big, white teeth.

'Don't you think the fact that the Vietnamese are ready to trust me is enough proof of my honesty? The other day the mother of the man we are talking about told me how she had been robbed of a large sum of money all because of the Cambodians. It seems there is a woman who trades illegally in diamonds. She is reputed to be half-Cambodian and to use all sorts of magic and talismans. The Vietnamese lady swore to me that she was tricked because this woman had put on her lips a magic rouge that gives her the power to convince anyone of anything. But even after this she trusts me, not because she likes me but because she knows that if I deceive her I shall not be able to make any more business here. The Vietnamese understand this sort of trust. And why not? It works very well.'

I said that in my case it wasn't a question of trust. I just didn't understand how it was going to work. Yem Sambaur sighed. He looked at the ring on his finger and twisted it so that the red stone reflected the light from the window.

'It is breaking my rules but I shall explain. I don't know, but maybe it will help. You know what the French taught us – to understand all is to forgive all. Everybody jokes about corrupt Cambodian colonels but how many people could afford to be honest living as we do?'

He smiled at me almost pleadingly, a demeaning expression for so big a man.

'It is very simple. We dress our, how shall I say? passenger in a Cambodian uniform and I take him to the military side of Tan Son Nhut in my car. That is where our planes come in from Phnom-Penh. The guards don't stop me, of course, and they expect to see other people in uniform in the car. The passenger stays beside me until it is safe for the plane to go. The Cambodian crew are reliable but you have to watch out for the other people who might try to speak to our friend in Khmer which of course he does not understand. But that really is the only problem.

'At Phnom-Penh my brother who is in the air force meets him and puts him in his car. It is the military side of the airport and everyone knows my brother. No one stops him. No problem.'

He spread his large hands open in front of me as if to prove that he was hiding no cards.

'In Phnom-Penh he stays in my brother's house until his papers are ready. This is where everything becomes quite elegant. From now on there is no more smuggling. It is almost legal. You see, there are many Vietnamese living in Cambodia and they have the right to claim Vietnamese passports from the Vietnamese embassy. My brother employs a Chinese who knows all the little bureaucrats in the city. First he applies for a Vietnamese passport. Our friend is Vietnamese. He looks Vietnamese and speaks Vietnamese. There is just the problem of a birth certificate to show that he was born in Cambodia. That costs a little money but not much. Everyone is frightened about the future. Everyone's price has gone down.

'So the embassy gives him an identity card as a Vietnamese resident and then a little later a passport. We pay the consul some money but it is now almost legal so not very much.

'Then he needs the visa to France. There are old Frenchmen in Phnom-Penh who are as scared as everyone else. They aren't rich enough to go back to France. How can they make a little money? My brother says to one of them – find someone to sponsor this Vietnamese student in France so he can apply for a student visa to Paris. He pays them dollars. Perhaps fifty. Anyway, not very much for they are old and frightened.

'Maybe the French think there is something wrong but the consular clerk is our friend and also they think it is right to help Vietnamese get out of Cambodia. Otherwise they think we will kill the Vietnamese when we get the chance. There is no problem with the Cambodian exit visa either. A little money to speed things up but at the ministry they are happy every time a Vietnamese leaves the country. It is all quite quick. Maybe three or four weeks. My brother's wife will cook good food for him. There is a big family. No one will notice him there. And then to Paris on Air France.'

He spoke with obvious pleasure about his scheme and the neat way in which each part fitted into the next. It was this as much as the details he described that made me think this plan, at least, should work. I should have left then but something made me ask him if he wasn't afraid he might be caught.

Yem Sambaur got up and walked over to the open window. He looked extraordinarily large and healthy. He took a packet of Kent from his trouser pocket and lit a cigarette with a heavy gold lighter. He had a thick gold chain round his neck. For a moment he seemed as self-assured as an expert surfer riding dangerous waves safely to the beach. But when he sat down opposite me again there was nothing self-assured about him.

'A year or so ago we had a big pageant in Phnom-Penh. It was held in the biggest sports stadium and it was all about our history and how glorious it was. That meant it was mostly about our battles with the Vietnamese. It ended with a scene that made everybody very happy. It showed the Khmer people rising up to drive the Vietnamese out of Cambodia for ever. We all cheered and the young men who were there started to believe that they were already heroes and that the battle with the Vietnamese communists was already almost over. I saw one of my young nephews there. He was with some of his student friends and I asked them whether they really thought it was so easy to defeat the Vietnamese. "Of course," they said. "After all, who are the Vietnamese? They eat dogs. That's all they are, dog-eaters."

' "Dog-eaters." ' He repeated the word and looked to see what my reaction was.

'What could I say to them? That they were silly, ignorant young men? They will have to learn that for themselves. But why can't we learn from what has happened in the past? You would have thought that we had had time to learn. How many people are forced to abandon their capital as we abandoned Angkor and then forget that they ever built it? You know of course that we forgot that we had ever built it. If someone had asked my great-grandfather about the ruins in the jungle he would have said that perhaps some gods had built it. He knew that Khmers could never have done anything like that.'

Yem Sambaur's voice had become shrill. He pronounced 'Khmers' with a look of distaste as though the word itself was ridiculous and shameful. I remembered how old Mr Do had also seemed to find it laughable, though he said it with pleasure, not the bitterness of the Cambodian.

'You see,' Yem Sambaur went on, as though talking aloud to himself, 'I don't believe that we shall survive. Do you think that a whole nation can get so tired it can no longer protect itself? I don't know. But my father, who was a wise man, took great care when he chose wives for my brother and me. They are both half-Chinese. My wife sometimes says that if she has a grain of salt in her it is thanks to that Chinese blood.'

I found myself embarrassed by this unexpected confession. The Cambodian must have seen me looking at my watch for he got up and apologised for keeping me so long. I told him that the money would reach Paris within three or four days. A colleague from the bank was going to Singapore and he had agreed to make the transfer from there. It seemed safer than sending a message directly from Saigon. Yem Sambaur said that with luck Thai could be in Phnom-Penh within a week.

Just before he opened the door he put his hand on my shoulder.

'Don't worry. My wife is the brains behind this business. It works very well. Our only problem is the timing. It's like cooking, I think. The knack is to know when to stop. Too soon, and we lose a lot of money. Too late and the whole dish is spoiled. But that's our worry, not yours.'

We walked together into the corridor. The door of the office opposite was open. There was a desk piled high with dusty files and a calendar that was a year out of date. The doors of a metal cupboard stood open to show shelves that were completely bare. Yem Sambaur shrugged.

The building seemed deserted. The consul's office was locked and a small dark man was asleep, curled like a shrimp, on a reed mat by the front door.

We shook hands.

'Maybe we shall meet in Paris. I sometimes imagine that I shall one day meet there some of the Vietnamese we have helped. It would be odd, wouldn't it? I wonder if they will want to recognise me. They will still feel superior, you know. After all, they will have a country to go back to.'

He stood on the embassy steps and watched me get into my car. Outlined against the doorway he seemed once more a reincarnation of the warriors of Angkor, but a brief and insubstantial one, a genetic echo that faded with each generation. A Vietnamese woman was selling sliced green mangoes from wicker baskets at the embassy gate. She wore a towel wrapped round her head to protect her from the sun and was laughing and shouting at her customers. There was about her a wily energy that the tall sad colonel could never match.

24

The visit to Yem Sambaur depressed me. After I'd arranged the details of the money transfer to Paris there seemed nothing more to do. It was too easy. Having decided to defy Gruson and Colonel Dinh I wanted to display my defiance but apparently would have no more chance to. Looking back I'd say it was a schoolboy's reaction, but it didn't seem so then. I thought it was a sign of maturity, which perhaps only shows how long it takes a certain sort of Englishman to grow up in the world.

I had gone to see the Cambodian on a Wednesday and the following Saturday I promised myself a solitary and rather greedy lunch at Au Maréchal. I lay in bed late reading old airmail copies of *The Times* and had just had a shower when there was a familiar rattling at the front door. My first thought was to pretend that I wasn't there. I knew it was Do. Only he shook the grille in that hesitant way.

Do grinned and asked if he could come in. His message was incoherent. There was someone I had to go and see. He was a clever man who could help Thai. He didn't live far away. Do would come in my car and guide me.

I was sure that this time Do meant to be incoherent, but there didn't seem to be any sense in calling his bluff. Whatever I managed to squeeze out of him wouldn't make it any easier for me to make up my mind whether to go with him or not. So I said yes; an unfortunate decision, it turned out later, for Do rather than for me.

He got into the car beside me with all the excitement of a young child, examining the dashboard and the door handles as though he had never seen such things before. I could not coax a single useful word out of him about the person he was taking me to see. All his attention was concentrated on giving me directions. The sleeve of his shirt, its colour as unconvincingly white as ever, flapped in front of me as he gestured in the direction he wanted me to drive. I was about to turn off Nguyen Du when I heard a familiar 'put-put-put'. I could see in the mirror the boy who mended bicycles pedalling for all he was worth to start an old Mobylette. He wobbled. There were heavy puffs of exhaust but eventually he picked up speed and stayed in view behind us.

Do directed me along Tran Hung Dao in the direction of Cholon and then we turned into a part of the city I had not seen before. There were old French buildings with yellow-washed walls and brown tiles speckled with age. The trees had once been carefully planted but were now as mangy as animals in a wretched travelling circus. There was less traffic and I could still see the Mobylette behind a brown Toyota saloon that had stationed itself between us. Although we made several turns both the car and the bicycle boy stayed in place behind us.

We turned into the courtyard of a building that must once have been some sort of government office. Steps led up to a door above which hung a long cloth banner with faded letters. Do translated it as the 'Catholic Youth League for Social Action.' The word Catholic told me what I should have guessed earlier. Do had at last managed to engineer my meeting with the priest he insisted was so clever. As we entered a large hall the Toyota drove in and parked at the opposite end of the yard. I paused and tried to see who was in it but the windows had been tinted against the sun and only threw back a reflection of the banner and the building.

The hall was bare except for a large desk behind which sat two young men in white short-sleeved shirts with a blue cross embroidered on the breast pocket. One of them had big spectacles and an almost pretty, child's face. The other was pale and strikingly ugly, a good candidate for Dinh's goon squad. He had small eyes in a flat face, and his hair had been cut in the crudest pudding bowl style.

The ugly one picked up a telephone when he saw us and bounced the receiver up and down. My attention was caught by a large painting behind the desk. Young people, boys and girls, holding hands or with their arms round each other's shoulders, marched out of the canvas towards me. There was something odd about them. Both the young men and women were extraordinarily thickset. Their arms were muscular, their necks like young treetrunks. They had body-builders' muscles under their shirts. They were all smiling and showed teeth every bit as large and white as Yem Sambaur's. I looked down at the pair of guardians. Their necks were childishly slender, their wrists no thicker than a rolled-up napkin. Did they think they looked like the young gods in the painting? I studied the picture again. It reminded me of reproductions I had seen of Russian paintings of revolutionary workers and peasants but that sort of optimism seemed extravagantly out of place in Saigon.

There was a cry from the top of the stairs and a figure in black waved at us to come up. I had been right about it being a priest.

Father Nguyen Dinh Lam – Do whispered his name as we climbed up – stood at the top of the stairs wringing his hands, a suitable gesture for a man who seemed to be in a permanent state of anguish. He was still young though there were already marks of grey in his hair, and had a tall, broad forehead and worried eyes. The anguish was signalled by the set of the jaw and the mouth that never relaxed, but was always ready to draw in air in pained disapproval. He was slender and light-boned: no better a candidate for joining the triumphant marchers in the picture than the two young doormen.

He shook my hand and pointed to a room down the corridor. It was the same as many offices that I had seen in Saigon, the sort of place that made you doubt that anything very efficient was ever achieved there. The filing cabinets looked as though they were seldom opened. The wall behind the desk was covered with hand-written charts. A crucifix stood on the desk beside a pile of old magazines. Father Lam brought forward some chairs made of woven pink plastic and we sat down.

I was next to a window and I could see the brown car still in the courtyard. The bicycle boy was across the road. He had propped the Mobylette against a tree and was squatting on the pavement, sucking an ice cream.

'Monsieur Do tells me that you have met many Vietnamese and have even travelled a little in the countryside. Perhaps that will make it easier for you to understand what I am going to say to you.'

The priest looked at me apprehensively. Do, seizing his cue, crooned out 'Yes, yes, Monsieur Michael has seen a great deal, a great deal.'

'It's an unfortunate business, a most unfortunate business.' He fidgeted in his chair and clasped his hands even more tightly.

'I'm talking about our mutual friend Thai. It is an unfortunate business. You see, it wouldn't be good for him to leave the country. He still has work to do here.'

I pretended not to know what he was talking about. I'd met Thai, I said, but I didn't know he was Catholic.

'I'm not talking about the Church.'

He sighed and looked at Do but found no help in that quarter. The old man was staring at the ceiling, far away in his own thoughts.

'I want you to understand.' Father Lam leant forward in his chair. 'I want you to understand why there are some Catholics who do not always support the government and who try to see things sometimes through the eyes of the other side. I think it is the special duty of a Catholic to do that for we bear much of the blame for the terrible things that have happened to our country.'

He saw at once that I did not understand him and impatience at last loosened his tongue. The words came rushing out now, like a confession that had been long and painful in the preparation.

'You must know that we, the Catholics, are responsible for bringing the French here. You have heard of the French bishop who helped our King Gia Long win the throne at the end of the eighteenth century. You've seen his tomb. It is near the airport.'

He was relieved when I nodded. That must have been the tomb the little taxi-driver Minh had shown me and which he held in such awe. I couldn't imagine him and Father Lam getting on together.

'You see, the Catholics brought us the truth of God but at the same time they used it to put us under the French. It became a poisoned truth and the poison is in us Catholics to this day.'

Do emerged from his own thoughts to murmur *'C'est vrai, c'est vrai.'*

I glanced out of the window. Two men had got out of the Toyota. One was a big fat man in baseball cap and dark glasses. The other was slight, and wearing a red shirt outside long Bermuda shorts. It was Tam Heo.

'We must ask ourselves,' Father Lam droned on, unaware that my attention had been distracted, 'we must ask ourselves if a truth acquired at such a price can be a truth at all. Or more precisely, we must ask whether the truth does not appear at different times in different forms. You see, I cannot look at one of my countrymen without thinking that perhaps this soutane that I wear is more like a jailer's uniform than anything else.'

He was pressing his hands together so hard that I would not have been surprised to hear the crunch of bones.

'Even though the Catholic Church brought French colonialism with it, it also brought progress. To this day those parts of Vietnamese society which escaped Catholic influence have remained backward, full of superstition and unenlightened customs. Have you ever been to a Buddhist pagoda?'

I nodded.

'Have you ever seen their plumbing?'

I was looking out of the window again. The priest saw my attention had wandered and repeated the question.

'Have you ever seen their toilets? They often don't have any toilets. I know for a fact that at the An Quang, where they claim to be such progressive monks, they may have two or possibly three. I myself have been to Tay Ninh to see the Cao Dai temple and they showed me their toilets. Two. Just two for the whole of that big temple.'

I barely heard his brief, sarcastic laugh. I had seen Tam Heo take something from his pocket and start throwing it from hand to hand. He was back to his trick with the grenade. I was about to interrupt the priest but thought better of it. Why hurry as long as Tam Heo was outside? And stopping Father Lam in the middle of what seemed more and more a confession wouldn't be easy.

'We must ask ourselves,' he went on, 'we must ask ourselves whether the truth is not now available to us in a new and purer form. In this new form it can bring us both more progress and at the same time the liberation which we could never expect from the West. I preached a sermon to my students here, not in a church of course, the archbishop would never have allowed that, but at one of the prayer meetings we have. In this sermon I took as a symbol of both progress and liberation the soldier of the National Liberation Front – what you call the Vietcong – who always carries in his canteen water that he has sterilised by boiling. For the villages he enters this is the new holy water, the cure to the sickness and misery caused by centuries of ignorance.'

Father Lam's eyes were shining. The anguish had gone. Do was leaning forward in his chair.

'And the soldier also brings liberation, because he teaches the people that they must fight for their own freedom. I said to my students that there have been many great martyrs for the faith in the past and in spite of all the guilt we share as Catholics those martyrs deserve our honour. But I asked them to reflect whether the true martyrs of today are not those young soldiers who bring progress and liberation with them. And I ask them whether their conscience as both Christians and Vietnamese does not tell them to join hands with those simple soldiers.'

Mr Do was so excited by this speech that I thought he was going to jump out of his pink plastic chair and start applauding. But the priest gave him a discouraging stare and the old man made do with his usual refrain of 'It's true, it's true.'

The priest too leaned forward in his chair.

'Mr Do has told me how you brought Thai into Saigon. It has nothing to do with me why you did it. The point is that Thai's friends are worried what may happen to him if he goes abroad. They think he may not really understand what he is doing and that people there may try to make use of him. If he was to stay here his old friends would see that no harm came to him. They understand that he has had a difficult time. They do not want to press him to do anything until he feels ready.'

I did not know how to react to this and my hesitation angered the priest.

'Thai has been infected by the wrong foreign ideas. He was at school in your country, I know, and perhaps there he learned to make a fetish of his "freedom", of his "rights" as an individual.'

He pronounced the words with contempt, as though they numbered among the most deadly sins. He stuck his chin in the air. The tone was self-satisfied now.

'The Church is a better school, a more severe school. It does not teach such self-indulgence. Thai should stay, and if he has to suffer then let him suffer. All these complaints that the communists won't listen to anyone else, that they are Northerners out to bully the more civilised South – perhaps there is some truth in them but at heart they are just excuses. Thai must recognise his responsibility, his father's responsibility, for what has happened to our country. Only the communists can save it now so Thai's duty is plain. He should not make too much of his own drama. It will not look dignified in the eye of history. Tell him that Lam, as priest and believer in progress, will never leave Vietnam.'

His chin went higher and his eyes flashed as he said the last words.

So this was the message of the communists. I no longer doubted that Do had been their man from the start. They had let Thai escape to Saigon, even helped him to without his knowing it. They had meant to play him like a fish on a line but he had slipped off the hook and they wanted him back on. I thanked God that Tam Heo and his friend were a perfect pretext for not answering Father Lam.

I pointed out of the window and remarked, as calmly as I could, that Colonel Dinh's men were outside. Neither Do nor the priest looked unduly surprised. They exchanged some quick remarks in Vietnamese and Father Lam got up.

'That's nothing to worry about. They often try to frighten us. You will be all right. They wouldn't dare do anything to you.'

He came with us to the top of the stairs. Under his and Do's eyes I had no choice but to act as coolly as they did. But Father Lam had vanished by the time we got to the bottom of the stairs. So had the two boys. Precautions were being taken after all. Only the young gods and goddesses striding out of the picture remained to defy the forces of evil and Colonel Dinh.

Tam Heo gave the grenade one more toss when we appeared in the front door and then stood still. When in doubt, I said to myself, behave as though nothing untoward is happening. We walked to the car and got in. Tam Heo put the grenade in his pocket and he and his friend got into their car. I drove off. They followed. When we came into the street the bicycle boy was pedalling hard to start his moped. He fell in behind the Toyota and we drove back to Nguyen Du in the same order in which we had left.

25

When we turned into my street I noticed a khaki-coloured jeep parked across from the corner where the bicycle boy conducted his business. It set off an alarm bell in my mind but I had barely time to think about it when I heard a car accelerating fast behind us. As the brown Toyota drew even with us Tam Heo, in the passenger's seat, wound down his window and threw the grenade. I saw his crooked teeth as he laughed. It hit the roof with a thump and I stamped on the brakes. It was all I could think of.

It was only when we stopped that I realised there had been no explosion. I got out. The windscreen and bonnet were spattered with something white and sticky. There was more of the white stuff on the roof and what looked like pieces of grey-green skin. I put my finger in a white patch and held it to my nose. The smell was as familiar as it was pleasant – *pomme cannelle*, the grenade-shaped custard apple. Tam Heo had thrown a piece of fruit at us.

It was humiliating to be frightened and made a fool of at the same time. I remembered the pig's head Dinh had left on Phap Long's altar. It was the same sort of joke, nasty but above all humiliating. Do looked at me as though I was making a fuss about nothing.

'It was a custard apple,' I said lamely. I suppose he took it in, I wasn't sure. After I had parked in the driveway he got out as though nothing unusual had taken place. He held out his hand, said he hoped to see me soon as though we'd got back from a picnic, and mounted his bicycle.

He pedalled slowly out of the gate and across the road towards the cathedral. I had turned back to unlock the front door when a car went by in the same direction. There was a clatter and a shout and the car seemed to pick up speed. I think Do was killed at once, for it only took me seconds to reach him and he was dead by then. He was lying on his side with blood coming from beneath his head. There was only a touch of it on his mouth. The front wheel of the bicycle was crushed but the back one was still turning slowly. I put my hand out to stop it.

There was no other traffic in the street. People were still eating or beginning their siesta. But to my surprise my neighbour, dressed only in a singlet and shorts, came out of his garden. He was a quiet, dignified man – a civil servant, people said – and we had never spoken more than the usual polite greetings.

'Did you see the car?' he asked. He seemed embarrassed by his clothes. He had probably been preparing for his siesta.

'I saw it. I was in the garden. It wasn't a car – it was a jeep, a military one. There was plenty of room on the road. The old man was riding along at the side. I think they aimed at him. And after they hit him they accelerated. They didn't turn round to look.'

He stared at Do who seemed to have shrunk in death, and asked if I knew him. I nodded, and to avoid being pressed for further explanation I suggested that we telephone for the police. He went into his house and I went to get a sheet to cover the old man's body. There were already flies on it when I got back. I drove them off and they settled on a piece of rotting fruit close by in the gutter. Their backs glittered in the sunlight like chips of mother-of-pearl.

A fat police captain arrived in a jeep half an hour later. He was neither interested nor suspicious. To my relief he didn't even ask me if I knew Do. He went through his pockets and found an identity card with a name I'd never heard of and an address somewhere in the Delta.

He gave a shrug when my neighbour told him about the jeep. An old man's death in a traffic accident, it said, couldn't be expected to take up much of a captain's time. Or perhaps that was just the impression he wanted to give. I couldn't help thinking that he was too unconcerned and that someone might have warned him about what had happened in advance.

He and his driver put the body in the back of the jeep and drove off. I was about to pull the wrecked bicycle into my garden when I saw a small figure running towards me. It was the bicycle boy who had followed us on his moped. He pointed at Mr Do's bicycle and said imperiously in Saigon guttersnipe's American: 'You give me.'

He must have seen Tam Heo throw the custard apple and the killing of Do. The jeep, without doubt the one I'd seen parked, would have passed directly in front of him. I stared at him and he stared back. 'You give me.'

I dropped the machine and he hoisted it half-way onto his back and began to drag it towards his open-air workshop like an ant pulling some monstrous trophy to its nest. I went into the house and was sick.

The physical traces of Do's death did not last long. It rained in the afternoon, the heavy but short-lived rain that now fell every day and sweetened the air for an hour or two before the heat returned and with it the feeling of being trapped again inside a tropical prison. I went into the street and could not see any sign of where Do had fallen or a hint of blood.

My resolve to stand my ground against Dinh, Tam Heo and all comers was beginning to look like adolescent bravado. I wasn't in danger. Do had been in danger and Ba's boy too. Thai, Ba and lord knows who else were still in danger. But I wasn't. They only needed to make a fool of me because I was too clumsy and too innocent to be a threat to anyone. It was a bitter moment, but even then I knew I didn't want to become like them. What was it Gruson had said about coming from a lucky country? Mine had been the innocence of the lucky and I did not want to lose it all. That, I like to think now, was my true moment of maturity. The lucky and the unlucky don't mix and what good does it do for the lucky to feel guilty about it? I went in and gave myself a strong whisky.

It couldn't have been long after six o'clock for it was starting to get dark. I often heard pedlars passing along the street selling fruit and snacks that my neighbours' maids and children liked to buy. At that time of the evening they liked to get things like sweet lentil soup and the pedlar, usually a woman, would squat beside the baskets she carried on a pole over her shoulder while she measured out her goods and watched them being eaten. There was also a woman who sold the same fertilised chicken and duck eggs that Maurice had tormented Gruson with at their first meeting when he took us for lunch outside the city.

The women knew I was not a customer for their food and no longer bothered to come into my driveway. But that evening I heard footsteps on the gravel and a voice called out, '*Ai an vit lon hon?*' It was the egg-seller's cry, but softer than when she passed along the street.

'*Ai an vit lon hon? Ai an vit lon hon?*' She repeated the cry, each time making it sound more urgent but no louder. I went to the door. She was an old woman, with the blackened teeth that Ba had told me were once customary in the North. She moved some of the eggs aside, took out a tightly folded note and handed it to me through the grille. Then she picked out an egg and held it up to my face.

'*Ai an vit lon hon?*'

She cackled at her own joke, put her baskets back across her shoulder and went out into the street where she called out in her usual way. The note, I guessed without opening it, was from Father Quan. The pedlar-woman was one of his displaced villagers from the North.

An hour later I was walking along the river front by the Majestic Hotel waiting for Minh. A police launch was nosing around two small freighters tied up for the night. The communists sometimes fired rockets into the city from the other side of the water where the lights of little huts and houses sparkled faintly like distant stars in a black sky. I had the unpleasant feeling that hundreds of eyes over there were fixed on my side of the river, so incautiously lit up and so absorbed in the pursuit of profit and pleasure, a theatre of fools in which I had become a bit player. I might not have kept the rendezvous had the manner of arranging it been less expert. The note was short but insistent, the hand unmistakably Father Quan's. He and his parishioners were a mafia I knew would not betray me and I trusted Minh to shake off anyone who might have followed me. At least I was sure that the bicycle boy hadn't. He was already dismantling Do's bicycle when I left. He raised his head to watch me but did not get up.

Minh drove up on time, grinning as though he was pleased to see me again. This time I tried to follow the way more carefully but again I got lost when we were near the airport. Perhaps he took me a different way on purpose. We went down crooked slum alleys that were all alike and through which it would have been impossible to follow us without being noticed. But we came out into the same open space by the little chapel. A boy opened the taxi door and signalled me to follow. He didn't take me to the office where I had talked with Father Quan but led me along muddy paths between shacks made of wood and cardboard and beaten sheets of tin.

The alley-paths were airless and most of the shack doors were open. Inside they were wretched places, with reed mats to sleep on, some cooking pots, and clothes hung from a nail in the wall. At the end of one alley someone had put a television set on a box and children and women with babies were sitting in front of it. The little grey screen showed pictures of grandly gesturing actors and actresses in magnificent Chinese costumes singing in a half-chant, half-wail. The audience was so entranced that no one noticed us when we walked by. The boy led me into a shack no different from the others but pulled away a piece of matting on the wall to reveal an opening. Beyond it was a larger room, lit by an uncovered light bulb hanging from the ceiling.

Father Quan was sitting at a table with Thai opposite him. Thai was looking at a young woman, dressed in a peasant's black trousers and white tunic. She held a naked baby which clung to her with arms and legs outstretched like a jumping frog. A familiar figure was kneeling in front of the mother and child. Mr Ba was poised professionally to take a photograph. The flash went off as I straightened up after stepping through the hole in the wall. The baby began to cry.

Thai looked round and smiled. The priest waved a welcome. Ba stood up, rubbed the dust from his trousers and hurried towards me. He took my hand in both of his and shook it vigorously.

'It's a good hide-out, isn't it?' he said. 'I told Father Quan that he could make a fortune hiding young men from military service.'

He laughed loudly. He was so plainly pleased to see me that I reproached myself for ever having doubted his reliability. In this little room at least, I felt, there should be trust. It would have been unbearable otherwise.

Thai beckoned to the young woman. She was his wife. I had seen many pretty girls in Saigon but she was beautiful, with a calm, strong face which one day would make her a handsome, endearing old woman. The little boy held on to her so tightly that he seemed part of her body. She brought me a bowl of tea, rocking the child all the time on her left arm. 'This is Vong,' she said, squeezing his cheek.

Thai was tired. He was every bit as thin as when I had last seen him. I wondered if he was not suffering from some infection he had picked up during his time in the *maquis*.

'They've promised that I will be able to leave in two or three days at most. It's quicker than I thought. I wanted to thank you for helping with the money and for everything else.'

I said I had seen Father Lam.

'Oh la la,' said Father Quan, giving his pipe stem a few quick sucks of pleasure, 'the poor Father Lam. He is the unhappiest priest I have ever met, that man. He carries around enough sorrows on his back for all the rest of us.'

Ba, not to be outdone, announced that he knew him very well. Some of his students had been arrested as Vietcong agents. Father Quan raised his eyebrows.

'Oh la la,' he said again.

Ba's revelation didn't surprise me.

'I suppose Father Lam gave you a message for me,' Thai said. 'I was waiting for something like that. They picked the right person. He suffers from the same middle-class guilt as I do. They wouldn't even have to tell him what arguments to use. Well, what did he say?'

I recounted as best I could Father Lam's sermon about the Vietcong soldier and his waterbottle. Thai interrupted me.

'But did he talk about guilt, too? He must have talked about guilt.'

He smiled when I said that the priest had called his soutane a jailer's uniform.

'Don't worry. I'm not interested in their message. They're too late.'

I asked Thai if he thought that Do had been working for the Vietcong all the time.

'It looks like it, doesn't it? I'm not very surprised. It makes me look a bit stupid, though, doesn't it, having them lead me almost by the hand when I thought I was being so clever in escaping.'

'But you did escape from them in the end,' Ba said.

'Yes, in the end.'

I told them what had happened to Do.

'That means Colonel Dinh feels frustrated,' the priest said. 'Someone like Do isn't worth killing. Dinh must be very angry.'

Ba stuck his chin out, a signal that he wasn't scared. Thai was staring at his wife. She saw I'd noticed and smiled.

'He's never seen me in peasant clothes before.' Her English was slow but clear. 'I've always worn Western dresses and things. Did he ever tell you about his cousins? The first time they wore peasant pyjamas was when they joined the guerillas. And now it's my turn, though I'm going the other way.'

When the time came for me to leave, Thai waved the baby's arm. 'Vong means hope,' he said. 'Do you think it's a good name?' Father Quan led me back to the taxi along the crooked, airless alleys. A familiar figure was sitting on its bonnet. The half-caste bicycle boy with the rusty black hair was absorbed in a game of pitch and toss with the driver Minh. He grinned when he saw me, jumped down, and gave a mock salute.

'He's one of our children,' Father Quan said. 'I asked him to keep an eye on you.'

The priest couldn't have known how much that hurt. My friends had set a little street urchin to watch over me in case I stumbled and made a fool of myself.

26

The meeting in Father Quan's sanctuary acted like a tranquilliser on me. I kept on remembering the scene I had come across in the room hidden by the piece of matting. The priest and Ba, Thai and his wife seemed to have been brought together like characters at the harmonious ending of an old mystery play. Virtue and innocence had triumphed. Evil – or perhaps just sinful, stumbling man – in the shape of Dinh and Gruson and the 'other gentlemen' could never penetrate to such a blessed place.

It was a strange feeling and it did not last long. One evening I went to a bookbinder's shop where I'd already had my *Dragon Book of English Verse*, a leaving prize from prep school, handsomely re-bound in blue leather. I'd bought some Somerset Maugham paperbacks in London – someone told me he was a good guide to the East – and I thought that nicely bound they'd make a good present for my mother. The bookbinder was an emaciated elderly man and he displayed his materials – marbled papers for the inner covers, gold letters for marking initials in various shapes – with an indifference that suggested he didn't mind if he sold anything or not.

The shop was usually empty. The owner would come out from behind a curtain, spectacles in hand as though he had been interrupted reading. But that evening there was already a customer in the shop. He was bending over the counter examining different sorts of marbled paper. The proprietor was watching him absent-mindedly.

I recognised the man at once. The light-brown trousers across the broad bottom and the bright blue shirt with sleeves buttoned at the wrists proclaimed Gruson. I would have walked out without saying anything but he heard me come in and, still leaning on the counter, twisted his head round to see who it was.

'Michael! I didn't know you went in for this kind of thing. Do bankers actually read real books?'

I put my parcel of books on the counter and looked at his.

There were several volumes of German poetry and novels by Dostoyevsky. He had chosen red leather for the binding and lectured the Vietnamese about making sure that the red of the marbled paper be made sufficiently bright. When he had finished he put his hands on his hips and looked at me.

'We haven't seen much of you recently, have we? What have you been up to?'

I didn't answer. He frowned and looked at his watch.

'Why don't you come and have a drink. I'm meeting Byrne just round the corner. I know you don't like him but he's not such a bad chap. Just a bit thick, that's all.'

I wanted to refuse but to my displeasure I realised that I still found it difficult to say no to him. I told myself that I was beyond his reach now. It ought to be me who had the upper hand for I knew things that he wanted to know.

So we walked out together and he led me towards Nguyen Hue where the flower-sellers had their stalls in the middle of the broad street. It was the time of evening when the last respectable Vietnamese were going home from their evening promenade and the Americans were coming out, exotic animals tempted by city jungle. Gruson marched through the people on the pavements as though they were invisible. None of the pedlars or street traders tried to stop him or sell him anything. Even the pimps seemed to realise that he was beyond any influence they could ever hope to exert and left him alone.

We turned down a side street and into the vestibule of what looked like a small hotel. There was a wooden counter and behind it the usual rows of concierge's pigeon-holes. A framed poster on the wall showed a strange figure in earrings and bare legs ...nking through bamboo from a tall pot. In wavy lettering it counselled:

'*Visitez Ban Me Thuot et ses tribus pittoresques.*'

Gruson stopped to look at it.

'Have you ever seen the fuzzy-wuzzies in the hills? The Viets treat them as though they were blacks in the old south. It's a shame. They're good chaps, those hill people, as straight as these people are crooked. Gurkha-types, that's what they are.'

The lecture over, he strode into the bar. Byrne was the only person there. He was sitting at a table at the far end. The room could not have been altered for many years. The wooden bar and the fittings behind it had the streamlined look of the 1930s. It was like being in an old ocean-liner condemned to the scrapyard. Black fans revolved under the ceiling. The bar led on round a corner into a restaurant where some noisy diners had already gathered.

Gruson looked around.

'Where's the barman? Boy! Boy!'

A head came up from below the bar, an ugly, malicious schoolboy's head except that it belonged to a middle-aged man. He lifted the flap of the bar and shuffled to our table. His supposedly white shirt and trousers were grey from years of half-hearted washing. He folded his arms and leered at us.

'*Bong shoir.*'

The words were spoken with such a heavy accent that I thought he was joking. But when I studied his face I saw that he had a cast in one eye that protected him from enquiring stares. He seemed to enjoy the impression he had made and when we ordered Pernod he turned away chuckling to himself.

'Well,' said Gruson. 'What have you been up to, Michael? We've been hearing all sorts of stories about how active you've been.'

I asked if he'd heard about old Do's death.

'Yes, I did hear something about him having an accident. I hope it wasn't your fault, was it? I'd hate to think that you were responsible for anything like that.'

Such obvious sarcasm surprised me. Gruson's style was lighter.

'I hear you've been having more trouble with your girl-friend.'

Byrne was wearing his heavy gold identity bracelet. It was loose and clicked as usual against his glass when he picked it up.

'If you want my advice I'd say girls like that are more trouble than they're worth. Very pretty, yes. Very tempting. But in the long run, trouble. By the way, I never touched her myself.'

He gave me what he may have thought was a companionable, understanding grin, but it still looked like the expression of a beast making up its mind whether to bite.

I got over-confident. Gruson seemed almost at a loss. Byrne, while scarcely pleasant, was perhaps being as nice as he could be. I wanted to make an impression so I told them Jeannette had been working for Colonel Dinh. It didn't have the desired effect. Byrne turned to Gruson.

'Told you so, didn't I? You remember that time I left her in my room and came back and found her going through my address-book?'

Gruson wasn't even interested. He waved his arm.

'Par for the course. What else do you expect? She was a bit-player. That was obvious from the start.'

Then both of them dropped the subject.

They were no longer interested, in Jeannette or in me or Thai or anything that had obsessed me over the past weeks. Gruson had invited me to the bar not in the hope of preparing me for another manoeuvre but for old time's sake, a coach who felt he owed a little of his time to an inexpert player for whom he had no more use. I couldn't understand why he had lost interest. He had not, however, lost his knack of guessing what was on my mind.

'Look, old chap, I want to thank you for your help and all that. It didn't come off as I'd hoped but you pulled your weight. Or you did at the beginning, anyhow. But we've had to write Thai off now. There's no point in wasting too much time on things like that. If it had gone according to plan it would have been different. He might have been an asset for us one day. But you've got to know when to cut your losses in this business. It was all getting a bit too complicated. Dinh and the Vietnamese were getting a bit upset, my American friend Wynant too. So we called it a day. At least we've spoilt it for the little red buggers. They're never going to trust him again. That's a plus on our side, you see, so it wasn't all wasted time. By the way, I don't suppose you know if he is still in Saigon?'

I didn't think it was a trick. He didn't seem the slightest disappointed when I said I didn't. At least I had sense enough for that. But I didn't have the sense to keep my temper. I thought of Do lying in the road outside my house and of Ba's baby son. I thought of Thai and his wife in the little hideaway in Father Quan's village, he on the verge of defeat and she, for all her love, unable to help him. I even thought of Jeannette, whose only hope was her brief prettiness, and of the anguished but unappealing Father Lam. All of them had been hurt in some way. And now Gruson had packed them up like a boy cramming his toy soldiers back into their box.

I don't know how much of this I managed to say for I soon began to stammer badly. Gruson gave the impression of not hearing what I said, but that I persisted in spite of my stutter did seem to impress him. It was the first time, with him, that I hadn't let it silence me. When I'd finished he took a yellow silk handkerchief from his shirt-sleeve, blew his nose loudly and called for another round of drinks. The barman grinned at me when he brought them. I think he had enjoyed watching me get angry.

'My dear Michael,' Gruson began. 'You are still very young though God knows it is almost time you started to grow up. You can blame me for the mess but tell me what mess can I create in this wretched place that its own inhabitants couldn't match ten times over? If they hadn't made such a monumental cock-up of the place people like myself wouldn't be here.

'And one more thing. Don't you waste too much of your time feeling sorry for yourself. It can become a habit, you know, and it's a pretty pathetic one. Let me tell you a good rule. When things get tough, pick a side and stick to it. You may not agree with everything it stands for but why should you have a right to expect that? If you want to get anything done you have to pick a side. Quite frankly I'd have had much more respect for your friend Thai if he'd stayed out there with the commies. I told you he was arrogant, didn't I? Well, it's the worst sort of arrogance, thinking you are so important that you have a right to stay innocent. No one has a right to stay innocent.'

He looked at me, raised his glass and winked, the gesture of a worldly uncle who has caught a young nephew out in some minor stupidity. I would have got up then and left if Gruson hadn't put down the glass he had half to his lips and said 'Good God!'

He was looking over my shoulder towards the door leading to the restaurant. I turned round. An old man was walking slowly towards us, though he wasn't so much walking as gliding. His feet scarcely left the floor. His body moved forward as smoothly as though it were carried and propelled by invisible hands. He was wearing black trousers, a white long-sleeved shirt and a black tie with a tight, tiny knot. The tie made me remember. It was the old Frenchman, Franchini, who had been in the *fumerie* when Thai escaped there. The *patron* had said he owned a small hotel.

In the better light of the bar Franchini's face looked as white and crumpled as a screwed up piece of paper. His eyes were small but shone very black. His mouth moved out and in. He was, nevertheless, a figure of dignity. His close-cut, crinkly grey hair, the stiff uprightness of the body suggested a distant military past. He stopped by our table. He held his hands towards us in a courteous greeting, said good evening and asked if we were meaning to eat in the restaurant. He did not recognise me. I didn't think he really saw any of us. He moved beyond us to the bar where the barman was picking his nose. Franchini went by him with all the dignity of a great ship passing an insignificant skiff and disappeared into the lobby.

'Who on earth was that?' Gruson said.

'It's the old boy who owns the place. He's an opium addict. Doesn't make much sense half the time.'

Byrne sounded bored but the old man's brief appearance had made an impact on Gruson. He turned to me.

'There are lots of different ways of living in this country. That's one.' He nodded towards the door through which the old Frenchman had glided. 'But it's not too different from what a lot of people here try to do. There are all sorts of ways of putting your head in the sand, as our young friend Thai is going to find out.'

He got up and the barman came over to be paid. He was grinning.

'*Patron très fatigué ce soir.*' He examined the money Gruson had given him and said once more, '*très fatigué.*' He found the thought so amusing that he laughed.

Gruson offered to give me a lift home but I refused. He leant out of the car window before driving off.

'I hope you've learned a few lessons, Michael. There's nothing worse in life than not learning an obvious lesson.'

He threw some coins into the street for the small boy who had appointed himself the guardian of the car and drove off rapidly through the cyclos and tiny taxis. It was the last time I saw him. I heard that he left Vietnam shortly afterwards.

I found a letter pushed under my door when I got home. It was from Maurice and the message was short.

'Our pigeon has safely flown away. M.'

I gave myself a celebratory whisky. For all Gruson's lectures we had succeeded where he had failed.

27

In the month that followed Thai's story began to fade like a dream. After receiving a packet of dollar bills I heard no more from his mother. I did not see Maurice or a single priest or monk of any kind. Even Jeannette had vanished from the swimming-pool of the Cercle Sportif. Perhaps Colonel Dinh had stood by his bargain and helped her and her mother get to France. I hoped so.

I half-expected to hear word that Thai had left Phnom-Penh and safely arrived in Paris. But when there was no message slipped under my front door, no sudden appearance by Maurice, I was not particularly disturbed. Sometimes a remark of Ba's or Gruson's would come into my mind. I did really dream of Mr Do a couple of times though in my sleep he got muddled up with the old school coach he once reminded me of and made his appearance on a cricket pitch, not in the derelict garden where I had first seen him or dead beside his ancient bicycle at our last encounter. Colonel Dinh, strangely, did not haunt me. I cannot say I worried much about Thai for I presumed he was safe.

I felt as though I were coming out of a long illness. The pain and the fever were almost forgotten but I would have to wait to discover in what other ways I had been damaged. As with many illnesses its effects might only make themselves felt years later.

The first thing to disturb this calm was news about Jeannette. I ran into one of her girlfriends from the Cercle and she asked me what I thought about the wedding. She was embarrassed when I asked what wedding and said Jeannette's. She was going to marry a journalist called Byrne. It hadn't occurred to me that he might present himself as her saviour. Of course it hurt my pride though I had no more claim on her and didn't begrudge her even this escape. But what hurt most was the realisation that Byrne could fit into a world I knew I did not belong to.

And then one evening, almost a month to the day after I got Maurice's note telling of Thai's departure, Ba turned up at the villa. He bustled in as he had always done, moved restlessly about the sitting room fiddling with his pipe and asking disconnected questions. But it was plain he was worried about something.

'Have you heard anything from Maurice?'

I shook my head and he frowned. He said he had been twice to Maurice's house in the past week for news of Thai. He should have left for France by now. But the first time Maurice told him he had heard nothing, the second time the house was locked. Even the maid wasn't there.

I tried to calm him but he was so down in the mouth that I suggested we go out and have dinner. I was a little surprised when he agreed but that might have been because I was at least shrewd enough to suggest that he take me somewhere I would find interesting. He could never turn down a chance to be someone's guide.

He took me to a restaurant close by in a street behind Le Loi. It was a simple place and scarcely looked like a restaurant at all, just a few tables in what had been a street-front shop. But unlike the restaurants in the more public streets in the centre it sold Vietnamese food. We ate *cha gio* that were brought to the table in long rolls almost a foot long and which the waiter then chopped into pieces with scissors. Ba asked for hot peppers which he consumed, seeds and all, down to the stem. He cheered up when he told me a story about the only foreigner he had known who could eat peppers like a Vietnamese, but for most of the time he was so patently out of form that I began to worry about him.

It was obvious, too, when we left the restaurant that he did not want to go home. We walked for a while and then he asked if I'd like to go to a nightclub. He said there was a place close to the town hall where a new singer was performing. She was said to be very good and all the young people were mad about her.

I didn't in the least want to go. I remembered the nightclub Maurice had taken me to. It would be too much like going back to the beginning of a book that one had no more use for. But I couldn't bring myself to disappoint him. It was close by and I couldn't imagine Ba sitting still for long anywhere.

The Queen Bee wasn't at all like Maurice's Pink Night. It was up steps from the street and we had to push past young men, some army officers among them, who were talking and smoking there to get to the entrance. They didn't seem very pleased to see me but Ba went in front like a tugboat clearing the way. It was a barn of a place. The audience was mainly young men. Some looked like students. Many, judging by their cropped hair, were soldiers out of uniform.

Ba persuaded a disobliging waiter to give us a table. We ordered whisky and Ba brought out his pipe. A girl in a miniskirt was on the stage with a band behind her. She was singing a French song. There was a great deal of talk among the tables. No one paid her much attention and she was only faintly applauded.

The band played a drumroll and a spotlight was turned on the stage. There was a surge at the entrance to the club as the people on the stairs rushed to get back in. The talk died down. A girl in a dark-blue *ao dai* walked onto the stage. She looked, I thought, like any other pretty Vietnamese girl, with straight black hair down to her shoulders.

But it was a strange voice for a girl who could not have been long out of school. It had a rasp that suggested she had already smoked and drunk more than was good for her. And as I studied her face in the spotlight I saw that it was made up to give the impression of childish prettiness. Her hair was parted in the middle and fell over the side of her face. The long fingernails were painted a pale pink. She sang the slow and lilting song standing quite still, her arms to her side and without in any way trying to play the coquette with the audience. But she made it sound even to my ears as though the words and music were the expression of her own life and she was singing for herself. I could understand why the young men came to hear her. This was innocence proclaiming it could not live for long, but not altogether resisting the debauched and worldly-wise life that was to come. And I recognised the singer. It was the same smoky voice I had heard outside Ba's house the night his child was wounded.

A thin young man at the next table leaned over and in broken English asked me if I understood the words. I shook my head and he pulled his chair closer.

'They are very important. We feel like this. It says a girl is alone. I think her lover is dead. Perhaps he is a soldier. The song is very poetic. It says the song will rock the girl like a lullaby for a thousand years. It is about death and war and loneliness.'

He stopped, exhausted by the effort of translating. He had something of Thai about him but there was a trace, too, of Father Lam's anguish. I had not expected to have their images conjured up for me again.

Ba pulled at my arm.

'Look over there.'

He pointed with his pipe to a table at the wall behind us. Maurice, in shirt-sleeves and tie, was sitting alone, a cigarette in his holder and a bottle of whisky and a bucket of ice in front of him. In those surroundings he might have been a creature from another planet. I tried to stop Ba but he was off his chair before I could lean across to hold him. Maurice didn't look as though he wanted to be disturbed.

Ba was back in a couple of minutes. He looked very serious. 'You must come over and talk to him.'

I didn't want to. I could see that Maurice was already quite drunk. The business with Thai was over and I was already feeling uncomfortable in this place which I realised belonged to a world I thought I had finished with.

But Ba was insistent. Maurice got up unsteadily to shake my hand. To the annoyance of the people around us he made the waiter bring chairs and glasses.

'Thai brought me here once,' he said. 'Of course, it's not the right place for me. I'm too old to understand what these young people feel. But Thai liked it. He laughed at it too, sometimes. He could see both sides, of course, but that was part of his trouble, wasn't it?'

He had drunk enough to darken his face and he looked shabby, scarcely recognisable as the almost dapper, self-possessed figure who had one evening arrived unannounced at my villa.

'We heard two days ago,' he said. 'I should have sent you a message but then I thought, why bother you. Thai's disappeared. He went out of the house in Phnom-Penh ten days ago and never came back. The Cambodians – our Cambodians – looked for him but couldn't find any trace. They are connected with the police, you know, so they know how to look. They said he might have been killed. But I think he's too clever to get into something like that. I think he disappeared because he wanted to.'

We got no more out of him than that. Later Ba and I sometimes tried to guess what might have happened. I wondered if Thai had killed himself. Ba was at first sure that he had gone back to the Vietcong – perhaps Father Lam's arguments had reached him after all – but then decided the communists had kidnapped him, having tracked his movements throughout. But he never showed up and when the news broke of the first big massacres of Vietnamese in Cambodia, the wretched Khmers' attempt to redress the balance of history, I wondered if he had not finally perished in them.

I heard only after I left Saigon that Thai's wife had gone to Paris with little Vong. Apparently she meant to wait for him there, and for all I know is waiting there still. The song we heard in the nightclub had got her future right.

It was, of course, defeat. Thai had been consumed. A fine piece of wood that should have been used to build something grand had been burned to keep alive a blaze that no one, whatever they pretended, was controlling.

Michael Bishop's Saigon

MAPS

The street names and monuments of the Saigon Michael Bishop knew before the communists took the city in 1975 signalled a past the flood of time could not submerge and which was ignored at peril.

Nguyen Hue. Named after a leader of peasant revolt turned emperor. A cunning victor over the old Chinese enemy, he united Vietnam at the end of the eighteenth century only to be defeated by Nguyen Anh, later the emperor Gia Long and founder of the last royal dynasty.

Vo Tanh, the street that led to Thai's hide-out, recalled one of Nguyen Anh's generals. Besieged for seventeen months, Vo Tanh asked for clemency for his troops and then blew himself up.

Marshal Le Van Duyet, whose tomb was contained in the temple Bishop saw on his way to Mr Ba's house, was another companion of Nguyen Anh and a friend of the Catholics, though not one himself. The marshal, it was believed, protected and guided his people even in death. The temple was visited by those anxious to know their future.

Phan Thanh Gian, where Gruson had his oddly decorated house. Named after a mandarin who cooperated with the French, regretted it, and committed suicide.

Tu Do, meaning 'freedom'. Vietnamese revenge for the street's earlier name, Catinat, taken from the warship whose bombardment began the final French conquest of the country.

Ham Nghi, the strect of which Bishop's bank was located. Named after the child emperor who began a hopeless revolt against the colonisers, and was quickly betrayed and exiled to Algeria.

The tomb of the *grand évêque* the taxi-driver pointed out when taking Bishop to his first meeting with Father Quan was that of Pigneau de Behaine, bishop of Adran. After asking Louis XVI to help Nguyen Anh to power he took matters largely into his own hands and helped his Vietnamese protégé build a victorious army, thus deciding the fate of modern Vietnam. The communists destroyed the bishop's tomb and other cemeteries after 1975. Almost two hundred years earlier Nguyen Anh had profaned the tomb of *his* predecessor.

Other streets were witness to a less disputed past:

Tran Hung Dao, which led Bishop to Father Lam to receive a message from the Vietcong. Named after a great strategist admired by all Vietnamese for his defeat of a superior Mongol army.

Le Loi. Named after the leader of a peasant revolt who founded the longest-lasting Vietnamese dynasty.

Nguyen Du, on which Bishop himself lived. A memorial to the country's greatest writer whose poem-novel *Kim Van Kieu*, a story of destiny and tragic love, expresses a restless people's spiritual world.

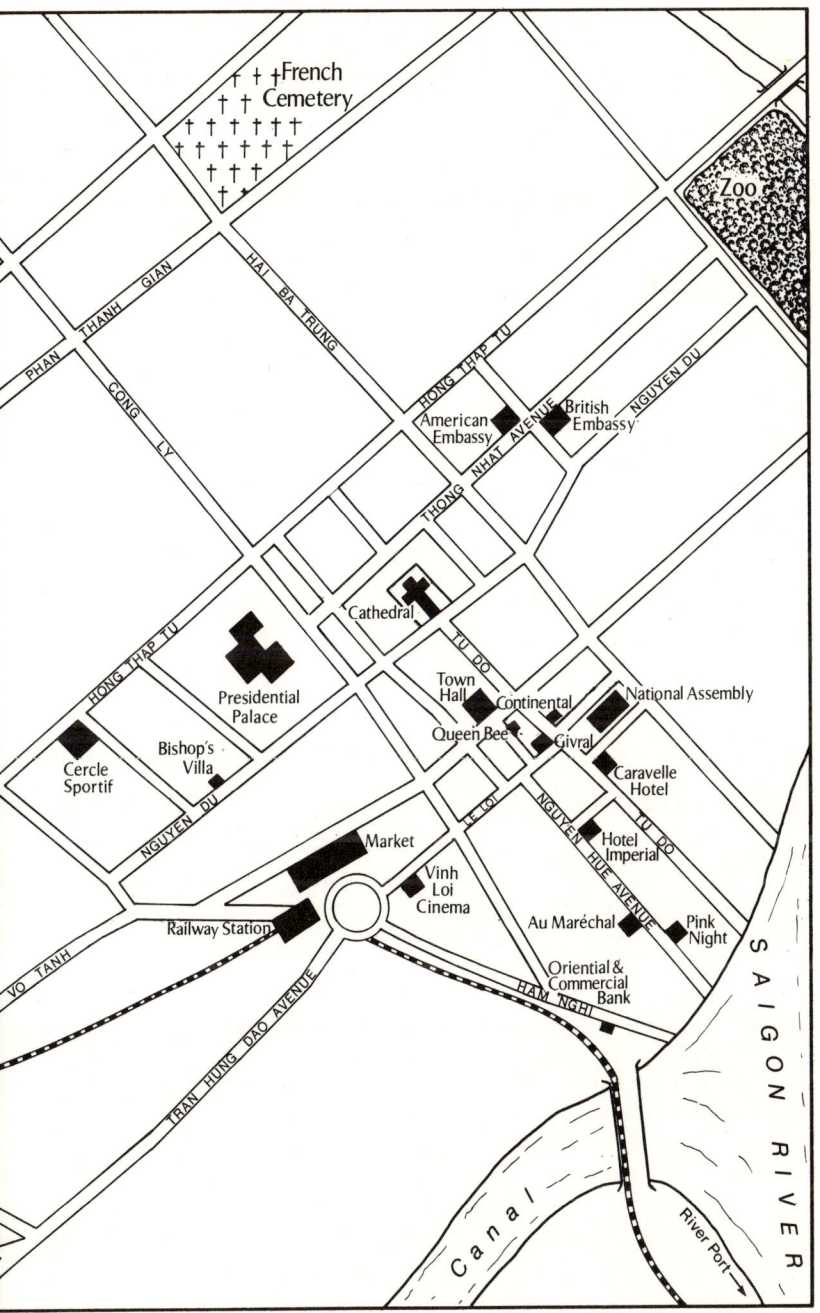

Central Saigon

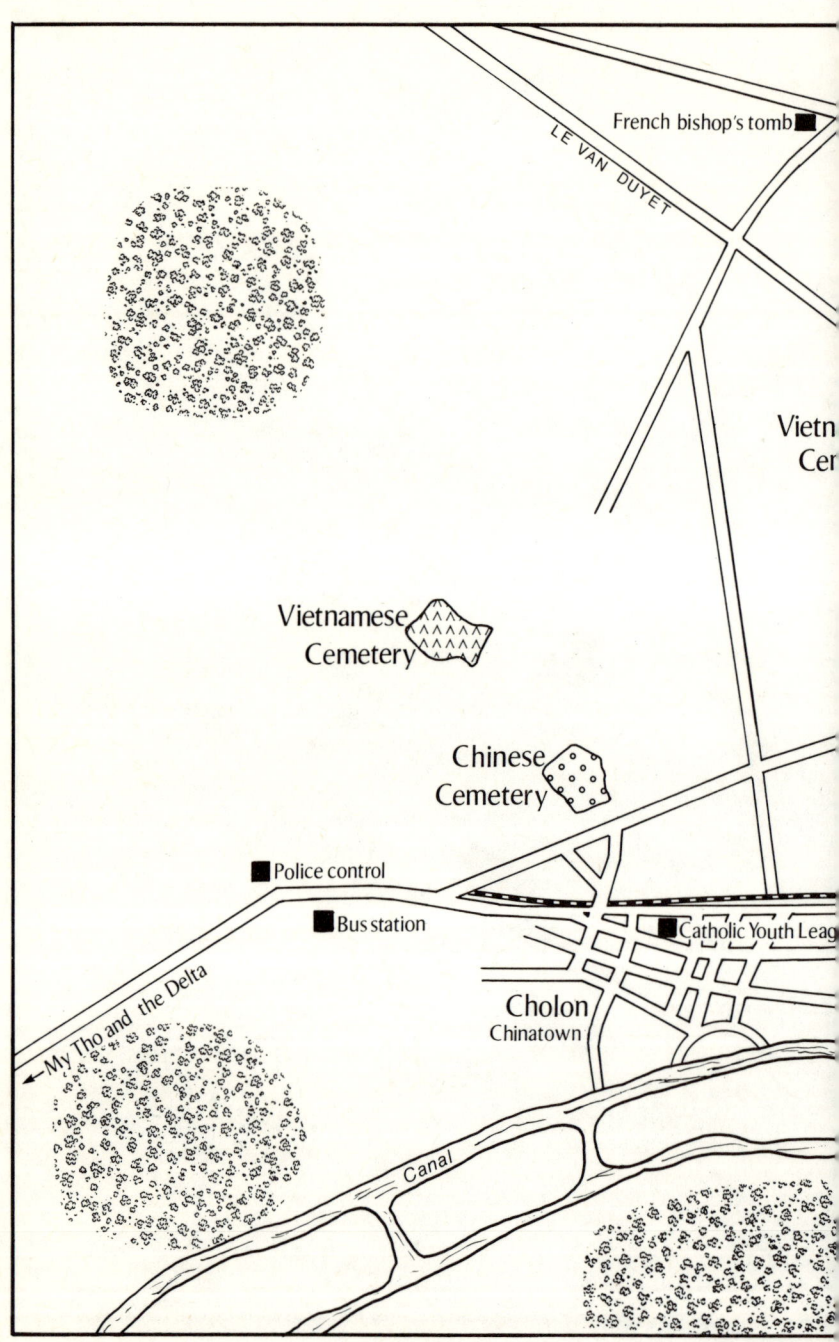

Saigon and Cholon